I0681770

NICK L. SHANE

SHOOt 'EM T'a HELL!

~THE GUNS OF INFINITY~
A Series In Big Action Western Novel

PROCLAMATION

OF THE

GOVERNOR OF MISSOURI!

REWARDS

FOR THE ARREST OF

Express and Train Robbers.

STATE OF MISSOURI,
EXECUTIVE DEPARTMENT

FRANK JAMES and JESSE W. JAMES,

THOS. T. CRITTENDEN.

SHOOT 'EM T'A HELL!

To my heart's inspiration (Diane)

"All the world loves an outlaw,
for some reason they remember 'em"
                                        -Jesse James

TO THE READER

The vast lands of the Old American West were an unchanging territory for many hundreds of years. In the 1870's it was still a harsh, and all too often unforgiving place for the settled eastern civilized; any land west of the Mississippi was still considered to be hostile.

The cruelty of the lands nature had caught many a man at unawares, bringing to light the savagery that still existed there, where men would rise up from its bowels, sculpted and chiseled to form like the very rock and dirt that lay upon the surface of the land itself.

Countless numbers would come looking to claim a piece of that land for themselves only to find that it would come with a high price, maybe even their own life. Men who were evil in nature, if not soulless, lay in wait there. Like vultures, anticipating the moment when they would close in on their intended prey, they would pick apart the flesh of the unsuspecting and feed the lusts of their own hearts.

The land took what it wanted from each allowing passage only to the strongest. The bones of dead unfortunates littered the desert lands and deep-canyon regions, remains covered over by time and the drifting sands. The Central Plains concealed the dead beneath a calm guise of swaying-grass-lands while the high mountain country of the Snow-Peaked Rockies laid claim to its victims as well. Ghosts still walked these unforgiving lands whispering cautions to those who may be next to leave their bones behind and be lost to the land forever...

. . . AND THERE WERE THOSE WHO REFUSED TO GO QUIETLY INTO THAT GOOD NIGHT. THEY WOULD LIVE ON TO BECOME LEGENDS OF THE LIKES WHICH THE WEST HAD NEVER KNOWN. MEN WHO WOULD FORGE THE COURSE OF THEIR OWN DESTINY, LIVING BY THE ONLY LAW TO SEPARATE GOOD FROM EVIL AND DEFEND THOSE WHO WERE INNOCENT—
THE LAW OF THE GUN!

Canyon de Chelly, Arizona - 1877

Yampah Canyons, Utah - 1877

The heavy Iron Gate swung open with a jaw clenching screech! Luis McCall stepped through the opening and turned an eye back to Huntsville Territorial Prison for the last time. It had been a long, hard two years behind those prison walls, but that was over. What he needed now was a horse and a gun! He hadn't forgotten; There were men needed killin' for the sins they'd committed, and the black hate he felt for a man named Clemens was about to be unleashed!

She was gone... A time that had slipped from his grasp, sifting through his fingers like the coarse desert sand. But, McCall was still dead-set to avenge her! He tipped his hat in the direction of Austin when he saw a dot on the horizon. A lone rider was approaching—a second horse in tow following along behind...

NICK L. SHANE
PREFACE

The night was black as pitch... pinholes of light were seeping through the dark Vail giving the only indication that he was still on earthy-ground and hadn't ridden off into a deep Abbys, or Black hole of some sort. He knew it was just the Mexico desert playing tricks on his mind, but the idea didn't set well with him, nor his Black Stallion, Nightmare.

Wreck Lawson was still madder than hell about the incident that had taken place back in Chihuahua a couple of days back. His head was still sore and bruised by the beating he'd taken from a band of Hell-bent-beaners in that damned cantina! It was his own damn fault for ever having taken that girl south of the border to begin with...

She was pretty, real pretty! She had auburn-red hair that danced like fire when the wind rushed through it. 'Reminded Lawson of a mid-summer sunset back home in Austin. Her teeth were pearly-white with a smile that would knock your socks off! And her body had curves a man would kill for if given the opportunity. She wasn't exactly the kind of girl you'd bring home to meet momma, but you could bet your last greenback dollar that the old man would'a been dancin' the jig!

He'd got'n in on a poker game (stud) at a little cantina called the *Spider's Web* and was doing pretty good with lady luck, and the cards, both seemed to be playing in his favor. But, the fiery li'l temptress, Marla who was accompanying him, couldn't help but notice the curvy black-haired senorita who'd slid in next to him at the table; she couldn't quite seem to keep her hands to herself! Lawson had caught Marla's eyes just as she was going into a back room with a tall and slender Mexican with long-wiery hair. The Mexican smiled through brown-yellow teeth as he followed closely behind her. The glare she threw at Lawson was cold; so cold the temperature of the room suddenly dropped and icy crystals seemed to, slowly form across the window panes inside the room. Lawson wasn't the first prey that hissing hellcat had played and he didn't know until just then that he'd been had! He was about to rake in another pot when one of the players (a beaner with a bad attitude and empty pockets) decided that the grinning gringo had reached his limit! 'Shame of it was; that pot was holding plenty and he'd worked hard and long at breaking them. Only one problem with the hand he was holding onto; Eights and Aces—THE DEAD MAN'S HAND!

Lawson made their call, flipped the table, then stripped both Colt's from leather blasting two of the men backwards across the room with .45 lead before they could blink. He planted the butt of one across another's forehead. That streak was short lived when a chair was shattered across his back knocking him to his knees and dislodging both Colts' from his grasp. Them beaners were madder than a swarm of pissed-off-hornets, punching and kicking him until they'd grown tired from it; well, that and the fact that Lawson had stumbled onto an axe handle leaning in a corner that fit his hand just right! He laid the stick across one's hand, shattering it at the wrist when the beaner went for a pistol'a. The next one to enter the scene was the wirey-haired Mexican. Lawson was in mid-swing when the Mexican came running out from a back room between some thin curtains and intercepted the baseball bat with his mouth. Lawson glimpsed the stick and found several teeth fragments embedded in the end of it like brown and rusted nails. During their delirium, Lawson was able to quickly gather his Colts', his Stetson, and make a break out the front door of the place. He booted stirrup, wheeled the stallion around and bolted out into the night as repeated rounds of lead buzzed past his ears until he had ridden out of their range of gunfire...

Only one thing Lawson wanted now... To ride back into Arizona and try to find his partner, Luis (Storm) McCall. He couldn't wait to see the look on McCall's face when he told him about that auburn headed gal he'd stolen from him back at the saloon in Santa Fe; after all it was McCall she'd been attempting to seduce from the git! Hopefully McCall would see the humor in it and they would both have a good laugh like always.

What Lawson didn't know was; McCall was already in Yuma and he was madder than Hell!

A coyote was yapping into the darkness of night as the lone rider and his horse made their way across the Abbys... Phantom shadows drifting across the vast, desolate terrain...

SHOOT 'EM T'A HELL!

CHAPTER 1

Yuma, Arizona – 1877

That damn Arizona Sun was hotter than Hell breathing down on the neck of a man like the very breath of the devil himself. Wreck Lawson, seldom sought gunmen from Texas, was poised in the street with his hand hanging in a claw next to his right side Colt .45 Peacemaker ready to strip leather on the son of a bitch who'd called him out; The man in the saloon who was to brave for his own good was now going to learn the hard way...

The blazing-orb, overhead, was glaring in Lawson's eyes. It hung suspended in the sky just above the loud mouth that was causing the imminent threat. Closing one eye reduced the glare, but the man standing only 20 feet in front of Lawson was still mostly an illuminated shadow shouting out a well of cursing threats. The loud mouth reminded Lawson of a cross-eyed-snake hissing out vulgarities over its forked tongue... fangs dripping of poisonous venom.

"Hey, boy!" seethed the coiling viper. "I'm 'bout t'a put a bullet right through that twitching' eye of Your's, so you'd best git t'a sayin' your prayers!"

Lawson had sustained an injury do to battle during the War of the States; At Shiloh a Yank' had rammed the butt of a rifle into his face splitting him wide under his left eye causing damage to the facial nerves. Lawson pinned the Blue Coat to the side of a thick oak tree. The bayonet fixed at the end of his rifle pierced through the Yank's chest like a bag full of sand. The Northerner had hung there lifeless, staring at the ground, a questioning look pulled across his face. His boots were two feet from of the ground. His shadow was cast where, Lawson still stood with hands fixed in a viced-grip on the wooden stocks of the long rifle as the Yank's thick-warm-blood oozed down the length of the rifle's barrel. When angered, Lawson's left eye would twitch; a sure sign to most to get clear of him, but some just couldn't read.

"Y'er drunk mister, exacted Lawson. I'm gonna ask y'a one more time t'a' walk away before I haf'ta kill y'a ."

"You ain't killin' nobody, boy!"

The stranger's hand swept to his side to unleash the holstered threat! The gun roared in his hand, but something was wrong. He felt a burning sensation in the top of his foot, and was being driven back by lead-like fists blasting deeply into his chest.

Lawson had unleashed his Colt with such blinding speed that the strangers threat never got clear of leather. The man had fired the Remington in the holster and blasted an acorn-sized hole right through the top of his own foot, the bullet traveling on burying itself deep into the hard-dirt beneath the sole of his boot.

...The Peacemaker thundered in Lawson's hand. flames spit from the muzzle as he slapped the steel hammer with the palm of his hand. Five black-red holes instantly appeared in the man's chest and gut; each bullet impact creating a "poof" of fabric at the man's shirt front. The blasted-fibers hung lightly on the air, suspended for a moment, then slowly began to drift away...

The foolish unfortunate clutched his hands tightly up against his chest, blood gushing from his heart, spreading between his fingers like a mufti-channeled river; a dammed-up levy that had burst and was overflowing from its muddy banks. A look of horror pulled across the hostile's face when he realized that his 1875 Remington Revolver was still holstered at his side, smoking, a former friend who had just betrayed him.

A nickel-sized hole instantly appeared in his forehead, the bullet splitting his brain in a wild explosion of crimson-red, bone fragments and brain matter from the back of his ruptured skull. His eyes rolled up to their sockets as if trying to look out of the shattered glass window that used to be the back of his head. He dropped into the street like a puppeteer had just cut his strings.

There was no doubt in Lawson's mind that the man was dead. He'd given him every chance to drop it and move on, but the crazy-eyed stranger would have nothing to do with it. Not willing to take the chance of being shot in the back at a future time, Lawson chose to end it right then and there. Lawson had learned a long time ago about turning his back on a wounded man. The bullet he'd taken in the back four years before in Wichita had left it's nickel-sized scar as a reminder. That bullet had nearly killed him. When he'd recovered he'd made a vowel to himself to never turn his back on a hostile man again—and he didn't! He showed no mercy when being challenged by another gun and he never gambled with his own life. In his mind there was a reason why the gun was called a six shooter; Apparently the one shooter of years past had needed some rethinking and, Lawson appreciated the odds that six bullets gave a man especially when staying alive was his main interest. He thumbed open the loading-gate on his Colt .45, turned the ratcheting cylinder dropping each smoking casing into the dust of the street. The brass casings chimed almost musically as they "pinged" one by one, and bounced around at his feet. A gritty dust blew in...swirled in circles along the streets length as the gunmen from Texas stood gazing at the dead man who was leaking a river of blood from the holes his .45 slugs had just drilled through the body. A crowd was gathering as Lawson emptied the spent casings from the smoking revolver and was replacing them with fresh ones.

"It was a fair fight!" Yelled a man from somewhere in the crowd.

"'Sure was, saw the whole thing!" shouted another gray bearded man, then he spat a stream of brown tobacco juice into the street and wiped his mouth on the sleeve of his shirt. Nearby, a group of women had gathered outside the church. One of them turned and ran away covering her mouth with her hands after having seen the dead man laying there in the street with his brains spilled everywhere.. looking like someone had just thrown a bucket of slop to the pigs. The dead man's eyes were slowly sinking in their sockets...oozing into the empty cavity of his shattered skull.

On the opposite side of the street stood five men. They were eyeing the situation standing in a group at the corner of a building where the wood of the boardwalk ended and were talking among themselves.

The Ferrell gang was headed up by West Ferrell and his

younger brother Trevor. The other three men were just trail riders who had drifted along the same path as the Ferrell Brothers a couple of years back. One of the men (an Englishman named Monty Langford was a bare knuckle prizefighter (fisted cuff) who had earned a reputation as a credible fighter. Not bad with the use of his fists, but hadn't earned any money as of late, though.

"Looks like Carter just had a bad day," said West Ferrell.

"Yeah, said Trevor, that stinkin' dog who shot him down is gonna git payback for what he just did to ol' Ben you can count on it!"

Just then a man with a sawed-off-shotgun came rounding into Lawson's view.

"Don't you move a muscle there slick... I've got you covered with a double greener—At this range I'm not gon'a miss!"

"The man called me out sheriff." (Lawson had just saw the star pinned on the tall man's chest) "He drew first and these good people can witness to that fact."

"Oh, I have no doubt it was self-defense! said the sheriff. That was Ben Carter. He's been causing all the trouble around here for about the past week now. I'd say he had it comin'. What bothers me though, he said, is; the first five rounds would've killed him clean, but you put another one between his eyes. In my book that makes you a very dangerous man. It also makes me very curious about who you are."

"The name is Lawson, Wreck Lawson. I don't take kindly to insults from strangers, or a badge if the man behind it ain't honest."

Several onlookers gasped after having heard the name, Lawson and began to step away. A lump formed in the sheriff's throat and Lawson saw the old man's finger twitch near the shotgun's trigger.

"Easy there, Sheriff, said Lawson in a calm voice. I ain't looking for any trouble."

Lawson held both Colts out to the sheriff, butt foreword.

"We don't need no more killing Mr. Lawson, so if you would just holster your guns and walk with me over to my office...

Lawson replaced The Colts back in leather as the sheriff held the shotgun steady, trained straight at the Texan's chest. The sheriff eased the barrels down, then the two men walked away toward the jail. The sheriff introduced himself to Lawson as; Charles Compton.

"I'll run some information on you up to Phoenix and see if you're wanted anywhere. It shouldn't take very long."

"If you find that necessary, said Lawson. "'Doubt you'll find anything though."

At the end of the street a small building came into view. The structure, cedar and brick, had two tall cactus on each side of the walkway that led to the front door. A sign hanging above the door read: YUMA JAIL

Deputy Billy Sutton (a young man of twenty years) had been sitting in the sheriff's chair. He jumped quickly to his feet when he saw Compton enter through the door. To, Lawson, Sutton looked more like a kid that had recently come off of his mother's tit than someone who should be carrying a badge and firearm.

"Billy, take his guns and lock 'em up in the Cabinet," said Compton.

Lawson unbuckled his rigs and handed them over to the young deputy.

"Take him back and lock him up with the other gent' we picked up last night, said Compton. I'm gonna run Mr Lawson's name up to Phoenix and see if he's wanted— shouldn't take very long."

The young deputy's eyes cut, quickly, locking with

Lawson's in a brief, but contemptuous glare. Sutton had heard the name before...

The sheriff proceeded out the door and crossed the street to send the telegraph. Billy Sutton opened the thick door that led to the holding cells in the back. The cells were dark except for some light coming from a small window. With a rattle of the keys the deputy swung the heavy-steel door open. Lawson stepped in and Sutton slammed the cell door behind him with an ear shattering —Clang!

Lawson spun and gave the deputy a cold glare, then turned away. The floor of the cell was hard dirt and smelled strong of damp mildew. Lawson let out a deep disapproving grown and set down on one of the wooden bunks. He wasn't too concerned about a warrant being out on him because he hadn't had any run-ins with the law for a while. Right next to him, in another cell, he could hear a man snoring. He knew it wouldn't be long before that would get on his nerves. As his eyes adjusted to the darkness he caught the outline of a man leaning in a corner. Lawson jumped up suddenly, clenched his fists.

"Who the hell are you?"

"Relax," said a man in a smooth-deep voice.

"Show your face mister, said Lawson. Or are you just gonna hide over there like a chicken shit?"

The figure straightened after hearing Lawson's words. The phantom stepped out into the thin-light-rays that were beaming in through the steel-barred window.

"Wreck... how ya been?"

As his eyes focused Lawson thought he recognized the man;

"Luis?" "Storm McCall?" "Is that you?"

"Yeah, it's me"

"Well, son of a bitch! How the hell..."

He stopped in mid-sentence remembering the last time he had seen McCall.

"I'm sorry 'bout..."

McCall threw a hard fist into Lawson's face, landing him on his ass on the hard-dirt-floor of the cell and seeing stars.

McCall (like Lawson) was a credible fighter. Standing at six feet, and weighing in over two hundred pounds, his chest was thick with lean-muscle, arms wide at the bicep. He had the temper of a rattle snake if provoked. Once he coiled up there was no doubt he would strike! His eyes were dark, hard and mean. It hadn't always been like that though...

"That's for Santa Fe, pard'!"

McCall stepped forward and stretched out his hand to pull Lawson up to his feet.

"Dammit Lou, that hurt like hell! That damn gal played on both of us man!"

"I know that now, replied McCall. But after you hightailed it out of there her husband came gunnin' thinkin' I was you, so I had to kill him. It was self-defense, but they're calling it murder in Santa Fe. He evidently thought I was messin' with his wife, but that was you..." said McCall with a raised brow. "Whatever happened to the girl?"

"I took her over the border into Mexico one night—Big mistake! There was this little Cantina... A card game was going on, stud, so I sat in for a spell. After I took all their pesos they got matter than a swarm of pissed off Hornets and decided they wanted the girl and they meant it! After one hell of a shoot out I rode out of there and headed for Yuma. Sure hated to leave her there like that..."

Somehow McCall didn't quite believe Lawson's last statement.

After a while they heard the front door to the jail open

and close.

"Billy", shouted Miller, free Lawson. He has no warrants I can find."

McCall was just getting ready to explain to, Lawson how he had ended up in the jail in the first place. After all he had knocked a man's front teeth out in a fight at the saloon; man by the name of Floyd Mathers. But, that story would have to wait for another time...

"Lawson, you're free to go," said Compton.

The steel door opened with a loud—Screech, and Clang!

Lawson stepped out and turned back to McCall..

"Don't worry pard'," he whispered.

The deputy, Sutton, was standing nearby and said;

"If that man is a friend of y'ers, you'd better hurry... Judge Neusome will be arriving in two days. The other man, there, in the next cell is going to hang this week. Were trying to fit y'er friend in on the same ticket. 'Don't see as how there's much you can do though..."

The deputy let out a chuckle underneath his breath that made McCall's blood boil. McCall stepped to the steel bars and whispered;

"You hurry Wreck... I've heard of this judge. His name is Neusome and he's earned a reputation for hanging. They call him "The Noose." He'll make me swing."

Lawson gave a nod.

"I'll see y'a soon Lou'.

He turned and walked out the door, retrieved his arms from Sutton, then exited the jail.

The streets of Yuma were beginning to crowd with the news of a double hanging. Lawson felt deep regret at having to leave McCall in that hot-stinking-jail, but he had no choice. No doubt about it; it was time to devise a plan. First he needed a drink and a few minutes to clear his bruised head. There was a sign hanging above an entry that read: DRAGON'S BREATH SALOON

He entered the saloon through the bat-wing doors. They yanked back and forth until the springs caught hold and brought them to a stop. Several heads turned in his direction as he entered the shadowy interior.

"Whiskey, bar keep," he said as he stepped up to the bar.

The bar itself wasn't very impressive, but they did have plenty of drink on the shelves and a couple of poker tables, not to mention the two soiled doves who were eyeing him from the end of the bar.

"Dammit!" he thought... No time for that right now.

"Howdy stranger, said the bar keep. I own this hear establishment; My name is Ralph Crepps, and the first one is on the house...

CHAPTER 2

Lawson threw back the whiskey, sat the glass back down on the bar, then pointed to it for a refill. The bar keep hesitated for a second having recognized Lawson as the man who'd killed Ben Carter out on the street earlier in the day.

"Yes sir, said Crepps (lump caught in his throat) that sure is a terrible way to die."

Lawson only gazed the man, looked down at the glass on the bar, awaited the refill of whiskey.

"If y'er referring to the man I shot today, that's over, and I don't wanna talk about it," said Lawson.

"No sir of course not," said Crepps. He continued to irritate Lawson when he said;

"That poor bastard over at the jail goin'ta get his neck

stretched... and now they even got some other sum bitch their going to throw in just to make the event draw even more spectators. Good for business if you know what I mean."

The twitch in Lawson's eye told the bartender he'd gone too far. Lawson pulled one of his .45's, grabbed Crepps by the front of his shirt and yanked him up onto the bar with the muzzle leveled right between the man's eyes.

"Shut up mister... you don't want to piss me off right now! That other gent' is a good friend of mine 'n he ain't goin' t'a hang—got it?!"

"Ye... ye...yessir... I meant no disrespect to you sir."

"Get out'a my face mister!" snarled Lawson.

He put the bottle down on the bar and shoved the man backwards with force. Crepps, slammed, clumsily into the liquor shelves rattling the glass bottles of whiskey displayed there, toppled a few of them over on their side.

"It's on the house mister," mumbled Crepps as he turned and quickly moved to the opposite end of the bar.

Lawson shoved the Colt back into its oiled holster, picked up the bottle and refilled his glass. There were three men in the bar, onlookers who had witnessed the situation, but they seemed very interested in minding their own business. Through the bat wing doors Lawson could see the light of day beginning to fade. The sun was setting to the West and it would be dark soon. One thing he wasn't going to do was walk through those doors and out into the dark of night like a blind idiot. He threw back the shot of whiskey just as the doors swung open—there were five of them.

The group of men eyed Lawson as they passed by. Two of them stopped at the bar as the others made their way to a table and sat down.

"Whiskey for my men!" shouted West Ferrell.

Crepps handed Ferrell two bottles of whiskey over the bar. Ferrell turned and walked back to the table, banged one of them down on the wooden top. He came back to the bar, slid in on the right side of Lawson and stood there. He popped the cork from the bottle and filled his shot-glass with whiskey, threw the shot back, then whacked the empty glass down on the bar.

"You really should think about leaving town, mister, said Ferrell. There's a U.S. Marshall coming in from Tucson tomorrow and he's one mean hombre. He's what you might call; a friend of mine. Like that man you killed out there in the street today, comprehend'e?"

Lawson said nothing; all he'd wanted was to have a drink and collect his thoughts for a moment, but his patience was beginning to wear thin. In the mirror behind the bar he could see the other men watching him. They looked mean and hard like they'd been in the saddle for a while— outlaws, no doubt about it!

West Ferrell had dark eyes, squinted when he talked. He and his younger brother, Trevor, wore matching Schofield .45's, tied down low. A much heavier gun than the Colt Peacemakers, Lawson preferred.

Monty Langford was a thick man with broad shoulders and long-swollen arms, red hair and a handlebar mustache. He reminded Lawson of an English Fisted Cuff.

Floyd Mathers (a big man with black hair and a full black beard) had a big-loud-mouth that was missing two front teeth (McCall knew that already)

Gene Antrim (greasy-yellow-hair) stayed mostly out of sight, but moved around a lot. The usual sign of a back shooter as Lawson viewed it. Without turning, Lawson spoke;

"I have some business in town, 'not leaving until that business is settled, comprehende?"

In the mirror Lawson could see Ferrell's men beginning to stand. They began, slowly, closing in from all sides like a pack of wolves surrounding their prey. Floyd Mathers came in and stood directly behind Lawson. Suddenly, he yelled out;

"You heard him boy! Now get scootin' before I start t'a breakin' you!"

Lawson didn't flinch.

"Why, you little..!"

Mathers threw his left hand down on Lawson's left shoulder in an attempt to spin him around. The whiskey bottle (already gripped at the neck in Lawson's right hand) came up, and around, exploding through the air when it shattered in the big man's face hurling him backwards with a mouthful of glass and more shattered teeth. Mathers timbered onto a table smashing it into a pile of broken boards underneath him and didn't move again. Before any of the others could react, Lawson had two .45's cocked and leveled on the man beside him—West Ferrell.

"Don't move that hand mister," said Lawson, seeing Ferrell's hand move towards the butt of his holstered Schofield.

"If you get me, my men will cut you down," said Ferrell.

"Maybe, said Lawson, but your skull is gonna' look like the Red River Valley after a dam just let lose upstream!"

Ferrell swallowed hard having seen the intent in Lawson's eyes. For a moment Ferrell's eyes shifted like a wild animal caught in a trap. Then, he said;

"Holster your guns boys he'll kill me..."

Ferrell could see a funeral in Lawson's twitching eye, and it was his own!

Floyd Mathers had regained consciousness and was attempting to get back up onto his feet when Lawson noticed him. The rest of Ferrell's men had holstered their guns and were backing away toward the bat-wing doors. Lawson caught movement in the mirror from the barrel of a 10 gauge sawed-off-shotgun that was being raised...

Lawson ducked underneath the bar as fire exploded from the greener, sending loads of lead lightning straight into Mathers, blowing his right arm and the side of his head completely off! He was dead before he hit the floor like a felled Redwood Trunk. Everyone went ducking for cover allowing for, Lawson to make a bolt toward the split doors. He quickly shot out between them and made the street. Luckily the 10 gauge was a single barrel shotgun.

"This ain't over you son of a bitch... you hear me... this ain't over..!" shouted Ferrell from inside the interior of the saloon. Lawson turned quickly into a dark alley and disappeared between two buildings.

McCall had been standing at the barred window when he'd heard gunfire. He knew the sound of a shotgun blast. A scene popped into his mind's eye; Lawson running around, tail waggin', Pro'lly just stuck his big dog nose where it didn't belong (he'd better not be dead he thought to himself)

McCall had been having a one sided conversation with the bald man in the cell next to him. The scum had told him about how he had killed a family nearby. They were settlers on their way to California. He was hungry and stumbled into their camp. They fed him and let him camp with them for a few days. On the third night he slit the man's throat and then had his way with the woman in front of their 11 year old boy. The next morning he shot the boy and took the woman along with the wagon full of everything they'd owned. Soon after he'd killed the woman, then drove the wagon in from the desert.

After having arrived in Yuma he'd gotten drunk at a saloon and began to run his mouth. People didn't like what they were hearing and they reported it to the sheriff. So, now he would get what he deserved—he was going to hang for it!

"I know that fella' is gon'a try t'a break you out of here... Lawson I believe? Take me with you mister. I won't be any trouble to you and I can handle a gun!"

"Sure..." said McCall, and that's all he said. But, in McCall's mind he had a rope flung over an Oak branch and was hanging that stinking piece of coyote-dung himself!

The sun had disappeared on the Western Horizon as the town was starting to come alive. Wagons were arriving on the outskirts, mostly vendors getting ready to set up for the *big* hanging party—this wasn't Yuma's first hanging.

Lawson had checked into a room at the DESERT MOON HOTEL with a front window that viewed the length of the Main Street. From there he could see anything that moved and he burnt no lamp to insure his silhouette couldn't be made in the window...

From the east side of town three riders blinked in from out of the darkness of night. They pulled up to the Sidewinder Saloon. Two of the men stopped and threw reins over the hitch post, then went inside. The third rider continued on stopping in front of the YUMA JAIL. He dismounted, then went in. After several minutes the man came out, swung up onto the saddle and rode back to the saloon. Only a moment had passed when, Sheriff Compton came out the front door of the jail and walked across the street. He stepped up onto the boardwalk heading toward the saloon. A moment later he disappeared through the swinging doors. Lawson saw that as the perfect time to go see McCall.

When he arrived at the jail he entered and was suddenly

staring down the barrel of a Winchester rifle. Lawson froze, instantly, and threw up his hands. The young deputy was staring into his eyes, a wide-eyed grin across his face as if daring Lawson to make a move.

"What do you want?" asked the young badge toter.

"Here t'a see McCall if it's not too late?"

"Well, it's late!" said Sutton with a smirk. It was silent for a moment... Then—

"Check in your guns, you've got five minutes."

The deputy pushed open the door that lead to the cells where McCall was being held. Lawson stepped inside and waited for a moment for his eyes to adjust to the dim lighting. Sutton closed the steel door with a clang! Then, he turned and left the area. On a small table was an oil lamp, the flame flickering, casting phantom-like shadows up the walls and across the ceiling.

"Is that you Wreck?" asked McCall.

"Yeah Lou', It's me."

"What the hell is going on out there!" growled McCall.

Shhh... damn, be quiet!" reacted Lawson. McCall just looked at him with a blank, wide-eyed expression on his face.

"Okay Wreck, said McCall (with deliberate sarcasm) I'll be quiet. What's the plan?"

"I'm workin' on it."

"Y'er workin' on it? Well, I'm a dead man—that's it!"

"Relax, said Lawson, y'er not gon'a die anytime soon if I can help it."

"Maybe you could think on that Wreck; about helpin' it a little?

"You just be ready when the lead flies!"

"Oh, I think I can handle that part just fine!" said McCall.

"I'll be back for you partner, said Lawson. We still got many a trail left t'a ride."

Lawson stuck his hand between the bars, McCall shook it.

"Be ready," whispered Lawson.

McCall gave a nod of his head and let go of Lawson's hand.

After Lawson retrieved his guns from the Deputy Sutton, he buckled them back in place around his waist. The ignorant greenhorn left him alone for a minute to check the cell doors to make sure they were secured. Out of curiosity Lawson slid open a drawer on the sheriff's desk...

"Well now, what do we have here—three tin stars..? 'Don't mind if I do."

He took a sheriff's badge from the desk drawer.

"'Always wanted one of these..."he mumbled to himself, then he slid the star into his vest pocket, turned and walked to the door. Just as he placed his hand on the handle of the door Billy Sutton entered the room.

"Hey Lawson... the sheriff is gonna want to talk to you about that shooting at the saloon today so make sure you're available. By the way, U.S. Marshal Henry Blake just arrived from Santa Fe and he's talking with Sheriff Compton down at the Sidewinder."

Lawson opened the door, then as he was closing it Sutton shouted;

"See you at the hanging!"

That worm of a deputy was really starting to crawl under Lawson's skin. But, now he knew who the man was that he'd seen entering the jail earlier. But, who were the other two? Probably hired guns out to make a name for themselves (That's the way Lawson had it figured anyway)

As he made his way back to the **DESERT MOON HOTEL** he stopped to roll a smoke. He leaned a shoulder against a thick post and began to twist up the quirly. The town was busy now with men on horseback, and wagons rolling in. He struck flame to a stick, then put it to the end of his quirly...

The first shot slammed into the post just above his head. A large chunk of wood disappeared exploding into splinters. Lawson hit the deck as rifle rounds thumped holes in the boards all around him. Suddenly, they stopped. He checked himself for ventilation and luckily found no leaks. He jumped up and disappeared into the shadows at the corner of a building. People in the streets ran for cover; a man was fighting to control his horse which was jumping and bucking, wildly, finally throwing the man into the street on his back.

The bat-wings at the Sidewinder Saloon slammed open, three men came running out into the street with firearms drawn. After seeing no immediate threat, they returned to the interior of the saloon. They were the same three men who had just recently ridden into town. Lawson stood silent in the darkness of the alleyway, his eyes searching rooftops for the shooter, but he saw no one. Then, he spotted, West Ferrell and his men. They were standing on a corner across the street. Another man suddenly rounded the corner and joined the others. Lawson took him as the shooter. Especially now, since they were all looking in the direction he had been before disappearing into the shadows. The thought of killing all of them right then and there was pulling at him, but he knew it wasn't the right time, but their time was coming! He stayed there in the shadows for a while watching as Ferrell and his men walked away. Something let out a low growl; 'sounded like a mad grizzly with a paw caught in a trap. He was hungry, had to eat now! He walked along the boards, cautiously, trying to stick to dark areas as much as possible. He made the front door of the HOLLIDAY DINER (named that after the famous Doc Holliday had killed a man there for blowing his nose at a table while the Doc was trying to finish his meal).

The place was full... mostly out-of-towners. To his surprise he was taken to a seat immediately which suited him just fine. He ordered the biggest steak dinner they had and a pot of coffee. He decided to have a beer while he waited. Looking around the fairly large room at the different faces. One man's face struck out—Frank Mcpheron! He couldn't believe his eyes for a moment. The last time he had seen McPheron was in South Texas. Although both Lawson, and McCall could both handle themselves in a scrap, they had seen firsthand the damage and punishment McPheron was capable of serving with his bare fists...

McPheron had killed a man in South Texas. The death was ruled accidental. After 49 rounds the holder of bets ran off with the prize money. It seemed the thief was an associate of the man, Frank had killed in the ring. Someone (most likely a law official) was paid to frame Frank for manslaughter and he served three years at Huntsville. McCall was there doing a two year sentence. They became friends, watching each others back on a daily basis. He'd told McCall that he wanted the man responsible, vowed to find him someday, and make him pay for his sins! For McCall the feeling was too familiar...

Lawson had finished his steak dinner and was enjoying his coffee when a big hand came down on his shoulder. He attempted to stand, but couldn't move from the force of the big hand holding him in his seat. Lawson looked up as the grip eased from his shoulder. Frank Mcpheron appeared, upside down, a crooked smile on his long face.

"Wreck, ol' boy, 'wondered when I'd ever see you again!"

Mcpheron stepped around, took a seat at the small table with Lawson. Frank McPheron had short-dark hair, thick neck. Had the jawbone of a horse, and a wide back lined with muscular definition. His fists were sledge-hammers and his cold blue-gray eyes weren't for looking into—unless you were considered a friend.

"It's good t'a see y'a Frank, said Lawson. How y'a been?"

"Been fine, just fine" said Frank.

Lawson got right to it...

"Me 'n Lou' got real problems old friend. I... well, we... shit, I don't even know where to start!"

"I already know all about it, said Frank. I heard about the wanted poster on Storm in Santa Fe. 'Got a friend there 'said Luis was headed west looking for you. The rest I learned after my arrival here in town."

"They're gonna try t'a hang 'im," said Lawson.

"I know, said Frank. I saw that U.S. Marshal and his two deputies ride into town this evening. And that Judge, Neusom? I've heard some stories about that one. He's a hanger—They call him "The Noose!"

CHAPTER 3

"I know, said Lawson. Luis told me he'd heard of him too. I've got to get him the hell out of that jail quick!"

They spoke quietly for a few more minutes, then paid the bill and left the diner. Frank had rented a room at the DESERT MOON HOTEL the day before Lawson had arrived. They decided to continue the conversation back in Frank's room.

McPheron pulled out a bottle of Bourbon Whiskey and poured both of them a glass. He told Lawson about the big prize fight coming up in Denver the next month. It was a best out of three with some heavy ranked fighters coming in to take a shot at the $5000 purse where bones would break and blood would spill!

Lawson began filling him in on a plan he'd been working on...

...After a final round of whiskey Lawson said goodnight and retired to his room. In his room he pulled back the thin curtain and took one last look up the length of the street below his window. He unbuckled his pistol rigs, then sat down on the bed, took off his boots and laid back. He slept with a .45 in his hand.

In the gloom of the jail cell McCall lay awake, thinking;

"These bastards are really gonna try'n hang me."

The thought was really starting to irritate him. 'Matters of fact he was getting downright madder than hell! He'd been through too much for it to end this way. He stood and went over to the barred window, gazed out at the dark-blue clouds concealing the bright glow of a silvery moon behind them. A coyote was yapping in the distance and McCall's mind began to drift away as he looked out at the heavens and earthy terrain possibly for the last time. The fullness of the moon was revealed as the curtain of clouds separated; its bright glow casting shadows at different point's about the open desert plain. He stared up at the ominous ball until his eyes became hazed over, then he went back to the bunk and lay back. He didn't want to think about her right now, couldn't afford too, but sometimes she just came upon him and there was nothing he could do to stop it.

"Sleep, he told himself, sleep..."

A different place in time...

Luis Daniel McCall had survived the horrific battles of the Civil War of 1861-1865. Having been forced to fight for the southern troops, against his brother's of the Northern Union Army, he had fought like a predator killing with precision and accuracy the same way he'd learned to shoot growing up in the rolling hills of South-Western Ohio with the rifle his father had left to him when he died in the winter of "58". Fighting as a soldier of the Confederacy had not been a choice he'd made of his own free will. Although his views differed from those in his native land of the North, his allegiance was still to the Union. That all changed when he was in route northward from South Carolina. He was intercepted by Confederate Troops and woven into the fabric of the Rebel Gray Coat Army. He avoided hanging by the neck as a traitor only by swearing to fight with them in their cause to defect against the army of the Northern Yankees. The next five years of his life would be spent on a wide battle ground of killing and bloodshed as his personal battle to return home to his native land in the north intensified with each bloody confrontation. Anyone who opposed or attempted to detour him from that, his most important mission, would die swiftly by the sword of his most inner free will. He had earned a new name given by his fellow soldiers; he would be known to them as *Storm* McCall among his fellow troopers. In the last year of the war, Luis had met up with a man by the name of, Lawson, from Austin Texas. Lawson became like a brother to him, and after hearing Luis's story he appointed himself an adopted guardian over Luis. Alongside him they cut a bloody path across many battlefields, confronting the enemy, forcing their way toward the north to Luis's native soil. Lawson was so determined to see him through the war that he became a wreckless and wild-eyed killing machine. It was not long before some of the fellow soldiers began to call him *Wreckless* Lawson. The man was deadly fast with his Colt Army .44 which he carried in a flap holster and was a superior sharpshooter with any rifle. There was little hesitation in his willingness to kill a man or in the methods he would use to stop the advancing charge of a potential enemy. Luis knew Lawson wasn't crazy. Like himself the man just wanted the damn war to end so he could get back to his home in, Texas, and he wasn't about to let one of those Yank' bastards stand in his path! McCall figured him for a man who had his own skeletons.

After what seemed like a lifetime journey, witnessing countless deaths and destruction, Luis McCall found his feet touching his home soil once again. It was the spring of 1865 and the war of the states was over. He had gone home, back to the farm he had grown up on in the rolling hills outside of Old Chillicothe. It was then that he learned of the deaths of his two brothers, both soldiers of the Union Army, their grave markers laid to rest beside their father in the family cemetery under the big shady oak where the three brothers had played when they were children. A time gone forever... living now only in his heart like a reel of scenes, black and white, clicking frames and silent images within the hazy corridors of his mind. The war had left its scars on everyone. With the passing of her husband and the deaths of three sons on the battlefront, the wounds had been too deep for Luis's mother. Lacking the hands required to physically work and maintain their land, alone, she could not manage. Her last hope had been for her remaining son, Luis to return home from the war. Three years had passed and still no word, leaving her to the final conclusion that; he too had fallen to the sword and that death had taken the last of her sons. She'd imagined His lifeless body laying beneath the drifting pillars of rifle and Canon smoke in a distant and foreign land. She died in the fall of 1863. Ellen Ruth McCall had kept a close journal which her only remaining son now held clasped tightly in his hands. It revealed to him all of her sufferings, and losses... Events he could not have foreseen nor foretold. At his feet were four headstones marking the graves of his father, mother, and two brothers: Robert Arlan McCall

Ellen Ruth (Harris) McCall
David Lee McCall
Robert Arlan McCall Jr

By 1867 Luis had rebuilt the broken property and had begun to establish some productivity again by farming the land and selling his grains to whole sellers and merchants in the local area and surrounding counties. Rebuilding had polished his skills as a carpenter. He hired out his labor around the county and soon earned a respected name as a quality builder, and crafted carpenter. With two full-time hired hands he was able to manage the farm and livestock while pursuing his work as a carpenter and developing his ideas in structural designs. In the summer of 1868 he became reacquainted with a past love. She was the daughter of a prominent doctor who had studied his practice in the Ohio region, but had moved away and relocated taking his family to Chicago ten years earlier. Although he had not seen her for many years his attraction to Jennifer Diane Fray remained the same as it always had been—instant. She had amazing wit, charm, and an amusing sense of humor; not to mention a beauty that was rare to behold. Everything she was filled his emptiness and what he had lost of himself during the war. For her, Luis was the answer to her heart and the man who would make her become a woman.

At first she had seemed a bit of a spoil to him having been raised in the lap of luxury with very little want. He soon found that she'd grown up in the shadowed background of a father and mother who had very little if any time for her. They were eccentrics, members of the social elite working, constantly, toward a higher position within the ranks of the social order of the community and those of political influence to them in the county and V.I.P in the states of Illinois, and Ohio—Not to mention growing interest in Washington D.C.—Senators—Judges etc.

Luis and Jenn were married on July 3, 1869 in Old Chillicothe Ohio. In that same year Luis developed a new building design that would soon revolutionize the farming industry. It was what he was calling the Grain Elevator. These "Elevators" that would touch the sky, could contain and store thousands of bushels of grains in storage bins and compartments throughout the upper levels of the towering structures. The buildings were massive in size and impressive to say the least. It didn't take long for the news to spread to the West. Farmers in North Dakota, Montana, and Nebraska were in great need of these new structures, and soon he was receiving offers to build them throughout locations in the Mid-West and North-West regions of the country. He hired the men necessary to construct the first design and then he and his new wife headed west to Nebraska. That year he erected five elevators which were being dubbed Prairie Cathedrals because of their massive size and what they represented to the western farmers. A man from Indiana, Joe Clemens, had heard about McCall's success. He was a former friend to Gerald, and Lynda Fray the "acting" parents of Luis's wife, Jennifer. Clemens had courted Jenn at one time, but that had ended when she'd refused his proposal of marriage. Not long after that McCall entered into her life. When Jennifer accepted his hand, Clemens was outraged and had set himself to interfere. One day Clemens had seen Jenn in town and had gone out of his way to harass her and had smacked her on her backside as she climbed into her buggy. She had asked him to quit behaving this way and that they could still be friends. Clemens would not leave well enough alone and told her that if he could not have her, then that Gray-coat-rebel trash and traitor to the Union, Luis McCall, would never have her! Jenn, knowing better, had chosen not to tell Luis of the incident with Clemens. Clemens was already turning some locals against Luis with his onslaught of fabricated lies. Even Jenn's parents were beginning to form judgments against the man—the same man whom they'd blessed with the hand of their daughter. The next afternoon Luis went into town. He heard about what Clemens had done and sought to find him. When he found Clemens standing with a group of men in front of the local pub he beat and nearly strangled him to death with his bare hands. Luis had warned Clemens on several occasions, but Clemens would not take heed to his advice. Finally, after having had enough of it...

Luis was a strong, physically capable man, and most would have avoided the confrontation. Clemens would not forget the incident and swore revenge against McCall. He would make it a point to discredit the name, Luis McCall at every given opportunity. After five years in the West, Luis sold, McCall Elevators, to Martin Owens, a man from

Montana. He named the new company, Montana Elevator Co. and continued to carry a good name and reputation (as Luis had intended) as he dotted the Western Scape with McCall's Prairie Cathedrals. The dream Luis McCall had envisioned and believed in. The time he'd spent in the west had had a profound effect on Luis. The open land and vast panoramic scape possessed a spirit of its own. Soon that spirit was calling him back. Though he had never been to Texas he'd heard enough about it to know that it was a vast land of cattle ranges, and land could be bought there dirt cheap. The way he looked at it; he'd done just about everything else so why not try his hand in cattle. Jenn loved the idea of a Texas ranch and began right away to help Luis in his planning. Come spring they would leave for Texas. They had only been back at the Ohio farm for a week when Joe Clemens heard about McCall's plans. Clemens enlisted two men to go out to the farm and cause trouble for McCall; "He was a dammed Reb traitor, and he deserved what he got!" Clemens had told the two hired trouble makers. Early the next morning, covered in black ash and soot, Luis brought their dead bodies into town. Both were killed by multiple bullets holes placed in their bodies. Jenn sat quietly on the perch of the wagon. She too was covered in black soot from the horrendous labor of trying to put out the blazing fire.

"They burned my house down and tried to shoot me in the back!" he'd yelled in the street. "Tell Joe Clemens when I find him he's gonna get the same...Tell him McCall said; he's a—DEAD MAN!" He rolled the bodies out of his wagon into the dust of the street as the towns people looked on. Three days later he took his wife and a wagon to carry their possessions, then started on the trail for Texas. Luis was financially secure. His business dealings had been sound, yielding him great returns on his investments. Taking the train had been an option, but both he and his wife had wanted to see the open country. Traveling by wagon would give them that opportunity. In Texas he would have a new start. And God knew if another man ever messed with his wife again—He would, no doubt, kill him!

After nearly three months on the trail, just twenty miles into the great state of Texas six men rode into their camp. With masked faces they took Luis at gunpoint. Jenn pleaded with Clemens not to kill Luis, but they shot him anyway. Clemens had tried to force her to leave with him; he'd even slapped her face red—still she refused him. In desperation she broke away from his grasp and went splashing across a shallow stream when a single bullet hit her in the middle of her back. She died there, face down, in that rippling stream. Her last thought being that of the man she loved—Luis McCall.

The other men riding with Clemens hadn't counted on this. They didn't sign up to kill no woman! All they knew was; A man named McCall had run off with Clemens's girl against her will, and Joe Clemens was going to kill the man and bring the girl back unharmed. None of them stuck around—they lit a shuck and they was gone! Some say it was pure chance that led the Texas Gunman, Wreck Lawson, along that winding stream that day. But it wasn't —It was fate; a course of destiny. A cross road that once, again, would lead the two men along the same path. Lawson patched the bullet holes, three of them in varied calibers, and brought McCall back from the grip of death. During the war of the states, Lawson had acquired a degree of medic skills from patching up the wounds of his fellow soldiers. The gunman took McCall to his side and began to teach him the law of the West—The law of the gun! McCall learned quick; he spent endless hours stripping his Colt .44 from leather until the iron became a part of him. He caught up with one of the men who'd rode in, Clemens's bunch just outside of El Paso, and put six bullets in him before he could cross over the Rio Grande into Old Mexico.

Ruled manslaughter, McCall spent two years behind prison walls thinking on vengeance and the endless depths of hatred a man could experience. He'd find Clemens someday, and the others, and when he did he'd put a bullet right through their—COLD YELLA HEARTS!

McCall was awakened early to the sound of hammering; only one thing that could be! This was becoming just a little too real. His heart raced and he swallowed a lump that was caught in his throat. He sat and placed his boots on the floor, then walked to the barred window and stood there as the sun was rising over the desert painting the horizon in red-rose mixed with turquoise, then the deep-purple of twilight. The colors faded as they reached to the upper heavens where the full moon was still visible in its ghostly glow. His memory drifted to places in his mind; the many miles he'd come to find a new life. He couldn't help but think of Jenn and how she had been taken from him. He thought of Death...

If Death really were an entity, dressed in black, heeling a sharp bladed sickle for his harvest of souls, then McCall couldn't understand why the Reaper would take her. She had never harmed a soul in her life. He thought of Death as a coward and he wanted to meet that bastard in the street, face to face, and put a bullet through his sadistic-yell'a heart!

Lawson was awake in the hotel room. He stood looking down from the window of his room at the men hammering on the wood frame of the killing machine. He felt an overwhelming desire to shoot them for that! Not that there weren't evil men who deserved to die that way, but, Luis McCall was no evil man and, Lawson had never known a better man, or friend. He felt better knowing that, Frank McPheron was in town and was willing to help before they got a chance to stretch, Luis's neck.

The streets were cramming up with wagons and people —most of whom were here for the big show; or "showdown" is how, Lawson thought of it.

A loud knock came upon the door. Lawson had both Colts leveled on the door, hammers eared back.

"Who is it?"

"Frank McPheron," came a voice from outside the door.

"Come on in," said, Lawson.

McPheron opened the door and stepped into the room with a big smile on his face.

"Show time, ready?"

"Yeah, let's go."

They made their way down the red-carpeted stair case to the main lobby of the hotel then exited the building. The streets were already alive with the thick of people, the place becoming almost circus-like as wagons and booths were being set up for peddlers selling their merchandise. One wagon was transformed into a makeshift stage where a man and woman were standing selling elixir and medicines of some sort in dark glass bottles. Another was presenting a show of puppets in some crazy re-enactment of a robbery and chase scene. Lawson, and, McPheron just looked at each other, shook their heads as they moved along the street.

"Wow, this town is going to get crazy real quick!" stated Lawson.

"I think you're right ol' buddy, replied McPheron. We should probably lay low for the next couple of days."

"'Couldn't agree more," said Lawson after a moment of thought.

Two days later...

The news of a *notorious* gunfighter being in Yuma was spreading fast; a double hanging, and a famous gunslinger all on the same ticket? Hell, who could refuse that offer? By the looks of the growing crowd not many could.

Lawson, and McPheron had stuck to their plan for the last couple of days, moving about the streets only when deemed necessary. Judge William Neusome "The Noose" was scheduled to arrive this morning on the train from Santa Fe. Lawson had kept an eye on the U.S. Marshal Henry Blake and his two "hired law dogs". They had made no secrets about the fact that they knew who he was also, keeping steady eyes on him whenever he, and McPheron passed along the streets. One question that had been on both of their minds was: Why hadn't they moved Luis and the other prisoner out to Yuma Territorial Prison. It was true that in the past the town of Yuma had held regular hangings, but for the past five years condemned prisoners were transported to the territorial prison for the handing down of execution. Lawson had a feeling in his gut. Something wasn't right... Hell, nothing about it felt right and McPheron agreed. At 9am Lawson, and McPheron had just came from seeing McCall at the jail, and were now heading to the HOLLIDAY DINER to grab some breakfast and a pot of coffee when Sheriff Compton rounded a corner, suddenly, and almost bumped, face to face, with Lawson. Lawson stepped back with a quick jerk, his left hand flinched toward his nickel-plated .45.

"Why, if it ain't Wreck Lawson. I've been meaning to talk to you..."

"What about, sheriff?" asked Lawson.

"That shooting over at the Dragons Breath the other day... I know you're not responsible, but I'm going to need you to fill out a statement. Seems you and the deceased man had had a prior disagreement of sorts. The killing is under investigation." Lawson tucked his hand inside his vest front and hooked it with his thumb and forefinger. Compton flinched back, quickly, thinking Lawson was going for a gun.

"When, sir?" asked Lawson.

"What?" asked Compton.

"When should I make the statement?" replied Lawson.

"Oh! Yes, of course. How's about right after the hearing today?"

"That will be fine sir," said Lawson gesturing as some sightly speaking gentleman (Lawson could be diplomatic on occasion)

Compton took a long stare into Lawson's eyes for a moment; the lawman had a slight look of confusion on his face.

"You wouldn't be having any crazy notions would y'a? I mean about yer friend in the jail there. 'Could possibly hang y'a know..."

"'Got no crazy notions sheriff, said Lawson. Just wanna see justice served is all."

"Well, there's plenty 'a law in town today. 'Hate t'a see anybody try'n bust that fella' out'a there—'Be a big mistake! 'Got'a get to the jail, he finished..."

Compton looked at McPheron, then back to Lawson again.

"You fellas watch y'er step."

Compton stepped around them and proceeded along the boardwalk toward the YUMA JAIL.

"What in Hell was that?" asked Frank with a wide-eyed expression while puzzling over the identity of the man he'd just, previously, thought was Wreck Lawson.

"Oh, said Lawson. I'm just practicing for when I run for the U.S. Senate," he said with a wide grin.

"Shit, you got'ta be kidding me!" said McPheron, then smacked Lawson on the back with his big hand. Frank laughed until he had tears in his eyes. Lawson didn't really think it had been all that funny.

What had started out as a slight glare, the morning sun was now turning into a white-hot-seer as it rose into the sky above the town. It was going to be a hot one in Yuma to say the least and anything caught out on those desert plains was going to get to know the meaning of survival real quick. As for Lawson, and McPheron, they were seated in a nice shady corner of the HOLLIDAY DINER having flapjacks, bacon, and hot coffee. The table where they sat was positioned in a corner away from the others (which is precisely why they chose it) making it much easier to discuss their plans without anyone overhearing. They took their time finishing breakfast, sipping coffee, and being casual as the clock ticked away another hour.

"What do you say we go down to the livery and check the horses? Asked Lawson. It'l give us a little more time to discuss things and get a feel for the town."

"Okay, sounds like a good idea to me," said Frank.

With that the two men paid their bill and exited the establishment stepping out into the dust of the Main street. Yuma had a courthouse; It had been established before the territorial prison had taken over jurisdiction in the region. It was a white two-story building with wide stairs leading up to a set of thick doors. On the side of the building a wooden frame had been built from 2x4 pine lumber—A killing machine capable of killing a man by the use of a rope and his own body weight when pulled tightly up around a man's neck, snapping it and cutting off oxygen to the brain. It would render the victim unconscious thus rendering death. A crude means of execution, yet for its time, the method was very effective.

...At the livery stables, Lawson had found that the horses were being taken good care of. His horse, Nightmare was being kept in a private stall away from the rest of the stock including McCall's animal, Red Horse. Lawson had had a good reason for naming that tall black stallion, Nightmare —that was one mean critter! And it didn't matter, horse flesh, or man flesh, it was all the same to that crazy animal! Except it wouldn't mess with, Red Horse much because that Red Sorrel had a temperament of its own. The two animals got along pretty well most of the time. But, when left alone they had to be separated from each other and any other livestock or some unfortunate cowboy would likely end up with a dead horse to tend too and nobody wanted that!

The middle of town was beginning to crawl with squirming maggots anticipating, as the hour grew nearer, that moment when they would, finally, squirm around the dead flesh of the two men who would be hanging in the sun—wilting... rotting...

As Lawson, and McPheron exited the livery stables, a clock high above the courthouse doors chimed, once, signaling the hour of the day: It was 9am. Within minutes the whistle of a train could be heard coming in from the distance. It grew louder... louder... until, finally, it came to rest at the station and released its steaming hot breath onto the platform with a loud sigh of relief. Lawson, and McPheron spun, quickly, to face each other—"The Noose!"

The first segment of the hearing was scheduled to begin at 10 am. At 9:45 am five men came out of the YUMA JAIL and began walking in the direction of the courthouse. Leading the pack was U.S. Marshal Henry Blake followed by McCall who was shackled in steel chains and irons clasped at his wrists and ankles. The Blacksmith had been called in to secure the bracelets with steel pins and an eight pound sledge. Both, McCall, and Kelsey had been custom fitted with the new jewelry. Walking behind McCall were two men dressed in black, both toting double-barreled 12 gauge shotguns which were poking straight into McCall's back. Tagging along in the back was the local law enforcement—Charlie Compton.

"Killer!" came a shout from a nearby crowd of onlookers.

"Hang that bastard!" yelled another man, throwing his fist up in the air.

The spectators who had come to town for the hanging were beginning to get excited.

"Thief!"

"Woman killer!"

Evidently the rumors had been circling town for the past several days. Hell, to them, McCall was already guilty, but it wasn't the first time the man had been persecuted for a crime he didn't commit.

From across the street Lawson could see that his partner was mad and he could tell that McCall had had enough of this shit! From out of nowhere a young boy came running up toward McCall, a wooden gun in his hand. He threw it out and pointed it;

"Bang! Bang! Bang! I'm faster than you mister!" shouted the youth. McCall turned quickly toward the boy, snarled loudly at him through clenched teeth. The boy jumped and stumbled back onto the seat of his pants stirring up a cloud of dust. He looked as if he were going to cry. He jumped up and ran away to the other side of the street where he fell down on the edge of the boardwalk and stared back at McCall in frozen silence. McCall and the armed escorts approached the courthouse. He was turned onto a brick walk-way and pushed to a side entrance of the building. The door opened and the group of men including, McCall, disappeared inside it.

"Well , I guess this is it," said Lawson.

"Yep, said Frank, it doesn't look good ol' boy."

"Nope, said Lawson, it sure doesn't. We're gonna haf'ta try'n change that."

The men walked across the street to the courthouse. Shuffling through the busy street, they made the stairs of the courthouse and entered the building. The court room wasn't very big, and most of the seating had already been taken, but there were still a few seats empty toward the back. The two men squeezed themselves in and sat down. The room was loud with voices, people talking back and forth. One of the stories going around was that McCall had murdered a man in New Mexico, then ran away with his wife whom he later raped and assaulted. Word was; somewhere along the trail McCall, and Kelsey hooked up... word was; McCall was in on the slaying of the family of settlers. But, if anyone had known McCall, they would have known that the man was innocent and he would have killed that no good piece of shit Kelsey himself if given a proper length of rope!

A crowd stood at the back of the room spilling out the

open double doors and onto the courthouse steps. A door suddenly opened from behind the judge's podium and three men entered into the room.

"All rise to the Honorable Judge William Neusom" stated the Bailiff. Neusome seated himself behind the judge's desk. The other two men, one being the prosecutor, and the other a defense attorney, seated themselves behind opposite tables. The prosecutor gave a curt nod signaling Neusome that he was ready to proceed with the hearing. The Bailiff was signaled and McCall was brought into the court room area with chains dragging the floor between his ankles. They made a, metallic, rattling sound as he limped, awkwardly toward the table where a man he'd never met before stated that he was there to defend him. McCall just looked at the guy, said nothing, and then seated himself in the empty chair next to his "newly found savior."

The charges were read; formally charging McCall with the crime. Then, the prosecution brought in their first witness. A woman was brought into the court and seated at the witness stand. She was wearing a black dress and had a veil pulled down over her face. She was sworn in by the bailiff and then told to raise the veil from her face. Lawson leaned forward, mouth open, and his eyes just about to bug out of his head at the realization of who this woman was—Marla Carlson! McCall was having the same reaction and Lawson couldn't believe what his eyes were seeing.

"Son of a bitch!" said Lawson, out loud, not realizing he'd said it.

"Order!" Barked the judge with a smack of the gavel and an intent eye glaring out into the audience right at Lawson. "How in the hell did she..?" thought Lawson to himself. The last time he'd seen her was during that shoot out in the Cantina in Mexico. He'd figured her for dead.

The prosecutor questioned her and she gave testimony to the fact that Storm McCall was the man who had killed her husband in cold blood in Santa Fe, New Mexico. She swore that she had witnessed the whole incident and stated that McCall was a cold-blooded murderer who deserved to die.

"You lying little tramp!" thought McCall to himself, his blood boiling. If she wasn't such a little floozy to begin with none of this ever would have happened!

Turning... McCall, found Lawson in the audience and threw him a hard glare. It was now apparent; this was how she would get even with Lawson for the incident in Mexico. She continued with her statement... glaring at Lawson,contemptuously, while pointing a finger at McCall, positively identifying him as the man who had murdered her husband.

"Why you two-timin'—bald-faced—lyin' little Hell Cat!" Lawson mumbled to himself under his breath.

McCall's Defense Attorney asked Marla Carlson only a few questions, which only further pointed a *guilty* finger at McCall. It was a set up designed to convict him and seal his fate. Finally, the judge asked her to step down from the stand. She pulled the veil back down over her face then stood, walked past McCall, and Lawson, without a single glance like "the mourning widow, dressed in black, on her way to bury the dead!" McCall got the feeling that it was his funeral she was planning to attend—and he was right!

...The way she had it planned; Lawson would be next in line for a dirt nap...

She walked straight down the middle of the isle and exited through the midst of people who were gathered around the front doors, and didn't look back...

CHAPTER 4

"Hang him!"

"Murderer!" came shouts from the, crowded courtroom.

"Order, Order, Order in this court!"

The angry voice of William Neusome elevated in the room as he slammed the gavel repeatedly against the hardwood top of the judge's podium. The hissing faded to near silence. The judge turned red-faced and stared, contemptuously, into the crowd of onlookers. McCall was asked to take the stand where he gave a short account of the incident that took place in Santa Fe. He knew that if he implemented Lawson, in any way, they'd both swing. From the witness stand McCall could see for the first time that Frank McPheron was seated right next to Lawson. McPheron just winked and gave a curt nod of his head. McCall was asked to step down and take a seat. After a few minutes of pause the judge cleared his throat and asked the defense attorney if he had any further witnesses. Lawson started to stand, but then sat back down, quickly. At this point he couldn't afford to be jailed for any reason. He knew that McCall would be lost to this hanging party, and he'd be next!

"The prosecution rests, then!"

"I object!" cried out McCall's attorney. "We have no grounds to close."

"Objection! Yelled the prosecutor. "They have no witnesses your honor!"

Neusome's eyes moved from the defense, then back to the prosecution...

"Well, then there's nothing left to do; we'll recess for jury verdict—that is all."

He smacked the gavel down onto the desk and everyone stood. The bailiff directed the jury into the back room where Neusome followed behind them, then he closed the door.

The court room was emptied with people flowing out through the double doors and onto the street. McCall was escorted back to the jail to await the jury's decision, but he already knew that that decision was going to be guilty and there was no doubt in his mind about it.

The two, hired law dogs (men in black) escorted McCall back to the jail poking him occasionally, in the back, with a sawed-off 12 gauge shotgun. The men were big, above six-foot in height. They both wore long black Slickers, and black wide-brimmed Stetsons that further shadowed the beard growth on both of their faces.

"They're gonna stretch your neck McCall and there ain't a damn thing you're going to be able to do about it," said one of the men. The other man just laughed at his partner's statement, then poked McCall in the back with a shotgun and gave him a push forward with the barrels.

"Yeah, guess you didn't know who that girl was back there in Santa Fe did you McCall? (It was the other man's turn to cackle now) You're just about a stupid bastard ain't y'ew, boy!"

"You don't know what the hell y'er talking' about, came McCall. 'Ain't killed nobody, yet..."

Both men looked at each other, then burst out in laughter!

"What the hell do you mean—yet?!" said the first man, coming to a serious and gritty tone of voice.

"You done did all the killin' y'er gonna' do mister! So shut y'er mouth and just keep walkin' before y'ew piss me off!"

"'Heard he was supposed to be some kind of bad ass with a gun," said the other man.

"Well, if he is he sure as hell don't look like it now, does he?"

"Nope, he sure as hell don't!"

Both men were laughing. One a cackling hyena, the other a braying jackass. To McCall they sounded like a couple of muley-mouthed farm boys; all mouth and no ass to back it! They reminded him of a couple of boys he knew back in Ohio when he was a young'n; It was summer... McCall was working on a farm bailing hay for the two boys' father. They'd been giving him a hard way to go. One day he'd finally had enough of it and kicked the crapp out of both of them right in front of their old man. After the fight their father told McCall that his two boys had had it coming for a long time and that he was proud of him for standing his own ground. McCall never forgot that day and right now he'd like to take these two to the school of hard knocks and teach them both some real manners. Yeah, they acted tough, but it wasn't anything a hard-knuckled fist through the front teeth wouldn't fix!

They arrived at the jail, then, once again, the cell door was slammed shut and McCall sat down on the wooden bunk. If something was going to save him it would have to be soon...

The Ferrell Gang Hideout

The gang members could be heard, talking from behind a group of large boulders surrounded by tall growths of thick brush. Five horses were ground staked at the edge of a hidden, narrow path leading to the inside where the gang was located. Smoke was rising into the air from a small fire, the gang seated in the midst talking amongst themselves.

"Hey, boss! Why in the hell did that U.S. Marshal and his two hounds haf''ta get in on the situation anyhow? Hell, we had it under control," said Gene Antrim.

"Yeah, that's what Carter thought too, replied West Ferrell. I guess they're just trying to keep everything official like so's they can hang the bastard without any legal problems. Either way they're gonna' hang McCall. Anyhow, that bastard Lawson is the one crawling under my skin right now. He's already killed two of my men."

"Well, actually it was that bartender, Crepps, that killed Mathers..." started his younger brother, Trevor.

"Shut y'er mouth boy! sneered the older brother. Lawsons' the blame! He's the sum bitch ought to be dead not Mathers! He's a piece of horse dung and I'm gonna make sure that he goes out in a box just like his partner, McCall! Speaking of which we need to pay him and that new partner of his, what's his name again..?"

"McPheron, replied Monty Langford."He's one mean son of a bitch; they don't come any tougher. I fought him once..."

There was a moment of hesitation in Langford's voice as

his mind searched those haunting images from the past...

"I've been looking for a chance to pay him back and It looks like the opportunity may have arrived."

A scowl came across Langford's face; a reel of images playing out in his mind; bloody, punishing, resentful images.

"That's not a bad idea now that you mention it stated Ferrell. We might just give you the opportunity to settle that score. And at the same time we'll put that dog, Lawson down for a permanent dirt nap!"

Yuma Jail

"Yep boys, it won't be long now," taunted Sutton. "Soon they'll take that length of hemp rope, then slip it up tight to the side of his neck... and then—Uhkkgg!"

Sutton (mimicking a hanging man) yanked his head to one side; tongue hanging out, eyes bulging. The young deputy thought he would have a little bit of fun poking at the two prisoners, but to McCall he was nothing more than a minor irritation that amounted to the likes of a mosquito bite on his ass!

Earl Kelsey had heard enough of his shit and jumped up, stretched one arm out between the bars and slashed at the cocky little deputy with claw-like fingertips.

"Shut up you big mouthed little' runt before I snap your scrawny little neck! Ain't nobody goin' t'a hang me! It's been tried before! You hear me boy—you hear me!"

Kelsey was mad to the point of insanity! Whining and growling like an animal that had its paw caught in a trap as he rattled the steel door of his cage with fury.

Just then the front door to the jail opened and the sheriff came in with the two hired hounds, both dressed in black.

"They've reached a decision!" shouted Compton. "Billy, open McCall's cell and bring him out!"

Meanwhile...

Lawson, and McPheron had gone back to the *DESERT MOON HOTEL.* They were going over the final steps of the plan they had devised to bust McCall out of the jail and get him the hell out of Yuma before they had a chance to stretch his neck. At Huntsville, Lawson had witnessed his share of hangings. He'd been given the duty of pulling the bodies down after the executions. It wasn't a pretty sight. It was a memory that Lawson had managed to push into the back of his mind. But, there in Yuma, right then, the memory was recalling itself back to him.

From outside the hotel window a commotion was rising from down in the streets. People were beginning to return to the courthouse.

"Well, that didn't take long," said McPheron, gazing out of the second-story window of the hotel room. Lawson joined him at the window. Looking to the opposite end of the street they could see McCall and the law-dogs in route back to the courthouse for the final words of damnation to be passed upon him and sealing his fate to a final doom.

"Wreck," said Frank, "I know you're madder than hell ol' boy."

"Frank, this is my problem. I never should have gotten you involved."

"Too late for that my friend, said McPheron, I'm already involved! so don't insult me if you don't mind."

After a moment of silence Lawson said;

"Sorry Frank, 'shouldn't have said that. I know y'er a friend and a good one—So does Luis."

"We're gonna' figure it out ol' buddy, you'll see, said

Frank. Besides, I came too far not to get a front row seat to the big show if you know what I mean?"

He smacked Lawson on the back, both men chuckled, lightheartedly, at McPheron's humorous statement.

"I know what I have to do Wreck, said Frank. Now is the time—let's do it!"

Lawson handed Frank a stack of greenbacks, Frank tucked the money in his pocket.

"Okay Frank, you know what to do right?"

"Yeah, I've got it!" replied Frank.

The two men stood at the window and watched as the Ferrell gang thundered into town streaming a trail of dust behind that was rising from the steel shoes of the various colored beasts that carried the men down the length of the street. The gang reined up in front of the saloon, then dismounted and tethered the horses to the hitch post. The huge cloud of trail dust the horses had created drifted in on the gang like a hot breath from the devils mouth. They pushed through the bat wings and entered the SIDEWINDER SALOON at the middle of town.

"I've got some unfinished business down at the saloon, Frank, I'll see you in a bit," said Lawson.

"I'll be there, said Frank with a nod of his head. You can count on it."

First things first though; Lawson still had to go back to the courthouse and attend for the verdict ruling, so he left Frank's room and made his way down the hallway passing the smiling doves (all of whom were eager to make his acquaintance) but, there was no time for that now. He was surely wishing there was though...

The court room was filling to capacity again and all of the seats were soon taken. Lawson stood at the back of the room just inside the entrance by the double doors. McCall was brought in and seated at the same table. Next came the jurors who found their seats, then sat down, quietly. Judge William Neusome "The Noose" entered the room, then sat down at the judges podium and smacked the gavel down on the wood top with a smack!

"Court is now in session! stated the Bailiff. All rise to the Honorable William Neusome!"

The judge turned his attention towards the jury;

"Have you reached a decision?"

The foreman of the jury stood and said;

"Yes, we have your honor."

There was a moment of silence, then the foreman spoke;

"Guilty—on all counts!"

The crowd broke out with cheers and shouting. Gunfire could be heard from outside the courtroom as people cheered the outcome of the verdict.

"The prisoner will rise..." stated the judge. "You have been found guilty... therefore I sentence you to hang by the neck until you are dead! May you burn in agony in the eternal flames of Hell for your sins! Now, do you have anything to say..?"

Neusome was staring down the end of his nose at McCall... the room grew silent except for some inaudible chatter...

"'Only got one thing to say," said McCall: "See you all at the party—And you're all invited!"

He stared, intently, into the eyes of Neusome, then turned around to face the sneering faces of the people who'd gathered in the room; ugly faces full of hate and contempt!

Lawson turned on one heel and slid out the door as the crowd's attention was on McCall who was now being shoved back toward the door from which he'd entered the court room.

The sun was simmering high above now, like a fireball in a blazing glow of white-heat and anything alive was trying to find shelter from its deadly assault. With both hands, Lawson pushed open the bat-wing doors and entered into the dim interior of the saloon. Tobacco smoke floated in thin sheet-like clouds about the room. Three men stood along the front of the bar and each turned to glance his direction as he approached its curved end.

Ferrell and his gang were seated nearby at a couple of tables cackling like a bunch of hyenas. The noise level at the tables dropped several notches as Lawson's presence became known to them, then came a still silence in the air...

"Whiskey barkeep," said Lawson, with an ice-cold stare. "And keep your hands where I can see 'em..."

The bartender approached him with a bottle of whiskey in his hand, shaking, like a lone-leaf on a tree branch that was clinging to the last seconds of its puny life. He almost dropped the bottle off the edge of the bar...

"Shot glass... " he said to the barkeep with the same, intent look. When the barkeep returned, Lawson said;

"leave it."

Lawson filled the glass, himself, as the bartender slowly backed away. Glancing back at the tables where the Ferrell gang was setting, Lawson almost choked on the whiskey when he saw the woman who was setting on West Ferrell's lap—Marla Carlson! She was giggling in Ferrell's ear. The rest of Ferrell's men glared back at Lawson like a pack of wolves. They looked meaner than a pit full of rattlesnakes ready to strike at any moment! Lawson gave a devilish grin, then turned back to the bar and filled his glass with more whiskey.

"Hang 'em high!" shouted Gene Antrim, then he let out with a laugh that sounded like a wounded coyote. The rest of Ferrell's men followed suit.

Lawson's eyes stayed fixed on the bartender. He kept his right hand near his Colt, watching Antrim as he moved across the room and took a seat at a table just behind him. In the big mirror that spanned the back wall of the bar he could see the faces of the men seated at the two tables. He threw back the whiskey, then hissed at the bartender (who was now quickly stepping away from him)

"It stinks of shit in this place" said Lawson, with disgust.

"What!" snapped Trevor Ferrell. "What the hell did you just say!"

West Ferrell pushed the woman off his knee sending her off onto the floor in a clamber.

"Get off''a me bitch!"

Marla Carlson rolled onto her rump, arms propped out behind her on the floor... hair tangled across her face and dress crumpled up to her waist showing the garter straps hooked at each thigh.

Lawson sniffed in, deeply, again...

"'Smells like shit!"

The three men who were standing at the bar began to find another place to be. The attitudes in the room were beginning to turn serious—real fast!

"Hey Lawson...'thought I told you to get out of town!"

Without turning, Lawson replied...

"Leave things be Ferrell. You'll get t'a see the sun rise another day."

"You threatening my brother you sum-bitch!" shouted Trevor Ferrell.

Trevor came sliding up, fast, on Lawson's left and began

staring, intently, at the side of his face.

"Yeah, what do you mean Lawson?" asked West.

"I mean; some things are just better left alone."

As Lawson was speaking, West Ferrell, and Monty Langford stood up from the table and began walking toward him...

"I mean... (continued Lawson) it's like a mad dog got his hackles raised and some shit-for-brains keeps pawing at his grub; sooner or later he's gonna get bit!"

"Well now..." said Trevor, cocking his head side to side like a chicken, wide-eyed and clucking as he spoke—"I don't see no hackles!"

Lawson turned his head, slightly and pinned the younger brother with a cold blue-ice glare.

"Make a move boy..." said, Trevor, tapping the butt of his revolver. That's when he saw the rage welling up in, Lawson's twitching eye.

"Oh shit!" said, Trevor, to himself, but, Lawson heard it too.

The glimmer of chromed-steel flashed in, West Ferrell's eyes. The big blade came down and pierced through the back of, West Ferrell's hand with a sickening shuck! The tip of the blade sunk deep into the wood of the bar-top pinning, Ferrell's hand to it, flattening it out like a frog that just got stabbed through the middle of its back. Ferrell screamed bloody murder when the blade of the big, Bowie nearly cut his hand in two. The blade flashed again when, Lawson withdrew it and came spinning around...

Antrim was going for his gun; he'd almost unleashed it when the shiny-steel-blade punctured through his larynx and continued through to the back of his throat stopping at the handle guards with a wet sounding—shuck! Lawson quickly released his fisted grip from the handle. Antrim's eyeballs were popping out of their sockets as he worked, clumsily with both hands, to dislodge the wicked weapon, the long razor-tip protruding out the back of his neck. He tripped backwards, crashed through the chair he'd just been sitting in, then landed on his back in the middle of the floor where he jerked and flopped like a fish on the shoreline of a river trying to find water.

Lawson had continued spinning to his right where Trevor Ferrell came rounding into his view... When Lawson's boot heels locked in place his left-side Colt was in his hand, cocked and leveled right between Trevor's eyes. The younger Ferrell brother had just cleared leather with his Schofield and was suddenly staring down the muzzle of a nickel-plated Peacemaker. His mind screamed—Noooo..! just as it was blown out the back of his skull! The big man, Monty Langford, ran out the back door.

West Ferrell was bent over at the waist holding his hand and bleeding like a slit pig. Ferrell dropped to his knees where his eyes caught the shadow of Lawson's big Colt painted black on the floor and pointed straight at him.

"Don't move boy!" growled Lawson through clenched teeth. His eyes cut quickly to the barkeep.

"You make one move toward that shotgun and I'll kill you mister!"

Ferrell looked up, his face contorted with dripping sweat.

"I'm gonna kill you for this Lawson," he said through clenched teeth.

"Maybe, but not today," said Lawson. "Now stand up—yell'a!"

CHAPTER 5

The bartender backed away quickly with his hands raised high over his head. Marla Carlson was running around the room as though she were trying to find a place to hide. She ran up to one of the men who had previously stood the bar and grabbed him by his arm, but he pushed her away and she stumbled back nearly falling down. She reminded Lawson of a vending monkey; the kind you'd find somewhere like, Italy, or Greece. Well, it was one of those foreign places. Anyways... he'd heard some strange stories about those funny acting little monkeys...

Her eyes were searching the room for someone to help her; the next victim to throw his soul into her tattered-tin-cup!

"Barkeep... get your ass over here!"

The man walked toward him, slowly, creeping.

"Reach inside my vest... pull the badge out and pin it on

my shirt."

The barkeep did as he was told.

"That's real nice," said Lawson, out loud, as he looked down at the tin star pinned to his shirt.

Crepps just stood there, staring— frozen.

"Now..."

Lawson leaned in and through a straight-right fist into the barkeeps nose. His head shot back and his body followed, the back of his skull whacked against the hardwood of a round column at the corner of the bar which knocked him out cold. His limp body sounded like a hollow log when it hit the floor.

Lawson looked at Ferrell and smiled—a devilish smile it was! But, then the smile disappeared.

"You're under arrest you peace of shit!"

A chill ran through, Ferrell's body as he stared into Lawson's ice-blue eyes, lifeless and empty. Out the corner of his eye Lawson saw, Marla Carlson running out the bat-wing doors.

"Where's y'er girl headed Ferrell?" asked Lawson.

Ferrell didn't answer, he just stayed there on his knees whimpering and bleeding all over the floor boards. So far the gunshot that Lawson had fired didn't seem to draw any attention from anyone outside the saloon. Guns had been firing in the streets for most of the morning and even now the occasional roar of gunfire could be heard coming from somewhere in town.

Just outside the doors of the saloon came several gunshots, and then a woman screamed. The shrill pitch pierced its way between the doors and into the interior of the saloon. Lawson smiled when he saw the concern on Ferrell's long face. He reached across the bar where a towel lay, snatched it up, and threw it in Ferrell's face.

"Damn you Lawson!" said Ferrell.

"Wrap that around your hand," said Lawson through clenched teeth.

Ferrell did as he was told, then was suddenly being hoisted to his feet from where Lawson had the shoulder fabric of the man's shirt twisted tightly in his fist.

The saloon had cleared out except for two men who had been playing cards at a table and were continuing to do so as though nothing had ever happened. Lawson whispered, snarling in Ferrell's ear;

"Okay, piece of shit, here it is! My friend is in the jail you son-of-a-bitch, and you're gonna' help me break him out— got it?!"

"You're supposed to be the big gunman, Lawson, said Ferrell. Why don't you just walked in there, shoot 'em all to hell, and be the big man everyone in town is saying that you are?"

"You know, that's not a bad idea Ferrell. But, if it's any of your damn business, I really don't take to killing people who don't need it. 'Long as they stay out of my way— Unlike you, piece'a shit...

He pushed the muzzle of his .45 deep into Ferrell's eye socket. Ferrell, froze... white as a ghost and stiffer than a damn California Redwood! With a vicious snarl Lawson said: "Now shut up and move—Boy!"

The man in the cell next to McCall had a name (if anyone cared) Eldon Kelsey had committed his last sin in this world and would soon be finding that his nightmare was only just beginning. Kelsey had spoken to McCall on occasion making sure that he wouldn't forget about him when he made a break for it. McCall had promised he wouldn't forget the man, saying; "I won't..." and that's about all he would say.

It was approaching noon when the thick door swung

open. In came, Sheriff Compton and Billy Sutton with shackles and chains. Compton dropped one set in front of McCall's cell as they went on past. The sheriff sorted through the key ring to unlock the cell where Kelsey was being held. McCall was relieved as the pounding in his chest subsided. As they shackled and chained Kelsey, McCall stared out the window. He thought of her; his heart ached with the guilt that he felt for having not been there to save her, he had always been there, he was remembering a time...

...McCall had gone to Wichita to build his Prairie Cathedral. Jenn had stayed home this time and she'd gotten sick with the fever. The doctor was saying there wasn't much chance that she was going to make it. After three days Luis received a telegraph explaining to him the seriousness of her situation. He boarded the first train heading east. He remembered how the thought of losing her had made him feel and he really didn't know if he could live without her. After a week she, finally, opened her eyes and found him setting there, at her side, as he had been for several days. The doctor had said that it was a miracle she'd survived and it was believed that McCall was the one who had brought her back from certain death. Jenn had believed it as well and had referred to him from that day on as "Her Miracle" always believing that he had saved her.

On the distant horizon, coal-black-clouds were piling high into the air. Flashes of, bright silver lightning webbed the sky, and a low rumble of thunder was rolling in over head...

"'Looks like a storm, thought, McCall to himself; perfect!
Kelsey was shackled and brought out of the cell into the

narrow hall. As they passed by, McCall's cell, Kelsey looked at him all wide-eyed and said; "Don't forget me..."

"I won't," said McCall, and that's all he said.

"Billy, you stay here until they're ready for the other one, instructed Compton. I guess they're goin'ta hang this one and then they'll have what they're callin' a "intermission" between hangings."

Gunfire was heard from somewhere in the street. Compton just figured it as someone excited about the hanging. Just as Compton opened the door to step outside of the jail with his prisoner, a woman screamed. At the same time, Lawson and his prisoner exited the saloon at the other end of the street. A crowd was gathering around a wagon hitched up to a team of horses. Ferrell glanced toward the wagon. He stumbled when he saw Marla Carlson's body. She had been mangled under the horses shod hooves, then thrown under a wagon wheel where her body lay twisted into the spokes like a pretzel. It was hard to make heads or tails of her.

"Damn Ferrell, I think she spooked from the gunfire, said Lawson. Looks like those horses must'a done the same." Ferrell didn't say anything.

"Yep," continued Lawson... "she must'a run right out those saloon doors and right into the path of those crazed horses. Damn shame I tell y'a, she seemed like such a nice gal..."

"Shut up you bastard! said Ferrell. Just shut up!" Lawson pushed the muzzle of the Colt into Ferrell's back forcing him forward and said;

"Get over it!"

It surprised Lawson that the shooting hadn't been detected. He had to take advantage of every edge being given to him if he was going to get McCall's ass out of

Yuma, alive!

A tall-thin man dressed in black and high-top hat was making his way between the people to where Marla Carlson's twisted corpse lay. It was apparent that every bone in her body was broken, including her neck, because her head was turned in the opposite direction looking down the middle of her own back, a puzzled look pulled across her face...

Lawson shuttered at the site of the mortician. He felt the same way as McCall did about them—Ghouls!

Lawson, hurried Ferrell to the front door of the jail.

"Now, talk and make it good or I'll splatter you all over the wall."

Ferrell swallowed the hard lump caught in his throat. His eyes searching, his mind trying to find the words. He cleared his throat and knocked on the door.

"Who is it and what business do you have?" asked Billy Sutton.

"There's been a shooting, and stabbing down at the saloon. My brothers' been killed!"

"Who are you?" asked Sutton.

"West Ferrell, dammit!"

Lawson listened as the lock-bolt slid away. When the door cracked open, Lawson shoved Ferrell through the opening right into Sutton. The deputy went flying backwards landing on his ass in the middle of the floor with Ferrell rolling away in another direction. The young deputy rebounded, quickly, getting to his feet with surprising speed. His right hand began slapping at his side holster, searching for the butt of his pistol.

"Don't do it boy!" demanded Lawson, but it was too late.

Lawson yanked his right-side Colt from its holster and had it leveled on the young deputy just as he was clearing leather with his own revolver. Billy Sutton was white as a ghost, all wide-eyed and shaking.

"I can't let you do this, said Sutton. Now put down your gun..."

"Shoot him, dammit! Shoot him!" shouted Ferrell.

The young deputy shifted his eyes and Lawson made his move. In a split-second the butt of Lawson's .45 smashed into Sutton's forehead, splitting him open—wide.

His body crashed in a corner with the gun dislodged from his hand. He lay there, still, out cold and bleeding.
McCall had heard the ruckus and gave a shout from the cell area;

"Is that you, Wreck!"

"Yeah, it's me, pard'."

"Get me the hell out of here!" shouted McCall.

Lawson stood over top of the unconscious, Billy Sutton. Blood was streaming down his neck and pooling on his chest. Lawson wandered if he had hit the young deputy too hard. He didn't look so good. Lawson was beginning to think that he may have killed Billy Sutton.

Again, McCall shouted out from the back...

Three men had been watching as the events were unfolding. They'd been watching every move, Wreck Lawson had made since their arrival into town. This was finally it—The moment Blake had been waiting for! The three men began the inspection of their firearms... ratcheting cylinders, checking cartridges. Shotguns were snapped open, shotgun shells dropping into the hollow barrels with a, popping sound. The U.S. Marshal knew Lawson; he'd had a run-in with him several years back. He wasn't going to take any chances with Lawson because he knew his reputation better than most. He had been sent to do a job on both, Lawson, and McCall and it was time that appointment got filled!

Lawson turned the key and the heavy steel door swung open with a loud—Clang! McCall stepped out quickly and moved around Lawson, making his way to the cabinet where his guns were being stored.

"Come on Wreck!" Urged McCall. Open the damn thing!"

Lawson was fumbling with the ring, trying to find a key that would fit the lock. Finally, a key opened the door and McCall reached for his arms. He buckled the holster that housed his black Colt .44 Peacemaker around his waste and tied it down on his thigh. He yanked the Colt from its greased holster and spun the cylinder to make sure that the gun was loaded. He also carried a Smith & Wesson Pocket .32---a Colt Third Model .41, he hid it back in its usual spot behind his belt buckle. He retrieved his 1873 Winchester .44.40, and the 12 inch Bowie that he carried; he slid it back into its leather sheath. Finally, the sawed-off 12 gauge shotgun he'd had special made by a "Smith" down in Austin a while back. The barrels had been sawed off at the stock and fashioned with a custom pistol grip. He usually kept the short cannon in his left side saddlebag loaded and ready to spit flames. That gun completed a most deadly arsenal, especially, in the hands of a man like Storm McCall.

Ferrell had sat, still, quiet. The towel he had wrapped around his hand was now a saturated blood sponge dripping crimson dots all over the floor. Lawson walked over and yanked Ferrell to his feet, then pushed him toward the back to a cell. He opened the cell door and shoved, Ferrell in sending him careening into a bunk where he hit and rolled up sideways into the wall with a hard—Thud!

"Shit, you sum bitch! I swear to god I'm gonna kill you for that Lawson!"

Ferrell screamed in agony, then sat whimpering as his lifeblood emptied onto the floor one drop at a time...

"Shut your mouth!" said Lawson with a hard glare, then he turned and locked the cell door behind him. When McCall turned, Lawson was standing over Billy Sutton, staring... he wondered if the boy's soul was leaving and where it might go. He really hadn't meant to kill the young deputy, but he had learned a long time ago about hesitation and the high cost that comes with it. Lawson knew Sutton would have killed him. But, that threat ended when the young man went for his gun.

Suddenly, in haste, McCall said;

"Are you gonna stand there in dreamland or are we gettin' the hell out'a here?"

Lawson snapped out of it. He walked over and dropped the key ring in the sheriff's crap bucket as McCall turned to the door... to freedom... to Hell and bloody freedom!

The wind was picking up due to the storm that was thundering its way into town. Dust swirled in the streets, shutters banged, back and forth, on the fronts of several buildings...

U.S. Marshal Henry Blake led his two Hell hounds (the men in black) out into the swirling winds. The men separated, walking three wide in the direction of the YUMA JAIL, as a dust devil spun up and cut across the street in front of them. A tumble weed rolled, wildly, along the building fronts, then the wind kicked it up onto a boardwalk and carried it away from site. Blake was a hard man with a reputation in Texas, and New Mexico. He'd started out as a lawman in Oklahoma City back in "62" and had made use of his most prominent contacts along the way. His hired deputies were mean looking wolves on the prowl for some game... noses sniffing, they detected prey and fresh blood at the jail. They breathed heavily, hackles raised, as they readied themselves for the kill...

At the other end of town, at the hanging party, the spectators were hissing and throwing objects at Kelsey. A woman threw a rock hitting, Kelsey in the back of the head, and shouted: "Burn in Hell killer!"

Others followed suit until Compton stepped up and shouted: "That's enough now, quiet down!"

Kelsey was shoved up the steps of the gallows. At the top a hangman's noose was slightly swaying in the, ever building winds. The sky overhead had turned to rolling-black-clouds. Electricity bolted down, in streaks, from inside their churning interiors. Kelsey looked up at the swinging rope, then into the churning black sky... his face went pale with horror when he saw the hangman standing there with his hand on the lever, and another, hooded figure dressed in black and pointing a finger at him...

"Nooo!" came a scream from inside Kelsey's head. Oh God, please help me! Then, another scream from deep within the corridors of his mind. Suddenly, a scream came out from deep inside of him...

"I don't want'a die!" Then, another... "I don't want'a die!"

People in the crowd laughed, aloud, then someone shouted

"Take your medicine murderer!"

Suddenly, a man crouched down at Kelsey's feet and began binding his ankles together with a thin leather strap. It was the hangman, George Maledon, of Fort Smith Arkansas. He'd been summoned in by Neusome because of his (recent) media credentials. Having been dubbed by the press as the prince of hangman. He would send over sixty men to their deaths before retiring from his illustrious career at a time nearing the turn of the century.

Kelsey stood, frozen... chest rising, falling again, searching the eyes of the people who would soon mock his death. Something caught his eye in the front row of the crowd. He saw a man... a woman... and a young boy staring up at him... their skin dirty, hair and clothes covered in fresh smears of brown earth.

"Nooo...This can't be happening—You're not real!" he screamed as the people in the crowd laughed and mocked him. The preacher walked over and stood beside Kelsey and began to read from the holy book. Kelsey's nightmare was now beginning...

At the other end of town things were much quieter; the only sound being that of the metallic jangle of spurs tilling the dirt of the street, then quieting as Blake and his men came to a stop in front of the YUMA JAIL. Just as McCall was opening the door, Blake shouted out; "Lawson... this is U.S. Marshal Henry Blake... You're under arrest for murder in Yuma today... I'm ordering you to surrender your arms and give yourself up! I know you have hostages in there... I'm going to give you 30 seconds, after that me and my deputies are going to open up on you! Now, come out nice and slow..!"

McCall eased the door shut, then turned to face Lawson.
"Who the hell is this guy?"
"We crossed paths down in El Paso a while back, before he was a U.S. Marshal. I'd rode into town after a long sit in the saddle. Apparently, he didn't like my looks 'cause he told me to get the hell out of town. I had just stepped down from the saddle; when I turned around he was standing there with his hand hanging over the butt of his

gun. I saw a glint in his eye, but before he could make his move my hog leg was hammered back and leveled between his eyes. Never thought I'd see 'im again... 'knew if I ever did I'd haf'ta kill' 'im."

"He says he's got deputies, said McCall. I'm figuring there are three of 'em. Watch my back..."

He opened the door and stepped out onto the wooden deck at the front of the jail.

"You're not Lawson," said Blake, a surprised look on his face.

"Nope, sure ain't," said McCall.

"Well, just who in the hell are you then?"

"'Names' McCall, and you won't be takin' my partner anywhere."

"What!?"exploded Blake.

He hadn't expected this. He'd been too busy thinking on revenge and how good it was going to feel to kill Lawson. Though Blake had been sent to Yuma to see it certain that McCall was hung, Wreck Lawson had been his personal motivation. He still got madder than hell every time he pictured that cocky little bastard, Lawson, beating him to the draw. Blake was anticipating that Lawson would try that again today. He'd stay in Yuma long enough to see the dirt shoveled in on top of both Lawson, and McCall.

A crackle of *brilliant* lightning exploded overhead causing one of the shotgun *toters* to flinch, nervously. Lawson came out the front door and, *smoothly* slid in on McCall's side...

"Blake..." said Lawson (in recognition to the Marshal) "I know you ain't here to arrest me; I don't feel like dying today, so   you'd best think about turning around and walkin' if you don't want to get filled with lead—Old timer."

"Old-timer! shouted Blake. You're pretty cocky there, boy!

I know you're fast, but you see these here shotguns pointed at you?" (one of the men shifted the barrels toward Lawson's chest) "You ain't that fast by god!"

"Well now, maybe I'm not Blake. But, I think I know somebody who is... damn shame of it is; you'll never know who."

"Yeah, and why is that?" asked Blake.

"Because you'll be dead is why" answered McCall in a smooth-level voice.

Blake's law-dogs burst out in laughter like a couple of cackling coyotes. Blake turned his head slightly and eyed the two men standing behind him. A cocky smile came across his face as he realized just how funny McCall's statement had actually been.

"Now, I'm going to tell you for the last time... said Blake, through clenched teeth; surrender those guns or I'm going to cut you down where you stand!"

A devilish smile pulled across McCall's face and Blake could have sworn he saw a twinkle of excitement in the man's eye. Blake's upper lip quivered like a snarling dog raising its hackles, then suddenly, his hand jerked toward the butt of his 1860 Colt-Army revolver...

The three men were, suddenly dancing to some strange-alternate beat as rounds of .44 and .45 caliber lead ripped, and drilled holes through their flailing bodies. When the dance ended the three men lay dead in the street, their hats cart wheeling sideways as the wind caught them and whirled them away onto the desert plain like mock tumbleweeds of a different kind. McCall snapped open the gate at the side of the smoking cylinder on his .44 and emptied the shells onto the wooden deck. The brass casings chimed, *musically* as they hit the hard wood. Tendrils of smoke oozed from the cylinder up the back of

McCall's hand, enclosing around it like the boney fingers of an unseen entity. McCall plugged fresh .44 rounds back into each empty chamber of the cylinder, then snapped the loading gate closed.

CHAPTER 6

Frank McPheron stood by with horses and supplies at the location he and Lawson had agreed upon. He had just heard repeated gunfire—it didn't sound like no celebration...

McCall, and Lawson bolted from the front of the jail glancing in all directions as they moved toward their appointed location with McPheron. Suddenly, a shot rang out; spinning lead hit Lawson high in his right shoulder drilling a hole clean through it. He grabbed it, stumbled, but continued running. They disappeared behind the corner of a building, then continued along its length, stopping at a rear corner where, Frank McPheron came into their view. He was holding the reins on two horses. With his help, McCall, and, Lawson wasted no time mounting the two grain burners, then they wheeled the animals around...

"I heard the shot—I'll take care of it!"

McPheron had seen a man moments before, snaking between two buildings, carrying a rifle.

"Thanks, Frank, said, McCall, we owe you for this one friend!"

"Get on out of here now and take care of him! There's whiskey in your bags and everything else you'll need."

"Thanks, Frank," murmured, Lawson, leaning forward in the saddle with his left hand pressed tightly up against his shoulder.

"You boys go on now—Ride!"

Frank smacked, Lawson's horse on the rump. The Black Stallion bolted like a gate had just opened from a chute at the Kentucky derby!

Frank made a quick dash into a narrow alleyway where he'd seen a man earlier holding a rifle. Several keg barrels were stacked up against the side of a building. Frank stepped in behind them, disappeared in the shadows and waited...

Eldon Kelsey stood at the gallows, his weight resting on a hinged platform as he lived out the last moment of his life. The preacher asked him if he had any last words...

"Where are they...? Where are they?!" I'm not supposed to die like this!" said the sniveling coward.

"Neither was them folks you killed out there in the desert —You Satan's follower you!" shouted a woman who was holding an infant in her arms.

A fat-red tomato came flying in from overhead and exploded right in Kelsey's face painting it an ominous looking blood-red. The big man shook his head, violently, from side to side after having been blinded by it. The preacher man was trying to wipe the drippy thing off of Kelsey's face as the sheriff read the death warrant out loud. All went to sudden darkness when a black hood was yanked down over top of his head and the rope was pulled up, snugly, in place at the side of his neck. Kelsey's heart pounded in his chest. The black hood filled like a balloon, and emptied in time with his panicked breathing.

"...And may God have mercy on your soul..." said the preacher.

The executioner reached for the wooden handle that would release the platform from under Kelsey's feet and drop him to his death.

Lawson was riding on fading from site as McCall slowed his big Sorrel and came to a stop behind a building. He yanked his Winchester .44 .40 from the scabbard and put an eye down the sights. Finding Kelsey's neck he centered the site, then squeezed off one round just as the executioner yanked the pin...

Monty Langford turned into the alley, moved quickly in McPheron's direction. He was running toward the sound of fleeing horses when Frank stuck his foot out and tripped him. Langford went down, hard, onto the dirt and dropped the rifle. He jumped back up, got to his feet fairly quick, and began looking for the rifle. When he spun around he was standing face to face with Frank McPheron.

"Well, said McPheron, what do you know—Monty Langford!" McPheron yanked Langford by his shirt front and pulled him into a killer right fist to the gut! No one could hear the beating, only Langford, and McPheron...

Kelsey's body dropped toward the earth like a bag of rocks. Suddenly, the rope yanked! In (what appeared to be) slow motion, the man's head was jerked completely off! The front row of spectators were horrified when Kelsey's head went flipping through the air. The headless body hit on its knees, then fell forward toward the crowd with blood spurting out the neck like a soda fountain painting the front row of onlookers in a bright shade of crimson red. Kelsey's severed head lay at the feet of the front row spectators who were quickly backing away from it. They were screaming and running around in a panicked frenzy realizing now that; death is never pretty no matter whom the victim may be...

McCall kicked the big Sorrel into a fast gallop as a grim smile of satisfaction pulled across his face. Lawson was just ahead, and McCall was quickly gaining ground on him.

Arizona territory

The rains came down... black-ink in the dark of night cascading from the clouds with the roaring of a great falls. Flashes of *blinding* silver shattered the black of night, thundering, quaking the world around them. Although the ground was dry and thirsty it seemed to be drowning, spitting the water back out, turning even the smallest of cuts and trenches into raging rivers. Yuma had faded from their back trail, its memory being slowly washed away.

McCall had suited himself, and Lawson with rain slickers just before the bottom had dropped out. He'd adjusted Lawson's hat and collar as to ward off the effects of the torrential downpour that was further plaguing them as they drifted blindly into the eye of the storm. Lawson was slumped forward in his saddle, his head bobbing around as if his neck was snapped and hanging from a stick. He fought desperately to stay on the black stallion's back.

"Hey, pard', said McCall, you alright?"

Lawson's left hand was pressed tightly up against his shoulder

"'Need to find shelter... get warm."

McCall grabbed hold of the reins of Lawson's black and tugged it to a stop. He dismounted, then stepped around to unbuckle a saddle bag. He reached inside it and pulled out a bottle of whiskey, re-booted the stirrup and slid back into the saddle.

"I'm gonna' find us some shelter if I can just figure out which way were headin'!" shouted McCall.

The rain was hammering the top of his wide-brimmed, Stetson so hard that he could barely here himself talk. He popped the cork from the bottle with his teeth then reached over and tilted the rim of it to Lawson's mouth. He took a drink and choked slightly, then took another. McCall pulled his Bowie from its sheath. He pulled back Lawson's slicker and made a cut across the fabric of his shirt exposing the shoulder wound, then tilted the bottle and let the whiskey pour out into the swollen black-red bullet hole. Lawson stiffened upright in the saddle, then slowly he relaxed once again. McCall replaced the long blade back in its sheath, then pulled the slicker back over Lawson's shoulder and the two set out across the unforgiving plain. They had ridden along the eastern shore of the Colorado River; it raged along its banks like thick-black oil, the terrain around them being spotted with deep pools of ink. The only thing McCall was certain of at that time was that they were riding north. Lawson needed medical attention, but that was out of the question. The bullet had exited clean missing the bones in his shoulder, which was good. He'd lost a lot of blood though, so shelter, or not, it was time to close and dress the wound.

The black terrain fell off and sloped downward at sharp

angles. McCall steered the horses toward the river's edge. The Colorado was raging along its banks and with each crash of lighting he surveyed the terrain for some kind of cover before Lawson would croak and become a permanent addition to the Arizona landscape. After about a mile or so something caught McCall's eye. It was an over-turned wagon. Its cover was ripped and blowing in the wind like a ghostly Rebel Flag storming into battle; its color's having been long faded from the relentless charge. For a moment McCall's mind drifted back to the southern battlefield, but a blinding crash of lightening snapped him back to his senses and he realized that a tree was burning just on the other side of the river. The flash had temporarily blinded him leaving spots in front of his eyes. At some previous point in time the wagon had rolled off of the side of an embankment and was at an angle to the ground—it looked promising to say the least. To find shelter inside of it seemed impossible, but underneath it? Well... like it, or not, it was all they had. He pulled Lawson down from the Black Stallion and positioned him underneath the platform, then began to enclose the shelter.

Arizona Territory
Camped along the Colorado River

Gale-force-winds were sweeping in from the south-west. McCall used the wagon's cloth cover as a wind break on one side of the vehicle's frame. Mature trees lined the river's bank, so he was able to locate some kindling to begin coaxing a fire into being. With a small tin of gun oil, and some dry shredded cloth, it wasn't long before he saw the first spark.

After he had detoured the wind from the makeshift

dwelling he'd placed blankets on the ground and had helped Lawson over beside the fire. He shredded the sleeve of Lawson's shirt, then emptied two .44 cartridges into the wound opening at the front of the shoulder, then the exit wound at the back of the shoulder. With the glowing-red tips of two sticks he ignited both openings. Lawson jerked and an agonizing grimace crossed his face, then he fell back into a deep state of unconsciousness. McCall cleaned the wound with fresh water, then dressed it with a clean wrap of bacon fat and cloth.

During the hours of mid-night the rains had begun to ease up, but the night was still alive with blinding streaks of lightening bolting down and crackling across the skies before making contact with earthy ground; the low-rumble of thunder slowly faded off into the distance.

McCall pulled the cork on a bottle, then put a glow to the tip of a thin cigar. He leaned back against a wagon wheel, raised his eyes and watched the light show. He and Lawson had survived. It wasn't their first close call and it most likely wouldn't be the last. The whiskey was sweet and it felt good to be free even if only for the moment. The task was done, now the hard part; wait and see if his partner would survive the darkest hours of the night.

McCall didn't sleep, he remained awake throughout the night inducing Lawson with regular doses of whiskey. The storms of the night had passed, but the gray-black clouds in the sky were still showing signs of possible threat. McCall had found a bag of coffee grounds during the night and was still adding whiskey to his cup when he heard a groan... he turned to see Lawson attempting to sit up from under the pile of blankets he'd stacked on top of him while he'd slept.

"'Don't think y'er ready for that just yet, pard', stated McCall. Best go ahead and lay back for a spell. Y'er gonna be sore, so you'll need t'a rest."

"I'll rest when I'm dead," replied Lawson, easing back down onto the pallet of blankets.

"I'd hafta' say you came mighty close to that last night."

"Who the hell shot me?"

"'Don't know... the shot came from a rifle on a building top. Frank said he'd take care of it."

"We got'ta ride Lou'. You know as well as I do there's a posse on the prowl. They get another chance and..."

"I can see everything five miles from that high point over there... them sons-a-bitches get within range of my Winchester and I'll drill 'em like swiss cheese."

"Just need... a little more rest... then we'll..."

A gasp of air exhausted from his lungs and he went limber. Once again the wounded Texan would succumb to, unconscious darkness.

On the Arizona plains

Sheriff Charles Compton was leading a posse of men north-east toward Phoenix. In Yuma the bodies of Henry Blake and his deputy dogs had been painted and propped up in pine boxes for photography. The pictures were scheduled to be released to the papers as soon as they came off the press. Compton was madder than hell! Them two side-windin' bastards were gonna hang if he had to track them all the way to Kalamazoo! The judge, William Neusome of Santa Fe, was not going to be made to look like a fool! He didn't care how far or how long it would take, McCall, and Lawson would swing at the end of a rope that he was now going to custom design personally for each of them! First his nephew Chad, and now Marla! First he'd hang them, then he'd burn them, then he'd personally scatter their ashes in pig shit! There was, however, one comforting thought in all of his rage; Cliff Rogan would arrive in Santa Fe later in the week and there was no doubt in Neusome's sadistic mind that if all else failed, Rogan would be his ace in the hole! He was deadly fast with a gun and had the disposition of a caged grizzly. There wasn't a man alive Neusome ever knew of whom could take Rogan—not by fist—nor by gun! Compton would telegraph by mid-day with a report; and it had better be of substance or Compton would soon feel the tightening of "The Noose" himself!

Judge Neusome had taken the body of his nephew's wife, Marla Carlson, and had her readied for the train ride back to Santa Fe for burial beside her husband. That poor girl's body was broken in so many ways she looked like a rag-doll that some displeased, angry, little kid had snapped and twisted violently, then threw back into a small pine box for return shipment!

It was mid-day by the river, and Lawson was still burning up with fever. The desert floor had swallowed the rains that, just the day before, had flooded it like a heifer was pissin' on a flat rock! It was getting hotter than Hell as the glowing-red orb of fire climbed higher into the sky, but Lawson would remain under the pile of blankets until the fever broke. Lawson was right, and McCall knew it—They needed to ride as soon as possible! McCall had stripped the horses of their saddles on the previous night. He'd led them into a clearing where long strands of green grass was growing on the side of the bank. He'd tethered them on a large branch of a dead tree that had fallen some years before, so for now they seemed content. The rains had receded and the sun was now popping out from behind the clouds. The only thing McCall knew to do at this point was to keep an eye on the surrounding terrain for the possibility of ambush and at the same time try to keep his partner's fever down by inducing him with whiskey as often as possible. At one point he had scouted a couple of riders off to the east. They moved on in that direction without ever having looked back. In the hill country to the north, however, he spotted what he was certain to be Redskins. There were only three of them, on horseback, but he could tell by the way they sat the bareback ponies and how they kept to the higher elevations that they were Indians. Eventually, they turned and disappeared over the rounded curve of a hilltop. Other than that not much was happening where he sat with his Winchester in hand on a large branch of a cottonwood that was looming just above the raging current of the Colorado River. At the time, McCall had no idea how extensive the man hunt for himself, and Lawson was going to become. The Judge, Neusome, had ties with powerful men back east. One of them in particular was dead set at bringing one, Luis (Storm) Daniel McCall to justice for crimes that he had committed against the good people of the state of Ohio. McCall knew nothing of this. His homeland of Ohio had become only a bitter sweet memory ever sense the tragic and senseless murder of his wife nearly three years earlier. McCall had already killed one of the men responsible for her death and had spent two years in Huntsville Territorial Prison for manslaughter. Four others remained... They had eluded McCall before he could pass judgment over them. One of those men was a man by the name of Joe Clemens. He and the four others had followed McCall and his wife west to Texas. Clemens was set on revenge because; even though Jenn wanted nothing to do with the man, Clemens had sworn to the others that McCall had ran off with his girl and he was heading to Texas to bring her back.

Clemens and his men had closed in on their camp and had shot McCall leaving him for dead. When Jenn refused to go back with Clemens a struggle commenced and Clemens became enraged. He began smacking and hitting her. She had broken away from his grip and was running away from the gang of men when Clemens pulled his pistol and shot her through the back as she went splashing across a small stream. When McCall awoke, Clemens and his men were gone. Lawson had rode in and found Jenn lying face down in the stream. McCall had taken three rounds from .45 —.44 and .36 lead. He'd survived it. And now, Clemens and the rest of his men were going to face judgment of Hell's fire and Storm McCall was going to be the one to judge them—even if it took all of eternity to find them!

He was thinking of her...

McCall didn't like being alone, but he was starting to get used to the feeling. He still loved her and couldn't stand the thought of leaving her, but she was gone and he was alive. The previous night, the thunder, the lightning and the rain was still churning in his heart and he could feel the fury of his given Southern Rebel name—A name that would once again bring fear to many a man's heart— Storm McCall! A single tear dropped, then trailed its way down along the lines of his dusty face.

CHAPTER 7

Second day
Camped along the Colorado River

The early morning sun painted a line of pink across the dark horizon. McCall sat down and leaned back against the wagon wheel; the glowing embers from the dying fire were still producing enough heat so that he didn't feel the need to add anymore wood to it. He hadn't had much sleep for the past several days and was beginning to feel the world around him slipping away as his eyelids grew heavier. Slowly, he began to nod off into the quiet darkness of sleep...

...It was peaceful there in the deep space of his dreams. And although he didn't want to leave that calm place, sounds in the distance were tugging at him, beckoning him back to this world... Opening his eyes, a shadowed figure was standing over him blocking the sunlight and casting a shadow across his face. In a blur the muzzle of his .45 flashed from its holster and was leveled, hammer snapped back, ready to spit flames!

"Whoa!" came a voice. The figure jumped back, both hands raised.

"It's me Luis... point that damn thing somewhere else!"

Recognizing the voice, McCall eased the hammer down and slowly slid the, Colt back into leather.

"What in the hell are you trying to do—give me a damn heart attack!"

"No, man, I just woke up and was trying to rustle up something to eat! 'Didn't mean to rattle you that way, 'just needed to feed this empty gut."

McCall smelled coffee brewing.

"How in the hell did you manage to pull that off?" asked, McCall, pointing to the brewing pot just above the ash embers of an earlier fire.

"Ahhh... it weren't nothin', said, Lawson. Remember, I can go left, or right when it comes to a six gun, or coffee. I'm what they call, Uhh... what the hell is that word again? Am.. Ambi... Ahh hell, I can't remember!"

"Ambidextrous?"asked, McCall, a smile pulling across his face.

"That's it! —Whatever, Luis. . ."

McCall pulled himself to his feet, raised his arms high above his head and reached for the sky as he let out a big yawn.

"'Looks like you feel a little better there, pard'," said, McCall.

"Yeah, but sore as all hell. 'You do the bandage y'erself?" asked, Lawson as he inspected the dressing on his shoulder with admiration.

"Ahh It weren't nothin,' said, McCall real casual like. I saved a wounded dog once and a couple of steers. What the hell makes you think you're any different?"

"Well, said, Lawson, thanks for including me in your long journal of doctor-patient records their, pard'."
McCall just smiled as he knelt down to pour himself a cup of coffee and said;

"Don't mention it. How's that shoulder doin'?"

"Well, said Lawson, bullet wounds usually make me feel like crap, but I think I'll live as long as there's plenty of whiskey!" He smiled.

"Oh, there's plenty of whiskey, said McCall. 'Bout five more bottles last I counted. How's about I rustle up some bacon 'n beans with some biscuits?"

"'Sounds good. 'Think I'll just sit back down and rest a little," said Lawson.

He eased back down on the blankets spread out underneath the wagon and pulled the cork on a new bottle of whiskey, then tilted it to his lips.

"Don't mean to rush things, said McCall, but how long do you think you'll need before you can ride?"

"I'm figuring on getting some grub in my gut, then saddling up. We can't afford to "hang" around too long in one place if you know what I mean," said Lawson with a raised brow.

"I've been keeping an eye on the area, said McCall. 'Saw a couple of riders off to the east yesterday, they kept moving in that direction. Saw Injuns in the hills to the north. They didn't seem interested in much, 'stayed in site for a few minutes then they disappeared back into the hills. You're right though... we need to get movin'."

Later that night

After they had had their fill of grub, McCall was telling Lawson that come morning he was going to go up on high ground and take a look around..."

"I'm just gonna lay back, sip on some whiskey, and get to healin'," stated Lawson.

Evening was setting in over the camp and the stars of the night sky glimmered within the panoramic bowl of the upper heavens. McCall lean back, his head propped up against his saddle. He'd already rubbed the horses down. He was having a smoke (Cheroot Sweet Cigar) and was sipping on a hot-tin of coffee. He'd wrapped Lawson's wounds in new cloth bandage and was surprised at how well the wound was looking. Although he was still running a fever he was doing quite well, considering. Lawson was sipping on some whiskey and made a gesture to McCall to partake of the bourbon.

"Hell, 'don't mind if I do," said McCall. He tipped the bottle up and took two swallows from it, then wiped his mouth on his sleeve and passed the bottle back over to Lawson. McCall took a draw off the thin cigar and dropped his jaw, letting the smoke gather, then popped his jaw back cutting loose a thick ring of smoke that turned up, then rolled backwards on itself. The ring of smoke slowed, and began to expand... He puffed the quirly again with Lawson watching, intently.

"There's the corral Lou'... now rope the Broncs!"

McCall popped his jaw sending three rings of smoke up toward the "corral" like he'd throw a wrangler's lasso if it were. They floated up to the hovering ring, then settled just inside the wide circle of smoke.

"Holy shit Lou'," shouted Lawson, "y'a got all three of 'em man!"

Lawson was laughing out loud and slapping his knee (his left hand)

"Yep, that's the damned best I ever seen it done!"

McCall cut a big grin.

They both burst into laughter as the smoke rings drifted away. The fire crackled and popped sending sparks of glowing red ash up into the night sky. The two passed the bottle for a spell and let their tensions come to an ease, and before they knew it both men were sawing logs. Things were peaceful for the moment...

...The grass lay thick, lush-green where they sat atop the rolling hillside... She was there; the sky above them deep-blue. Cotton-like clouds floated over head, seemingly, motionless toward whatever destiny lay ahead on the horizon. She was gazing into his eyes... her golden hair glistening, flowing in motion, crossing her face from the passing of a gentle breeze as the sun's brilliance danced upon each waving strand. She smiled... contentment aglow about her face like that of an angel. No words were spoken, none were needed. They just sat there, side by side, looking up at the warm summer sky; just sitting together looking to eternity...

"I love you Luis... I always have..." she whispered, softly, into his ear. Then, she was gone. The sky darkened, suddenly, to an ominous merk... The sun wilted to black... He stood alone on the withering grass beckoning her to come back to him as the world around him began dying...

From somewhere, McCall heard his name... Faintly, from

a distance, then closer. He opened his eyes and jumped back quickly!

Lawson was gazing down at him, but jerked away at the same instance!

"Sorry pard', 'didn't mean to startle y'a, but it sounded like you was talking to somebody"

"Dammit, would you quit doin' that!" said McCall.

Next Morning

"I'm gonna saddle up 'n ride up to the north. I'll find some high ground. If there is a posse out there I'm gonna make sure I see them first.

"Make sure you come back Lou'... I'd hate to have to fight these bastards all by myself."

"I'll be back in a few hours. Keep y'er eyes 'n ears open"

He grabbed his saddle and walked over to where the horses were tethered, hoisted the saddle up onto the big horse's back. He patted the horse on its long face... "That's a good fella. I need you to take me for a short ride, 'think you can do that for me?"

The Sorrel horse shook its head and nickered.

Lawson's black stallion, Nightmare, turned to look at Lawson with a curious look.

"We're not going this time, boy, said Lawson to the black. But, we'll be riding soon enough..."

McCall tightened the saddle straps, booted a stirrup, and turned up onto the saddle. He maneuvered the horse up the side of the muddy embankment, then hit level ground and tore out for the red hills and mesa's that were protruding up out of the desert plain just a few miles to the north.

Phoenix, Arizona

Compton had rode his nine-man posse hard...

The rains had finally eased up and Compton was Hell-bent for Phoenix. He and his posse arrived there during the mid-night hours and had checked into rooms at the SILVER MINE HOTEL. Monty Langford didn't look so good. His lips were purple and swollen. He was missing a front tooth, and his left eye was a swollen slit painted in black. It looked as though Frank McPheron had done some handy work on the ol' boy back in Yuma. Compton entered the Phoenix sheriff's office. He'd already placed his men at strategic points in town, but had decided to take Langford along with him. When he entered the office an older gent' stood up from behind a desk...

"What can I do for you fellas this morning? (then he noticed a badge on Compton's vest) Or sheriff I mean, sir."

"My name is Charles Compton. We're looking for two men who are wanted for murder in Yuma."

"Yes sir, I do believe I remember receiving your telegraph stating that fact now," said the marshal.

Compton hesitated in his speech as he handed two wanted posters over to the Phoenix marshal.

"These two men (continued Compton) are extremely dangerous killers and are responsible for the deaths of eight individual persons, one of them being that of a woman, said Compton cocking his head to one side and squinting as he gazed into the marshal's eyes. Compton had intended to insinuate that McCall, and Lawson had been up to foul play with a member of the female persuasion.

"Didn't you fellas hang that son of a bitch, Kelsey yesterday?" asked the marshal.

"Oh, we tried too, sneered Compton, but that bastard, McCall shot and killed the son of a bitch before we could git'er done!"

The Marshal chuckled, lightly, at the statement, but then adjusted his attitude seeing that there was no sign of humor on the irritated face of Charles Compton.

"Storm McCall was to hang yesterday, but somehow he slipped out of the noose. He's going to hang, by God! And that dirt slinging Texan, Lawson, is going to swing right beside him! Have you seen these men, sir?"

As Compton spoke he sounded more and more like a politician than a local town sheriff. As with Lawson, Compton must'a been practicing his speech for the time when he'd run for U.S. Senate.

Marshal Benjamin Miller looked over the wanted posters, then scratched his chin;

"Nope, can't say that I have sheriff." The marshal raised his eyes and locked gaze with Compton.

"But, if you do while you're in my town you 'n y'er posse, just remember who has jurisdiction here. You are under my authority. So, you 'n y'er men keep y'er noses clean 'n we'll have no problems between us, understood? By the way... how's come you folks didn't hold the hanging out at the territorial prison down there in, Yuma?" asked Miller, pinning Compton with a questioning look.

"'Just wasn't time for that, replied Compton. The judge had personal interests in both of these men and wanted to see to it personally that McCall was properly executed for the murders of his niece and nephew in Santa Fe.

"Well, I don't always understand everything, and don't guess I need too, said the marshal, so good luck catchin' y'er men sheriff."

Compton gave a curt nod of his head.

"I have a few more of these posters. Would you mind if I have my men post them here in town, marshal?"

"Do as y'a please, sheriff," said Miller, weaving his fingers together at his belt buckle.

"Thank y'a kindly," said Compton, touching the tip of his narrow brimmed Stetson. He turned to the door... Langford followed closing the door behind them.

Phoenix was a growing city with a train station and a stage route that made its way into town twice a week. There were numerous saloons and gambling houses, hotels, banks, blacksmith shop, and several new frames under construction. Other things were growing there as well, like; a young lad with a big attitude!

Compton was a, wily, old son of a bitch nearing sixty years of age. He'd seen his share of times and sorrows through the years and he really wasn't the kind of man you would call soft—He had sand! But, his age was catching up to him and he could feel the years beginning to take their tole. He really didn't believe that McCall had deserved to hang either, but he was a man of the law, and McCall, and Lawson had disrupted his town and undermined his authority as a lawman. He couldn't let them get away with that—and he wouldn't! He exited the jail and headed back toward his hotel. He'd kick back for a few and rest his bones while the rest of the men headed on toward the DRY SKULL SALOON to knock back some of the trail dust they had carried in with them from the desert. Sheriff Compton had sent instruction with his men to gather information concerning the outlaws he was chasing. Later he would post his watchdogs at strategic points in town. Compton made his way up to his room. He dragged a chair over beside the window and pulled the thin curtains apart with a pinch of his fingers. He opened up the case he had retrieved from his saddle bag before entering the hotel. Retracting the scope he began spying out across the open desert, watching... yearning... waiting. If McCall and Lawson rode into town they would be riding into Hell's fire judgment! The two men would be shown no mercy. Compton (tight jawed) growled a deep-throaty sound under his breath... "Come 'n get your medicine boys..." he mumbled to himself as he gazed through the lens. It was wrong what had happened to his deputy; Young Billy Sutton was to be avenged!

Phoenix, Arizona
Same day

Marshal Ben Miller was scratching his head... He wondered why Compton hadn't telegraphed ahead in his pursuit of these dangerous outlaws. His mind pondered over the whole damned thing. "Why a hanging in such a small town?" he asked himself. "'Seemed they would hold an event like that closer to a court that had territorial jurisdiction." Though he had known about the hanging, he'd been informed earlier that it was to be a single execution. Something just didn't make sense in the big picture of things. He got up and walked out the front door of the sheriff's office. It seemed, maybe time to do a little inquiry of his own into the facts of this somewhat complex situation that had just landed itself in the town of Phoenix. He went to the post office to send a telegraph down to Yuma. But, after two attempts, he'd gotten no response. He decided to send it to the office of the Governor of the state of Arizona.

SHOOT 'EM T'A HELL!

Message:

—This is Sheriff Benjamin Miller of Phoenix Arizona—Stop.

—Requesting information on all officials directly involved in execution sentence of one; Luis McCall, two days ago in Yuma Arizona including name of judge—Stop.

—Please forward information to myself—Stop.

—Am awaiting your response—Stop—Thank you—Stop.

Miller thanked the clerk and instructed him to fetch him at his office upon reply from the Governor. Miller went out the door and turned onto the boards of the walkway and was heading back to his office when his eyes beheld a curious sight. Leaning against a wooden post just ahead of him was a young man, head down, staring at a piece of paper he held pinched between his fingers. This kid was going to be trouble someday and Miller knew it. He knew it as sure as he knew his own name. Jimmy Potts was seventeen at the most, but acted much older than the other boys in town who were his age. He was a scrapper this one was and had earned a reputation as a rebel who refused to heed to any respect towards the law whatsoever. As Miller approached the youth he recognized the paper in the boy's hands—A Wanted Poster. On the front of the poster was the face of a man Miller had been hearing a lot about recently—Storm McCall.

"Don't go gettin' no funny notions there Jimmy, said Miller raising a brow. That man is a dangerous killer who'd chew you up and spit you out with a quickness!"

Jimmy Potts rolled his head over his shoulders, then straightened and released the wanted poster. It floated down, laid face up beside Miller's boot. The young Potts turned slowly and squared off with the sheriff. His right hand dropped to his side as he pinned a penetrating glare into Miller's eyes.

"Jimmy Potts you'd better not even think about..."

The sheriff's words were cut off instantly when Potts yanked his Army issue revolver from its holster, cocked and leveled, pointed right in Miller's face.

"You mean fast like that old man?" said Potts, turning the gun from side to side... displaying it like a prized trophy. Miller couldn't speak. His heart was pounding in his chest and he was frozen with shock staring down the black muzzle of the large caliber revolver leveled just inches from the tip of his nose.

"The name is no longer Potts... It's Phoenix—Jimmy Phoenix!"

He spun the gun back and slid it smoothly into its holster, intertwined his fingers, cracked them at the knuckles, then turned his head and looked away from the Marshal. Miller stood there and watched as the cocky showoff walked away. Potts turned and disappeared through the bat-wing doors of the VIPERS DEN SALOON.

...He was fast with that gun, and everyone in town knew it. One thing was for sure; the Marshal had seen some quick draws in his time, but none the likes of what he'd just seen with Jimmy Potts. Miller was truly shaken, but at the same time his pride was hurt and it pissed him off!

"...Damn greenhorn, mumbled Miller to himself. Fool kid ain't ever even killed a man!"

Miller didn't know about Abilene...

The Marshal moseyed on back to his office and scooped some coffee grounds into a tin pot, placed it on the wood burning stove, then took a seat behind his desk and sat, staring down at the wanted posters spread out on the desktop. He scratched his chin as he looked over the faces of, Lawson, and McCall and several others including; Jesse James, and Dave Rudabaugh. Something about that failed double hanging in Yuma just didn't make sense to him and he wondered just what the hell was really going on down there. When the coffee had brewed he filled his tin cup and took a couple sips of the black liquid, then re-seated himself behind the desk. The thought of the encounter with that Potts kid hadn't left his mind—He was still pissed! With the Woosh of a hand he cleared the desktop.

Jimmy Phoenix... Just who in the Hell did that wise-ass kid think he was foolin'! He had half a mind to go back down there and show that cocky little shit who was boss, by God! A swift kick in the ass would work for starters. And, then, he'd...

He took in a deep breath and exhaled. Hell, who was he kiddin'... He wasn't a young man anymore and even if he was he could never match Potts on the draw—'Damn kid was just too fast with that gun! But, fist t'a fist... He'd'a kicked shit out'a that wise ass greenhorn any day of the week—Including Sunday!

He kicked his boots up onto the desk and crossed them at the ankles, then leaned back in the chair and closed his eyes for a moment and tried to just let it go..."

Nearly an hour had passed when a young lad about ten years of age came barging into the room out of breath and wielding a slingshot in his hand.

"Marshal Miller?!"

"Yes son, what is it?"

"You've received a telegraph over at the Post Office, sir!"

"Why, thank y'a Tommy I appreciate it," said Miller with a wink.

"You're welcome sir, said the young'n. The young man turned and started for the door.

"Oh, Tommy! jumped Miller. I'd best not here about you shootin' any more windows out with that thing or else were gonna have us a little problem you and I—Got it?"

"Yes sir," said the boy, his head down and pawing at the floor with his bare foot.

"Okay then, you can run along now."

He bolted out the door like a flame was attached to his backside. Miller just smiled and shook his head... "Young'ns..."

CHAPTER 8

When Miller arrived at the Post Office the clerk moved over behind a small desk and sat down.

"You've received a reply from the Governor, Ben."

"Go ahead with it, Curly," said Miller.

The clerk put the tip of his index finger to the lever of the machine and began tapping... After a moment a message came in.

Message:

—Identify yourself—Stop.

Marshal Benjamin Miller of Phoenix here—Stop.

I am speaking on behalf of the Governor of the great state of Texas—Brice Alderman—Stop. Your inquiry has been forwarded to our office, sir, and has been read by the Governor himself—Stop. McCall and Lawson have been recorded in the state of Texas as former convicted felons.

Both served time in Huntsville Territorial Prison, but at different periods—Stop. Luis Daniel McCall was sentenced to hang for murder in Santa Fe' by one; Judge William Neusome—Stop. U.S. Marshal Henry Blake and two deputies were sent to Yuma by said Judge for reasons unknown at this time—Stop. Blake and both deputies were killed in the line of duty by the hands of McCall and Lawson—Stop. Federal warrants have been issued for both of these men—Stop. It also has come to our attention that; William Neusome and Henry Blake were cousins—Stop. The man McCall killed in Santa Fe' was Neusome's nephew—Stop. That is all we have, sir—Stop. Thank you and good day—Stop—End message.

Thank you, replied Miller.

The communication ended.

By evening Compton was starting to get antsy. His ass was hurting from sitting in front of that window for too long. He decided to go on over to the Vipers Breath Saloon for a stiff shot of poison to pour down his gullet. The tinkling sounds of the rickety piano drew louder as he approached the split doors. He entered the saloon and to his surprise the interior was most impressive. There was a large mirror that covered the back wall and spanned the length of the bar. Above the bar hung four wagon-wheel chandeliers. The wood work glowed with a rich luster bringing out the grain of the dark mahogany. There were four gambling tables in the middle of the room. A roulette table was arranged in the far back corner where two of his men stood watching the ball drop and roll before dropping into a numbered slot. Lavish paintings lined the walls, mostly busty-women in the flesh, eyeing the patrons of the saloon, seductively, in an alluring temptuous invitation of sorts. Two card tables were running, four men at one, three at another, and two saloon girls (soiled doves) were busy making their rounds working the *tricks* of their trade. Tobacco smoke floated about in flat ribbons.

Compton pulled a pouch from his shirt pocket and walked over to the bar. He ordered whiskey and a beer, then began putting together a smoke. He stuck the quirly between his lips and struck a flame to the end of it. He blew out a rolling cloud that slowly thinned and became flat ribbons of smoke. He ordered another whiskey, threw it back, then turned and motioned for his men.

"C'mere boys," he said.

Slowly, the men gathered around him.

"I'm headed back towards Yuma. You can come with me or stay—the decision is yours. But, if I were you, I'd go. It's a long ride back and we'd be better in numbers if y'a ask me."

"Well, I'm stayin,' said Langford in a cheery voice. 'Gonna have me some rough and tumble fun with the woman folk," he said, glancing back over his shoulder at one of the sultry saloon gals who were sitting at a table smiling, and winking back at him.

"Me too, said another man, Ned Bartley. We ain't seen no sign 'a them two yet, 'n pro'lly wont!"

The rest of the men agreed to ride back to Yuma with Compton.

"Alright then, said Compton. Those of you riding with me, we leave in one hour".

The men turned from Compton and resumed their previous interests.

Compton finished what he had to say then turned towards the doors. He'd taken about three steps when someone spoke from the back of the room...

"What's th'a matter, are ya all, yella?"

The Piano player stopped the music on a sour, off-key note. The place got real quiet.

"Who the hell said that?" asked Compton, spinning around on the heel of his boot.

"I did..."came the voice again from a table positioned in a shadowed corner. At that point all eyes in the room turned their attention in that direction.

"Who are y'a?" came Compton with a loud-irritated tone of voice.

Ned Bartley pushed his way through the men and, declared;

"Nobody calls me a coward, mister! Now, show ye'r face or I'll blast y

a right where y'a sit!"

"Alright, alright, came the person sitting at the dark table. But, y'er makin' a big mistake."

The dark figure stood, slowly, and stepped from behind the table, then entered into the dim lighting of the bar room. Compton's men stepped back, cautiously.

"The names' Phoenix—Jimmy Phoenix."

"Hey look, choked, Langford—It's just a kid!"

Compton's posse of men laughed simultaneously at the revelation,as did several other patrons in the room.

"You'd best run on home now boy, I think I hear y'er mommy callin' for y'a!" laughed Bartley, obnoxiously, causing the other men to laugh even harder.

"Say that again mister 'n I'll shoot you in your big mouth!" said Jimmy Potts cutting a hard glare at Bartley. Jimmy was young, but they should have known age didn't matter in those parts. Boys grew up fast and some became hard and mean—and deadly!

"You called me a coward, boy, and now y'er gonna pay for it!"

"No, I didn't, replied Potts. I called you yell'a, and the

rest of y'a too for runnin' away from a fight."

"Well, I don't see anybody runnin' now, do you?!" stated Bartley.

Bartley's hand inched toward the butt of his 1875 Remington .44 revolver...

"I wouldn't do that mister if I were you!" said Potts, jerking his hand quickly to position next to his sidearm.

"Not in my place!" came a shout from behind the bar where the bartender stood with a raised shotgun.

"Take that shit outside! You can kill each other in the street, but not in here!"

"Well, yell'a, came Potts, whats it gonna be?" A devilish grin crossed his face as he said it.

"Oh, you wanna draw on me, boy!" yelled Bartley, starting to back towards the doors, kicking a table and flipping a chair over as he moved away.

"Stop this, now!" barked Compton, stepping in and shifting his eyes to Bartley.

"He'll kill y'a Ned..." whispered Compton. He shifted his eyes back to Jimmy Potts —"I can see it in his eyes."

"Shut up! screamed Bartley. He called me out like a man —Now he'll have to prove it!"

"You've had too much t'a drink Ned, pleaded Compton. For God's sake man let it go!"

"Ain't got nothin' t'a do with God, Charley! scoffed Bartley, looking the Yuma Sheriff in the eye. 'Can't let it go..."

Bartley pressed his back up against the bat-wings, parting them. He turned and stepped to the middle of the street, then spun around and called for the mouthy greenhorn.

"I'm here boy! Bring y'er iron 'n let's dance!"

"Well, he's called me out boys... Fair fight now 'n y'er all gonna witness it."

"He's had too much drink son," said Compton, sounding merciful.

Phoenix went to the bar, grabbed a bottle of whiskey (already setting there) turned the bottle up to his lips and rolled three bubbles to the bottom of the bottle as he swallowed. He placed the bottle back on the bar, shook It off, then squared eyes with Compton.

"Now, so have I Sheriff—Now were even-steven!"

Phoenix adjusted his pistol rig, then reached into his belt and pulled out a thin-black glove. He slid the tight leather cover over his left hand and stood there, staring between the bat wings where he knew Ned Bartley was impatiently waiting to get it on. Phoenix went to the doors and pushed them open. He stepped across the boardwalk, then down the steps. Dark mud squeezed out from under his boots as he walked to the middle of the street, spurs jingling to the rhythm of his steps as Bartley circled him to his left... his body hunched over, sidestepping, left hand held out to his side, his right hand a claw ready to stab at the butt of his pistol. Phoenix stopped and squared off with Bartley... legs spread wide in his stance. He rolled his head around from shoulder to shoulder, cracked his knuckles, then he stepped back onto his right heel. His hand moved in to position next to his Schofield ready to hook and draw.

"I'm gonna kill y'a kid for what you said to me," stated Bartley, his eyes mean and serious.

"You sure are gonna look funny mister, said Phoenix. I mean.. all yella' with red spots... just like a clown—a dead circus clown."

Bartley drew a deep breath, then through clenched teeth...

"Draw—Boy!"

Ned Bartley yanked his gun from the holster, but the pistol exploded in his hand...

Phoenix's first round hit the Remington's cylinder blowing the gun apart. It ripped the back of Bartley's hand open—Wide. He screamed out and grabbed at the wound.

"That's for being stupid enough to draw on me mister," continued Potts.

The next round drilled Bartley above his left knee, dropping him into the wet mud of the street.

"That's for walking out into the street against me y'a dumb bastard!" snarled Potts.

Reaching out with both hands Bartley tried to speak, but made no sound... His eyes—cue balls, his mouth gawking wide with sheer terror.

Ned Bartley stared into Phoenix's blackened pupils as the boy, turned killer, quickly approached him. Potts put the .45 muzzle up against Bartley's forehead and pulled the trigger with a cold, blank-faced stare. The gun thundered shooting brains and flames out the top of Bartley's head! Ned Bartley's body flung back into the mud with tremendous force. He lay jerking, bloody tissues pooling in the mud around the gaping wound... bubbling like lava oozing from the mouth of a volcano. The man's heart erupted when Potts popped two more rounds into his chest and Bartley's body jerked with each impact.

Potts spun around on his heel, gun in hand, leveled, and said: "Anybody else wanna try?"

The men backed away with the young gunslinger who was randomly pointing the gun at each of them.

"We could take 'im, said Langford, there's still eight of us and he's only got one round left in that gun."

"Yeah... you could take me, stated Phoenix, but I'm gonna' kill one of y'a, so who's it gonna be? Maybe you big man..."

Langford backed away. No one cared to step forward and accept the challenge.

With *iron balls* Potts emptied the spent cartridges into the street and began thumbing in replacements as he gazed the body of the man he'd just killed lying dead in the mud of the street. He suddenly laughed out loud... He couldn't help but think how much Bartley looked like a clown—A dead circus clown in yell'a with red polka dots! The blood that encircled Ned Bartley's mouth resembled a painted-on frown.

...A gunshot rang out from somewhere in town...

Miller made the street just in time to see Jimmy Potts walk up to a man that was on his knees with hands held out in front of him. Without hesitation Potts put the muzzle against the man's forehead and pulled the trigger. Before Miller could blink, Potts fired two more rounds into the man's chest. The young gun was reloading when the Marshal came rushing in with his Schofield drawn...

"Jimmy Potts—Drop that gun boy—Now!"

Potts continued on with what he was doing as if no one had spoken. He spun the gun back and shoved it into its holster. Only then did he acknowledge the Marshals presence.

"Oh, howdy there Ben. You wouldn't mind pointin' that gun somewhere else, now, would y'a?"

The young-gunny was staring so intently into Miller's eyes that the boy almost appeared cross-eyed.

"I said... Point-That-Gun-Somewhere-Else—Ben!"

"Gi'me y'er gun Jimmy—I'm not gonna tell y'a again!" stated the trembling Marshal.

"It was a fair fight Marshal," said Compton. As much as he hated to say it he couldn't deny the fact.

"That man was one of mine. He called this young fella' out. 'Cant say as t'a when I ever seen such cold-blooded killing though..."

"Well, there y'a have it Ben!" said Potts. I ain't done nothin' wrong and these men even said so."

"Jimmy Potts... I want your ass out of town before sundown! You're no longer welcome in Phoenix and I've had enough of y'er shit t'a last me a life time!"

"Told y'a before Ben... The name is Phoenix, said young Jimmy pulling the glove from his finger tips one at a time. Potts looked down, then gazed out across the open desert.

"Ahhh hell, I wasn't stayin' anyhow Ben. Besides, this town ain't big enough to contain a living legend like me. I'll leave tonight, but not 'til I'm good 'n ready."

With that, he turned and walked, slowly, past the posse, shook his head with disapproval as he stepped up onto the boardwalk and re-entered the saloon through the double doors. Inside he was greeted by the two saloon gals. With one on each arm he started up the staircase to the second floor where the girl's working rooms were located. Potts stopped halfway up and turned. He flipped something shiny with a metallic "ping" into the air. The object hit the floor with a whack, then rolled across the wood floor on its thin edge... then over to the bar where it hit and stopped.

"That's for the whores 'n whiskey! You can bring the whiskey up to the room."

The bartender leaned over the bar top and eyed the coin; It was a Twenty Dollar Silver Eagle.

"Okay Jimmy, I'll have it sent up to y'a!"

The two gals with him could be heard giggling until they faded and disappeared down the hallway where a door opened, then closed.

In the street, Miller looked at Compton and said:

"I want you 'n y'er men out'a my town. 'Somethin' crooked goin' on with y'a and it don't smell pretty! Oh, 'n don't forget y'er man there, Sheriff!" said the Marshal referring to Ned Bartley. He holstered his gun and turned, then walked away in the direction of his office—He'd had all of the bullshit he could stand!

Compton's men wrapped Bartley's body in a blanket and threw him over a saddle. The rest of the men mounted their horses, then turned them back out onto the searing heat of the desert plain while the hole in Bartley's head dripped a bloody trail behind them as they rode out of Phoenix. Each man, pointed horse face, south-west in the direction of Yuma.

Jimmy Potts pulled the thin curtain back and watched as Compton's posse rode out. The thought of cutting the first notch in his handles excited him. 'Matters'a fact he'd go ahead and notch one for Abilene while he was at it! He'd been told to leave town, and he would, but first he had some unfinished business with ol' Ben. He'd seen the Marshall when the lawman had exited from the telegraph office... Potts wondered what he'd been up too. He wasn't about to let that old man ruin his plans. No, he would make sure ol' Ben didn't find out anything! His thoughts were, suddenly, interrupted when he was pulled back by the naked gals;

"C'mon, cowboy... let's see how long you can stay in the saddle!"

Potts just grinned as the two *gigglers* yanked down his trousers, then pushed him back onto the bed.

Third Day
Scouting for signs of a posse

The desert floor was beginning to heat up, heat vapors rising from the desert floor rippled the air cracking the face of the earth in millions of shard pieces like shattered pottery. Up ahead, to the north, was a Mesa sticking up like a sore thumb on the, otherwise, empty horizon. There were a few rolling hills here and there, but that big piece of rock was the only landmark for him to follow.

After an hour's ride McCall arrived on the southern side of the Mesa—It was a tall chunk of rock. At its base lay the corrosion that had slid, and fallen from above forming at the same angles found in typical canyon regions. McCall dismounted the Sorrel's back and tethered the reins around a large-flat rock. He grabbed his Winchester, then turned and walked to the edge of the Mesa where it angled down to meet the earth. He placed his boot on it... 'didn't sink like mud. He took another step up onto it... 'boots pushed in just enough for good traction without slipping or sinking. He began to climb, placing each step sideways, leaning in, digging his fingers into the mixture of dirt and fine rock to balance himself. He had to stop several times to rest, but finally made it to the place where the fine stuff he'd climbed met against the hard rock of the Mesa. Turning, he planted his boot-heels in deep and leaned his back against the solid rock wall that reached upward toward the sky behind him. At his estimate; he figured he was standing about a hundred feet above the desert floor. Red Horse was staked just below him on the south side of the Mesa. From where he stood he could see points, south... east... and west, and was able to survey the entire area up to at least 10 miles. For the first 15 minutes or so he saw nothing. Then, a black dot on the horizon caught his attention. It was moving, slowly, tracing a thin-black line behind it as it moved in a north-easterly direction. McCall watched as the train slowly faded from his site...

He turned his attention towards the sky where an eagle was circling. Wings spread, wide, it soared in and landed in its nesting place high atop the Mesa. In the distance a herd of Pronghorn Antelope were moving south-west across the open terrain; most likely heading toward the water source of the Colorado River that was snaking its way across the land, its length narrowed to a point on the distant horizon. McCall's eyes searched the terrain below him... west... south... then to the east. Between east and north his eyes caught a hint of movement. He continued to watch as an apparent presence drew closer... He could see the slightest hint of movement at its front tip—Horses! And where there were horses, usually, meant men.

"'Posse, more than likely," said McCall to himself.

It was too late to try and descend back down the grade. He bent his knees and crouched down, low, levered a live round into the chamber of the Winchester.

"Oh no, the horse! If they see me I'm dead up here...

CHAPTER 9

Steel-shod-hooves rumbled over the desert floor. McCall froze, motionless, against the sheer rock as the riders approached the Mesa from its eastern side. The group of men slowed the horses, then came around until they were directly beneath him and brought the horses to a stop. McCall put the butt of the rifle up against his shoulder and drew a bead down on the lead rider with finger lightly pressed against the trigger. McCall's Red Sorrel was staked just around the next bend just out of their site. McCall could see the men and he could see his horse; The riders were pointing in varied directions, apparently discussing which direction they should ride next. McCall noticed that on one of the horses' back was a man face down across the saddle, figured him for dead. The riders seemed to reach a decision, and all at once they bolted south-west towards the Colorado. McCall withdrew the rifle from his shoulder and began to make his dissent back down to the bottom of the steep grade. There were nine riders in the posse. McCall had no doubt in his mind that they were from Yuma and the lead rider was none other than Charlie Compton. At the bottom of the grade he grabbed his water canteen, tilted it up, and chugged several long drinks down his throat. He did the same favor for Red Horse, splashing several soaking bursts of water into the big animal's mouth. Then, once again, he was on the grain burner's back cutting a thundering line, south, back towards the camp—the same direction he was certain Compton and his vigilante posse were heading...

Back at the river Camp

McCall, upon the big horse, thundered back into camp. He pulled reins and brought the animal to a stop with trail dust swirling and drifting in on them. He dismounted quickly and left the horse by the river's edge where the roar of its course was beginning to calm. The flood waters were slowly receding, reducing the river back to its natural flow.

"They'res a posse out there... last I seen of 'em they were headed this way, stated McCall. We ain't got much time before they'll be on top of us—I'm sure it's Compton. Sorry pard', but we got'a ride out'a here real quick like!"

"How many?" asked Lawson.

"Nine all together. They can't be more than a few miles North of us. 'Looked to me like they were headin' towards the river."

"Yeah, 'sounds like they're gonna follow the water's edge and scout for signs of track—smart move..."

"Well, they're gettin' smarter, I guess, but that's the first thing I'da done."

McCall was quickly gathering gear and packing it into saddle bags as they spoke; Lawson was doing what he could, but his shoulder ached with every movement he made.

"Looked like they were coming from Phoenix, so we'll make sure not to go that direction, said McCall, over his shoulder as packed his saddle bags.

"By now there's a bounty on our heads and wanted posters are circulating," said Lawson.

There was a moment of silence between the two men... They'd both had run-ins with the law in the past, even did hard time together. But having a bounty on your head meant something entirely different. Anywhere they went, from now on, they'd be hunted by men of all creeds with only two things on their minds; the two things men would surely kill for or die for... riches or fame, it was all the same and that's just the way it was.

It was time to ride!

With a little help, Lawson made the saddle. The two hi-tailed it out of that river ravine like the devil himself was comin' down to lay his claim on 'em! If he was, he'd better hurry, the Reaper was already in the and game dealing out Eights and Aces!

Within a mile, the Colorado cut wide in front of them and dropped off into a deep-banked gully. They began looking for a way to cross, but the cliffs of the river were too steep. Going east would mean riding toward Phoenix and that was out of the question.

"What do y'a think, Lou'?"

"We got'a cross over. 'Might haf'ta border California 'n

trail north for a while," said McCall.

"'Was thinkin' the same thing; either that, or get up into those mountains, find high ground where we can hole-up for a spell and get this posse off our backsides."

"'Got'a do somethin' pretty quick or were gonna run headlong right into Compton and his bunch. We got no cover out in the open like this."

"Higher ground it is!" hooted Lawson as he wheeled the black around and kicked the animal into high speed. Without another word both horses were stomping up a trail of dust toward the mountains that lay only a couple of miles ahead...

"...It's them alright! shouted Compton as he watched the two riders through his looking glass. We got'a git 'em a'fore they git on high ground!"

With a high degree of haste he closed the glass and dug his heals into his horses ribs sending the animal rearing into a high speed gallop that the rest of his men were having a hard time keeping up with.

...Several shots rang out...

Turning in their saddles they could see that they'd been made—It was Compton! Lawson and McCall had a fair lead on him, but that old son of a bitch of a sheriff was leading his own men by about the same margin and was throwing down a hail of gunfire from a Henry rifle just as fast as he could jack ammunition into the chamber! Both, Nightmare, and Red Horse, knew the sound of gunfire. They also knew the sound of lead spinning past their ears and what it meant to get hit by one of those; no more grazing in the pasture on a lazy day... or those special sweet fall apples... or the company of a fine Thoroughbred Mare! (when those rare occasions would present themselves) Nope, no one needed to coax those animals into running faster. Sheer determination to see another fine day alive was all the motivation them two animals needed! Those thundering beasts poured on the power like there was no tomorrow!

Just ahead of them lay a structure on the desert floor; 'looked like a bridge spanning over the river and a perfect place to cross! Shod hooves quaked the structure as the, racing animals turned onto bridge's the span. There was barely time to react, but both men managed to pull reins and halt the stammering steeds at the edge of the snapped and broken boards where half the span of the bridge had been violently twisted off and washed away by the recent flood. Having no other choice, they wheeled the horses around and quickly dismounted. They led the exhausted horses down the steep bank and onto the rocky shore next to where the river was raging. It was dark underneath the trusses where the sun had no angle at that time of day. They stashed the horses behind some large rock cover, then made a break for the shadows under the bridge where the rocky-dirt sloped down from above at steep angles. McCall had grabbed the sawed-off shotgun from his saddle bag and a box of shells. He was running and punching shells into the empty tubes. He snapped them closed just as he'd made the shadows beneath the structure. That place under the bridge was damp and cool. Anyone (or anything) who'd been out on that blistering desert would have thought this a perfect place to shade themselves from that broiling burner overhead—And it did!

McCall heard the rattle and could see the thick Diamondback viper coiled and ready to strike at the side of his leg. He jumped back from it as .45 lead blasted the striking snakes head off! Lawson was standing there with smoking Colt in hand and said, "Dinner" McCall was relieved because that fanged killer was the biggest snake he'd ever seen!

Lawson found a place within the thick 10x10 lumber and wedged himself in where the frames joined in a **Y**. They sat, quietly, as the rumbling sound of a horse approached. After a moments time a shout came from above the rim of the river gully;

"This is Sheriff Charles Compton of Yuma—I have two warrants! I know who you are down there so throw down yer guns and give y'erselves up or go face down over a saddle—Choice is y'ers!"

McCall and Lawson looked, intently, at each other, but made no sound... only listened and waited for someone to make a mistake, and they would, and it would be their last! The ground above them quaked as the other riders in the posse made the rim edge and dismounted from their horses.

"You killed a U.S. Marshal and two deputies in Yuma!" came Compton, again. He heard no reply. The only sounds were of the Colorado as it raged along its banks. Men were moving along the upper rim, levering rifles and positioning themselves for a shootout with the two outlaws. Then, McCall spoke...

"We didn't kill anyone that didn't try to kill us first; and we ain't guilty of any murders of innocent people either!"

"Well... You've been tried and convicted of such, so the law stands—and the law says y'er guilty! So throw down y'er arms or I'm sendin' my men down there! Now, what's it gonna be..?"

"Go home, sheriff! shouted Lawson, nobody needs t'a die here today! Just leave it alone 'n ride out peaceful like 'n we'll do the same!"

The shouts echoed along the steep walls of the gully. The

roaring current of the river ripped and tital'd along its lower banks as the tension between the men mounted. While Lawson was speaking, Compton was quietly signaling his men and positioning them for a shootout...

Around a bend in the river a man came sliding down the dirt and loose rocks on his back side, quickly, working his way to the bottom of the gully. The other men lay out flat at the rim edge gazing down rifle sights that were trained on the shadows at the bottom of the bridge structure. Two men found the wit to try and sneak out onto the broken structure and take position from above. The lumber that spanned the crossing was considerably thinner than the truss material that was used on the frame. The two men separated, then knelt to one knee and awaited the signal to open fire...

Thin streams of light pinpointed where the boards were spaced in the otherwise black ceiling of the bridge that loomed above McCall and Lawson. That light was enough to give away the positions of the two men lurking above on the bridge's upper edges.

"Hey Compton! shouted McCall, you've already got one man across a saddle, 'seems t'a me you'd be satisfied with it and take y'er losses back for buryin' before there's none of y'a left t'a take 'em back t'a Yuma!"

A puzzled look came across the sheriff's face. He was wondering how the hell they knew about Bartley... But, his anger replaced his curiosity.

"Die then y'a sons a bitches!" he shouted in a voice that echoed and carried along the heat rippled airwaves like it had came straight out of the mouth of Hell!

There was just no way around it, they were going to have to shoot their way out of there!

Muzzles began flashing, lead spinning, exploding chunks of wood into needle-like splinter fragments all around

McCall and Lawson. The sound of it was deafening. Lawson detected movement within the truss' right over top of him. He pointed his rifle on it, then he saw it again and began jacking round after round into the firing chamber of his Henry. Pinholes of light appeared in the lumber as his bullets thumped through them. A man screamed out and stood when lead found his knee. The next two rounds from Lawson's Henry rifle penetrated upward... through a leg, a cheek of his ass, and continued on burying itself deep into his upper torso. The third round drilled him clean, spinning deep into the middle of his back.

A rifle came over the top, then the man followed toppling over in a clumsy mid-air roll. His body met the rivers current at an odd angle creating an enormous splash where it hit, then was quickly swallowed by the river's current, and carried away, never to be seen again...

McCall caught sight of the man who'd slid down the gully wall and watched as he ran and ducked in behind some rocky cover next to where the horses were staked. He squeezed off a flurry of lead from a pistol—hitting nothing. He was stabbing new cartridges into the revolver's cylinder when Lawson's black, Nightmare, turned its long neck around and pinned a "critter gone wild" gaze on the unsuspecting stranger. McCall knew what was coming next...

Before he could finish re-loading the horse's eyes bugged out, lips curled back exposing the claw of horse teeth ready to take an enormous bite out of someone's ass! That crazy animal bit down hard on the man's left shoulder, and yanked, snapping the bones and tearing loose a hunk of horse-bite-sized flesh. The man screamed and grabbed his mangled shoulder;

"IIEEE! It bit my goddam arm off—Oh God!"

The maimed man came running out from between the two stallions, nearly got kicked by the red horse as it attempted to stamp both of its rear shoes upside the back of his head. He tripped and fell, got back up and ran straight into the shadows where Lawson and McCall were hold up...

The shooting had stopped as everyone was re-loading. A sudden shrill scream halted the men above the rim in their tracks. All eyes were fixed on their man at the bottom of the gully...

In all the excitement he must'a forgot where the hell he was because the last thing anyone would have figured on him doing would be to run straight into that dark cave where two angry bears (McCall and Lawson) were cornered!

In the dark cover of the wood frame the man stopped and leaned back against the thick lumber, then looked back over his shoulder into the gleaming-bright light of day. In the darkness stood McCall... blacked out by his surroundings he watched the man, and so did Lawson, like two deadly rattlers ready to strike on a frightened desert rodent. The man turned, slowly, letting his eyes adjust. Suddenly, as if smacked in the face, he realized what he'd done. His heart raced into a panicked beat.

"Shhh... drop that gun mister," said McCall in a low-even tone. The sawed-off was leveled at his side with both hammers eared back, left hand cupped over the top of the barrels in a viced grip. The man's eyes widened, flashed like shiny silver dollars. He stepped back, his thumb fumbling for the hammer on the pistol...

"I'm not gonna tell you again..." said McCall.

The hammer, suddenly, locked back. With a swift motion he threw the pistol out and attempted to level it.

"'Told y'a not t'a do that!" barked McCall.

Fire flashed from the pistol muzzle lighting the darkness up like a camera flash, then it was dark again.

He heard the blasting roar, and a swarm of angry bees came flying out of an orange-blue cloud of smoke that sailed right into his face—There was no time to duck—it was instantaneous! The swarm tore into his flesh, and there was an instance when he felt the skin on his face shredding away with bone, everything blurred into a high-pitched ringing... then, silent darkness.

CHAPTER 10

McCall had squeezed off both triggers and watched as the man's head disintegrated with a loud "POP!" when the blast hit him in the face. The body lay fifteen feet from where it had stood, arms stretched out in front, legs kicking as if trying to find solid ground to stand on. Then, slowly, the limbs relaxed and the body died. McCall dropped two fresh shells into the smoking tubes, then snapped the steel barrels shut.

Having watched the whole of it from above the rim, every man up there was now set on killing those two for the cold blooded murder of their friend! There would be no trial—Not for those two!

A hail of lead suddenly came down from the heavens like a storm of biblical proportions being unleashed on Pharaoh by the, inescapable, wrath of God's hand. And although that thought could have seemed fitting for the part, the only wrath being inflicted on them right now was coming from a bunch of pissed off "oath vowers". They'd have to run out of ammunition sooner or later...

"Christ All Mighty... save us from this treacherous enemy that has enthralled itself upon us..."

"What..?" said McCall. McCall was tucked down in a corner watching Lawson with a brow raised.

Lawson sat between the rafters looking up and preaching as if he'd just found some kind of Holy Spirit that, until now, was completely alien to him. He went on with it as the roar of gunfire continued from up above the rim; the thundering of it periodically drowning out the voice of his own reasoning.

"...And I will not forsake ye nor abandon ye on that day when your enemy does approach! I the Lord will be your defense and..."

As suddenly as it had started the gunfire ended; except for a couple of straggling rounds from the men with slow attention disorders. Lawson began laughing out loud while Compton was pushing new cartridges into his Henry rifle.

"Whats'a matter, tinny? Ha ha ha... Y'a can't seem to hit about shit with them rifles... Maybe you'd have better luck with a slingshot!"

Lawson laughed hysterically for moment, then stopped, suddenly, silent, looking above with wide-eyed curiosity— The same thing McCall was doing...

"Save us from this treacherous enemy you say, huh?" asked McCall, looking up at this stranger who was once his partner.

"Don't ask me, replied Lawson. It worked didn't it?"

Something had happened... that much was certain! Just exactly what it was that had happened McCall wasn't really quite sure about...

SHOOT 'EM T'A HELL!

Without warning McCall jumped to his feet. He bolted out from underneath the structure and cut a jagged line to his horse. He pulled his Winchester from the scabbard at the side of his saddle and jacked a cartridge into the chamber. He rolled out quickly and bolted out from between the two horses; dust popping up at his feet from rifle rounds as he dove to cover behind a mound of hard dirt, then laid his sites down the length of the barrel of his Winchester.

"I am going to see both of you hung, or shot down, whichever comes first!" shouted Compton.

"Why wait, tin-man? shouted McCall. We're here and now —Let's do it!"

Just then a man came up to one knee and began levering rounds down at the point where McCall's voice was coming from. McCall squeezed the trigger on the Winchester and put a bullet through the middle of the man's chest, dropping him. He fell over the side of the gully wall where his body slid, then rolled to the bottom, his rifle slid down, slowly, behind him...

"I'm gonna get more men! shouted Compton. I'll track y'a to the gates of Hell if I have too!"

"Yeah, you may find yourself standing there alone Tinny! shouted McCall. Hell's a little too warm for me, 'got other plans—Sorry!"

"Either throw lead or get the Hell gone!" shouted Lawson.

Suddenly, a man shouted out:

"Tell Frank McPheron the next time I see him I'll kill him! Tell him that's from Monty Langford!"

The accent was definitely of English origin.

"We'll tell 'im, you can bet y'er next broken jaw on it!" came Lawson.

"Just tell him!" replied Langford.

A few horses whinnied, then shod hooves were

pounding the earth; the sound faded off into the distance...

The two waited for a short while before they came out from underneath the dark cover of the bridge.

"Holy shit! said Lawson as he stepped back out into the light of day. Thought we were for sure goners that time."

McCall said nothing, just walked from body to body checking the dead with the heel of his boot. He checked the pockets of the three men and to his surprise there was about $280 between the three of them.

"'Gonna' haft'a bury those poor bastards, said Lawson. 'Ain't no sense in poisoning the coyotes."

McCall was busy watching, keeping a peeled eye on the upper rim above them. He snickered at the statement Lawson had just made and said:

"Yeah, we'll bury 'em alright..."

Lawson just shook his head as he gazed down on the headless man lying at the foot of his boots.

"Yeah... I guess we will."

Lawson didn't have to guess, he knew the method McCall used when burying the unfortunates who were foolish enough to oppose him. It wasn't really a proper burial, but at least they'd be planted beneath the ground—Drilled and planted!

McCall scaled up the wall at the same point where they'd first led the horses down into the gully. At the top of the rim edge he popped his head up to take a look around. He saw nothing except vast open space as he looked out across the open desert. Then, he heard a horse blowing and nickering over near the edge of the broken bridge span. Something was rope-tied across the horses back... a man, dead. Upon closer inspection McCall could tell it was the same horse he'd seen from atop the Mesa earlier that day.

"Well, well... Looks like Compton forgot one of his own," thought McCall.

Red-Faced-Buzzards were circling overhead...'nothing McCall hated worse than those demon birds (as he called them) He levered off two shots into the air that sent the birds fleeing off in all directions. The horse bolted to the south with the burden of the dead man still attached to its back. McCall slid back down the steep rise and began looking for a place to bury the dead unfortunates—he found it. He dragged each body to a place along the ravine wall where the earth protruded out like a mouth rendering a hollow spot underneath it just big enough to swallow the bodies of three dead men. McCall took the honors upon himself to perform the burial ceremony; He stepped up onto the steep dirt embankment and stood over top of the makeshift grave. Without another word he began stomping on the hard brown formation of dirt and rock until it began to collapse. Then, suddenly, the embankment caved in sealing the tomb and the fate of the men inside of it forever. McCall rubbed his hands together with a look of contentment upon his face like he'd just completed a job well done—And that was that!

Lawson had readied his horse and was booting a stirrup while McCall finished his good deed. McCall booted a stirrup and turned himself up onto the back of the red horse, and with that they forced the animals up the steep grade and back onto the desert floor. They turned horse face, north toward the dark hills and set them at a even gate, then began to put Yuma even further behind them.

California had sounded sweet, but it wasn't in the cards. It was well above a hundred degrees, where they were now, on the Arizona plain. Just west, over the river, was a land—It was No Man's Land. That place was so deadly it had earned the name Death Valley. Many a man had already died in that scorching desert furnace. McCall and Lawson decided they weren't going to be the next ones to die out there like a couple of stupid longhorns that had strayed the trail.

Santa Fe, New Mexico

"I want them low-down, murderin', sons'a dog bitches, dead! Do you hear me...?—Dead!" barked Neusome, jumping to his feet and pounding his fist on the thick desk top in the den of his Santa Fe ranch.

Cliff Rogan, bounty hunter, fellow lawman, and long time friend had just arrived from Kansas City the night prior. He hadn't expected the judge to greet him this way.

"Bill... Bill! burst Rogan. Calm the hell down old friend'.

He lay his hand lightly on the judge's shoulder.

"I've never seen you like this before."

Neusome pulled out a hankie and swiped it across his forehead. His face was flushed to red and he was perspiring.

"I know... I know Cliff, said Neusome in a more settled tone. I sent Charley Compton up to Phoenix. He should have been on their trail. All he did was get one of his men killed—and by a damn kid at that for crying out loud! Who is going to step up and regain authority over these territories before..." (a chilling revelation came to the judge and he pondered the possibility) ...before more like that damn kid in Phoenix decide they can kill whoever they want whenever they want!"

"It came to my attention that Compton's man drew on the kid first," stated Rogan.

"He was a man of law with family! It never should have happened!"

"He was riding with a posse, Bill. He was only sworn as an acting deputy and the kid knew that, stated Rogan. A

Deputy Sheriff holding an official office never would have called that kid out. No, make no mistake about it, it was legal by the "Code Duello" and that kid knew exactly what he was doing! He killed that poor bastard in cold blood I heard. But, all the same, he did it by the code. What was that kid's name... Jimmy something..?"

"Jimmy Phoenix... That's what they're calling him! came Neusome. Compton said he's cocky as hell and bent for trouble at the drop of a hat. Enough about him! I want those two that killed my niece and nephew! You know I just buried her out there early this morn', he said, jerking his head toward the window indicating the fresh grave mound in the earth. Neusome walked over to the large paned window and stood, staring out into the family cemetery...

"'Poor girl never would have harmed a soul."

The judge dropped his head, sniffled, but a tear never came; probably because he was lying! He knew that girl was trouble the day his nephew married her. The girl had an itch she just couldn't quite seem to scratch by herself. It was no secret to the old man that she'd driven her husband to the point of murderous jealousy because she was rolling in the hay every time she got that itch—and it wasn't with her husband!

"What do you want me to do, Bill?" asked Rogan.

Neusome raised his head slightly and pinned a look on the Bounty Man;

"Kill 'em—Both of 'em!" I'm upping the bounty on each of their heads to $5000. The new posters are already printed. I want you to circulate them between here and Tucson because that's where you're heading. The train arrives tonight, be on it! All of your expenses are covered."

Neusome reached inside his long jacket and retrieved $500 in greenbacks. He handed it over to Rogan. The bounty man dropped the bundle of bills inside his jacket pocket.

"Consider it done, Bill," said Rogan. He turned and walked to the door without another word.

Santa Fe
Evening at the train station

Cliff Rogan led his Chestnut Bay up the loading ramp and into the livery car. There were two other horses inside... nothing special, just a couple plain hammerheads and the strong smell of hay and horse apples. He handed his ticket to the usher and boarded the train; "Not many souls aboard he thought to himself." That suited him just fine. Rogan wasn't much on socializing; he preferred keeping to himself on most occasions, especially when traveling by way of rail.

The train had been under way for nearly an hour with the endless clamber of rail sections under the mega-steel wheels of the train car clicking out a steady rhythm. The sun was setting in a orange blaze across the western horizon as the train chugged along on the span of, seemingly, endless steel rails. Rogan tipped his hat down over his eyes and leaned back against the studded-velvet padding of the back rest; He'd arrive in Tucson 'middle of the week, but for now he was gettin' some shuteye. The windows of the passenger car went black with night as the locomotive engine spewed its exhausted breath out...A swirl of smooth amber cream against the silky satin sky...

Camped somewhere in the Arizona hills

The white-meat of the Rattle Snake was good... McCall had never had it before but took an instant liking to it; 'thought it tasted a little like chicken.

Both of them had taken their fill of the skinned and roasted reptile, laying on the salt and pepper at regular intervals. When they'd finished they kicked back beside the fire and sipped on a tin-cup of hot coffee. Compton's posse was headed back to Yuma, so for now that threat had ended.

The two had ridden fairly deep into the hills before making camp. McCall had seen some redskins early that morning, but the Indian wars were over, but the two still stayed on guard. The U.S. Government had been placing the Native Americans on what they were calling "Reservations" all across the country. It was well known that groups of hostiles were still making attacks on military installations and people traveling in short numbers. But, so far they'd seen no sign of any.

"I was thinkin about what, Langford said back at that bridge, said Lawson. I been puttin' it together; I think he's the sum' bitch who put lead in me."

"What makes y'a so sure?" asked McCall.

"Well... you remember when I was hit? Well, Frank said he'd seen a guy with a rifle moving between the buildings, 'said he'd take care of it... Well, he must'a took care of it I'd say! He pro'lly put a poundin' on Langford's head for him to be so fired-up mad like that."

"I think y'er right about it, said McCall. Maybe he'll show in Denver next month."

"Maybe.. 'I ever see him again I'll kill 'im for puttin' lead in me!"

"I think we'd be best t'a stay on the hoot for a while... stay out'a the light 'a day 'til we get t'a Denver, said McCall."

"Y'er right... snakes crawl at night though, Storm"

"Well, now, as you can see we know what t'a do with snakes don't we? 'Gonna' shave my face clean come mornin', 'suggest y'a do the same, said McCall. The less we look like those wanted posters the better."

With that McCall pulled the blanket up across his chest.

"How's the shoulder?" he asked.

"It's fine, Lou', Just fine. I'm gonna watch the fire for a little while."

McCall, knowing what Lawson really meant, said:

"Already had y'a figured for as much."

Lawson smiled and left it at that. He stood and walked outside the glow of the fire, Henry Rifle in hand. He saw the shadow outlines of some large boulders and made his way over to them. It was a good lookout point. From there he would be able to see anyone if they were to try to sneak into the camp for a sudden ambush. He climbed up the large rocks, stepped from one to another, then took a seat and peered down on the camp where the glow of the crackling fire painted the surrounding area a deep-orange blaze against the flickering shadows of the night. The black hills were too dark and rugged for anyone to travel at night. They'd stick to these hills until they came to level ground, then they would travel by night with the Hoot-owl and make their way toward Colorado to meet Frank McPheron in Denver. It would be a long, and hard ride, but they really didn't have much choice in the matter; The two men were judged guilty of crimes they hadn't committed, and by now half of the country was getting the news about the killings in Yuma. It wouldn't be long before a lot of men would come to see them as a solution to their "individual lackings"

Hunting men for money could earn someone a decent purse; and it wouldn't be long before they'd come sniffing. The smell of greenback money had a tendency to carry a great distance and the alluring scent was enough to entice the senses of most men. They'd come from hundreds of miles to track them—and try to kill them if they had the nerve. It was 1877 and most outlaws of the time *were* guilty of the crimes they'd been accused of. Including men like; Jesse and Frank James; Dave Rudabaugh; John Wesley Hardin; The Youngers'; and a whole hell of a lot more. Some would mention Doc' Holliday on that list, but Doc' was a gentleman. Holliday never robbed or killed a man that hadn't earned it. He was also a most loyal friend; as Wyatt Earp had found true of Doc', Wyatt had been adopted!

Men, with genuine heart and generosity like that of, Doc' Holliday could never be guilty of the same—Ever!

McCall really wasn't sure why he hadn't killed Joe Clemens and had had the deed buried from his mind a long time ago, even before Huntsville. But, his hatred for the man had been so strong it had given him a reason; A reason to live for the day when he would stand over Clemens' bullet-ridden body and piss in his curs'sed lying mouth! That's the reason he had never gone back to Ohio —All the god'am gossip and lies! A month had passed since his release from Huntsville and he'd had enough of being patient—Enough of standing by the damn river waiting for Clemens to come floating by! McCall's blood was going to boil soon... and when it did, come Hell or high water, nothing would stop him from killing Clemens— Nothing!

There were still a lot of things he, and Lawson didn't know, but one thing he knew for certain; Neither himself nor Lawson was going to lay down in the dirt for anybody!

CHAPTER 11

10 miles south of Phoenix
Nightfall at a ranch beside the Gila River

The Ranch hand never knew what hit him when he stepped into the barn to tend to his last chores of the day... Jimmy Potts needed a horse, a good horse, and he was going to get one! He'd studied the place thoroughly for sign of anyone he'd consider a threat... Gazing through the windows of the house he saw an older gent' of about 70 years, and a woman of about the same. He'd crept along the back of the house and stopped at a corner where he could see the barn more clearly. Potts had just stepped out when the ranch hand exited the barn about fifty feet from where he was standing. He jerked back behind the corner before the man caught sight of him. When he passed, Potts made a run for the open barn doors.

The interior was dark except for the glow from a low burning oil lamp hanging from a nail that had been driven into the thick-truss-lumber. As his eyes adjusted, Potts sighted an Axe handle leaning in a corner. He picked it up, then hid in an empty horse stall, watched between the spaces in the wooden gate and waited for the hand to return. When he did, Potts slithered up behind him and whacked the oak handle across the back of the man's head. He stripped his saddle, then dragged the man and pushed him up across the back of his horse. Inside one of the stalls he'd found a horse, but not just any horse; It was a horse of the likes which he'd never seen before. A Grulla Stallion with white stockings and a diamond patch of white on the bridge of its long face. A majestic animal bred from the best of bloodlines. He led the horse out of the barn and attached his saddle to its back then crept out leading the hammerhead, the ranch hand tied belly down across its back. When he attempted to mount the Stallion it backed away from him several times before he, finally, booted a stirrup. Then, with a yank of the reins, the horse submitted to his control. Within a mile of the ranch, Potts shot the man dead, then rolled his body down into a deep ravine like an animal he'd never planned to harvest, but had done the spineless deed for no other reason than for the thrill of killing. The power he felt enthralled him to believe that he was born to rule over other ordinary men who weren't destined to the same greatness he was. He would have to prove himself even if it meant killing everyone who tried to stand in his way... Sheriff Ben Miller, of Phoenix, found that out when he opened his eyes and found Jimmy Potts standing above him... A length of hemp bound between in his hands. Though Miller fought and kicked from behind his desk, Potts had proven to be too strong for him and strangled the Sheriff to death as he'd napped at his office desk. Potts hid Miller's body in an empty flour keg situated on the bed of a freight wagon, it being just one of several other barrels. The empty kegs were transported weekly to Casa Grand'e, a good day's ride from Phoenix. Potts thought of how funny it would be when they opened that barrel and found Miller inside; upside down and powder-white like a ghost. An evil grin crossed his face at the idea of it...

Potts re-mounted and continued to ride, south, toward Tucson. There he would gather the information, then he would track and locate Lawson and McCall. But, he'd never tracked a man before, especially men like those whom he was seeking. He rode on into the night occasionally yanking the Schofield from its holster, spinning the gun around on his finger, then he'd replace the iron, smoothly, back into its leather housing strapped to his thigh, thinking... envisioning... anticipating... He leaned forward and eased into the saddle and began whistling to the tune of *My darling Clementine*.

The Gray Stallion resisted but, finally, gave in to the will of the young stranger who was now straddled across its back.

Two days later
Tucson, Arizona 1877

The streets of Tucson were rutted with deep wagon track due to the onslaught of flooding rains. Muddy water still lay in pools in varied spots; the sun's rays gleaming off the murky surfaces like old and faded mirrors. Cliff Rogan mounted his horse and turned it out the livery car door. He walked the horse, slowly, down the middle of the muddy road, taking his time, studying the faces of the men as he passed them by. He didn't notice anything that would catch his attention except a cocky looking kid leaning against a post where some wood steps came down to meet the street. The kid didn't look very old, he thought, maybe seventeen or eighteen at the most, but there was something in his eyes—something cold and empty and Rogan didn't like it. After a minute of matching glares with the ballsy little shit, Rogan tired of the game and turned his head to spit a long stream of sticky brown tobacco juice onto the street...

The lanky gun toter didn't know who the man on the yellow colored horse was, but he didn't like his looks. He was going to find out who he was though. He figured he'd keep an eye on him and see what he was doing in town. If no-one else in town knew who he was, well, then he'd just walk right up to him and ask him himself!

As Rogan rode on, a thought crossed his mind...

"That kid was wearing a gun, and Phoenix Arizona wasn't more than two days ride from Tucson. Could that have been the one their calling Jimmy Phoenix?, he thought to himself."

Rogan glanced back over his shoulder for another look, but the kid was gone. He turned back in the saddle... to his right was the GOLDEN GLIMMER HOTEL. Just up a ways, on his left, was the VULTURES NEST SALOON. The saloon would have to wait. Right now he needed a room. He pulled up and threw reins over the hitch post, then entered the hotel.

Rogan awoke from the three hour nap. He'd been on that train for nearly two days and sleep hadn't come easily. He walked to the window and peered down on the street... It was dark and only a few people were moving about along its length. Several horses were tethered at the saloon, but for the most part Tucson seemed pretty peaceful this evening. He'd thought it out carefully; There was no way McCall or Lawson could ever identify him. So, in Tucson he was just another passing face just like everyone else.

It was time for a drink!

He checked his sidearm for load, then, content with his findings, he replaced it back in its holster. Within a few minutes he entered the VULTURE'S NEST SALOON. The interior was about the same as any other place he'd seen. Two men sat at a table playing rummy, and three others stood the bar; one of them being the kid he'd seen at the edge of town earlier in the day. He ordered a beer and went to a table and sat down. After a few minutes he pulled out a wanted poster and unfolded it on the table.

"I'm looking for two men, said Rogan. Their names are, McCall, and Lawson."

He held the poster up for the patrons to see...

"There is a $1000 bounty on each of their heads. If any man can tell me where they are, I'll give that man $500 upon their capture."

The men took turns leaning in to check the faces. One of them, a cattle granger from Kansas, said he'd seen a poster of the same two men a couple'a days back... up in Raton, but as far as their whereabouts he had no idea. The other men shook their heads as well, none having seen either of the men.

Rogan was finishing his beer, and was just about to put the poster away, when the tall-slender kid with collar length blonde hair pushed a piece of paper right up along side of the one he possessed—It was a poster of the same two men.

"I take it y'er a bounty hunter, said the kid. What's y'er name?"

Rogan just looked up at the kid, then said:

"What's it to y'a? 'You usually go around asking strangers about their business? 'Sounds like a good way t'a find trouble if y'a ask me."

"Well, I didn't ask for all that other stuff you just said... all I asked was y'er name. 'Figured we had somethin' in common. You see... I'm a bounty man myself."

Rogan was raising his mug to finish off the last swallow of his suds. But, when that wet-eared newcomer said that Rogan choked spraying his mouthful of beer across the table...

"You got'ta be kidding me!" said Rogan, finally, after choking on the suds.

"You think that's funny mister!" steamed Phoenix, his hand jerking up to rest next to his holster where a .45 was resting. The young man's pupils went black and Rogan stiffened gazing into them.

"Who are you boy?" asked Rogan in a calm-even tone.

"Oh, so that's it huh? Now he wants t'a know my name" said the youth with a snarl. "And don't you ever call me boy again..."

The other patrons in the bar had cleared the area when the lad's hand moved to his side. Rogan was regaining his composure, but his eyes were filled with watery-tears and his vision was momentarily blurred.

"The name is Jimmy Phoenix and you'd be best t'a never forget it!"

Rogan's heart skipped beat upon the revelation of the kid's identity.

"Whoa there son! I can't see a damn thing with all this water in my eyes. I'm afraid if I move you'll shoot me..."

Rogan wasn't afraid of the lad standing in front of him, but he couldn't see! He knew if he moved, Phoenix would, no doubt, kill him.

"Let's just call it a day Mr. Phoenix—Wad'a y'a say? You

have my sincere apology."

Phoenix was impressed. The man had handled his situation well and he was actually considering not killing him. Besides, he'd called him mister and that was the first time in his life he'd ever been addressed with the label of a man.

"Whats y'er name mister?" asked Phoenix."

"Rogan, Clifford Rogan, but most call me, Cliff."

"Well now... see! It sure would'a been a whole lot easier if you'd just done that from the start, Cliff. I'll tell y'a what, said Potts as he holstered his gun; You follow me up t'a Colorado 'n I'll give you $500 t'a watch me kill 'em both!"

With that, the young-gunny turned and walked out the swinging doors of the saloon. Rogan cleared his throat and dried his eyes, then walked to the bar and ordered a shot of whiskey. A confrontation like that would have shaken most, but Cliff Rogan was seasoned with years of confronting men and he knew the best way to handle those situations was to keep a cool head. He threw back the whiskey and returned to his former, lax state of character. Shortly there after he went back to the hotel. As he approached the stairs he overheard a conversation between the desk clerk and another gentleman. Seemed there was going to be a prize-fight next month in Denver. They were saying that a man named, Frank McPheron was ranked as the number one contender in the, best out of three, bouts. One of the other contenders being that of a man by the name of Monte Langford. Rogan had found a section of newspaper and had taken a seat on a red-velvet covered Settee and continued to eavesdrop on the conversation that the two men were having—they went on with it...

Apparently Monty Langford had fought McPheron before with McPheron being the victor. There was always bad blood between the two after that and now they were going to get a chance to re-kindle the fire in Denver. A couple of days back, word had come from Yuma that Langford had shot Wreck Lawson as he and McCall were making their escape. It was also stated that McPheron had assisted Lawson and McCall in fleeing from Yuma (not proven) and after they'd gotten clear of the town McPheron beat the stuffing out of Langford. Langford was now swearing for revenge in Denver. Rogan was ecstatic, and intrigued, by what he was learning; 'Seemed that Phoenix kid wasn't as dumb as he looked. Come morning he'd catch the next train to Phoenix, then on to Flagstaff. He'd leave the train at Gallup and go north by stage up to Durango. From there he'd ride east a couple of days and try to make Trinidad at the "OLD BACA HOUSE" where his travel would be near closing. Another week and he could rest. But, right now he couldn't rest if he had too— He wanted to be on that train! The only thing he wanted now was to locate and kill those two animals before they could harm anyone else. Soulless-devils like them had to be banished from the lands in order for the territories to grow, expand, and prosper among other civilized states of the union. Rogan didn't represent the law anymore; He represented the voice of a people who insisted on a swift form of justice—and he intended to speak very loudly on their behalf!

Two weeks later
South- Eastern, Utah

Coal-black thunderheads were piling on the horizon as the Utah terrain closed in around them... They had been on the trail for two weeks since leaving Yuma and had put a lot of miles behind them. They had seen a few "redskins" off to the distance; They would follow for a while, mostly out of curiosity, then they would be gone.

Traveling across the Arizona Canyon Country had been a task in itself and it was no wonder that the only travelers in the territories were mostly outlaws and Redskins. Thunder rumbled across the sky, echoing down the walls of the Green Mountains and deep into the valley floor where McCall and Lawson were riding, phantom shadows of the night. The winds were picking up, rustling the leaves in a nearby tree line...

Lightning flashed, constantly, in the blackened sky like a strobe rendering man and horse to appear, almost, *mechanical* in motion. A light patter of rain began to tap out a rhythm on McCall's Stetson. It quickly turned into the drumming beat of a downpour. Rain drops shredded through leaves like liquid daggers hailing down, the thin branches trembling from the assault. Lawson was the first to rein up and dismount. He opened a saddle bag and grabbed his rain slicker, threw it quickly over his shoulders. McCall did the same pulling the color up high around his neck and tipping the brim of his hat down to protect his face. They remounted and rode for higher terrain, cutting trail up on a muddy hillside into the dense timber and pines. They rode higher along the tree line on the face of a sheer-rock ledge until they sighted an overhanging rock on the hillside where the rain was cascading over. There was no cover for the horses, but the trees and pines would help block the rain, somewhat. They picketed the horses and dashed quickly underneath the big rock. It was small inside with only enough room for them to sit.

"Dammit!" exclaimed Lawson as they sat watching the lightning flashes that revealed the valley floor far below them. The horses blew and whinnied... heads down, pawing at the muddy ground and, seemingly, pissed off about their situation; at least that's the way it seemed. Those two horses were standing, side by side, staring at the rock where the two riders were taking shelter. They were looking hateful as hell!

"I think the horses are pissed," stated Lawson.

"Yeah, they do seem to be a little upset," replied McCall.

"Awww, they're horses, they'll get over it" said Lawson.

"I sure as hell hope so; I don't want that crazy-ass Black of y'ers tryin' t'a chew my damn arm off."

"Well, pard', if you happen to dose off you might wanna keep your hands and arms inside the slicker. You'd look pretty funny with your Colt tied down and no hands to use it!"

Lawson began to laugh... so did McCall.

"Hey! blurted Lawson, they'd hafta' call y'a the no-armed kid! Hey Lou'... y'a think you could learn t'a hook 'n draw with your foot? Now that would be somethin' t'a see!"

Lawson laughed so hard his stomach hurt. McCall just sat staring at him and shaking his head—It wasn't that funny, really...

"Where in the hell do you come up with this shit?" remarked McCall.

"I don't know... It just comes over me sometimes," chuckled Lawson, wiping tears from his eyes.

McCall reached inside his slicker and found his shirt pocket, retrieved a pouch of tobacco. He opened it and began to prepare the fixings for a smoke. He fired it up with a stick match. He handed the pouch over to Lawson and he did the same. They smoked... and watched... and listened as the thunder echoed down through the valley, the rains washing down over the rocks on the side of the mountain where they were holed up for the night.

Morning finally came in, but the sun was blocked behind

a cloud of gray-white fog that had settled into the valley. An occasional opening in the thick mist would reveal the valley floor that lay far below them. The rains had slowed to a steady sprinkle, misty-fog creeping along at the base of the pines on the slow morning breeze...

They were both tired, but with nowhere to stretch out and rest they'd been forced to weather it out. They managed to rustle up a few small twigs that were dry enough to burn, and started up a small fire for some coffee and sliced bacon. The horses seemed forgiving enough as they grazed, chomping on the moist sweet grass of the new morning that was covered with little beads of watery dew. After filling up on the fried bacon they sipped coffee and began the task of drying their rain soaked gear the best they could. The drizzle eased as the sun rose overhead and began burning the fog away from the surrounding atmosphere. They folded the slicker's up and put them away, then mounted up. Each took his turn emptying his tin of coffee into the hot coals of the dying fire, then they wheeled the horses around and headed down the steep slope, then back onto the Big Mountain Valley.

Deep-rocky canyons to the west had accompanied them for most of the travel. A week before, just north of Flagstaff, they'd crossed over the Little Colorado River at which point Cliff Rogan's train had rolled into the station there. Rogan had no idea at that point that only 30 miles separated him from the men he was pursuing. He took the train on, east, up to Gallup.

CHAPTER 12

Arizona Territory

The body of the dead ranch hand was found rotting in the bottom of a rocky ravine. The man had been drilled between the eyes with a .45 bullet. The horse that had carried him there was found nearby; the other five bullets spent on the lesser animal. The murder was reported by the ranch owner, Myles Forte', to the local law enforcement which was some 20 miles south from the location of the ranch. Myles Forte', a Frenchman who had come to America in 1848 with the interest of breeding and selling Thoroughbred Horses, had gathered several men and were following two sets of tracks—one of those tracks being that of a prize-winning thoroughbred bloodline. The other being that of the man who was not only a horse thief, but also a cold-blooded murderer. Forte' and his men had been able to track the killer for some distance, but the

Frenchman had decided the best thing for him to do was to ride to the nearest town and report the incident to the authorities; feeling that that would be the best way to apprehend the man who'd killed his ranch hand, the same son of a bitch who'd stolen his prized possession! It had taken Forte' decades of breeding to produce such a bloodline, and that Gray was to be the last of his prized stock before he was to retire as a, well respected breeder of thoroughbred horse flesh. Forte' was well to do, financially, having connections in the circuit from, Pacific California, to the Eastern Atlantic Coast... New England areas, and Kentucky. Once word got out on that horse it was just a matter of time before the man riding it would be looking through the loop of a hangman's noose...

Jimmy Potts had ridden out of Tucson with a piece of valuable information; He'd learned that Frank McPheron and Monty Langford were to fight in Denver the middle of October. He was sure that that was where he would find Lawson and McCall giving him, just about, four weeks to arrive in time for the big show. The ride would be long and treacherous, but he rode on in spite of the distance not allowing the thought of it to intimidate him. He was thinking about the man he'd met in Tucson—The bounty hunter—Cliff Rogan. Potts (now Phoenix) knew he'd caught the man off guard, but that's the way he liked it, and the element of surprise was his edge! He'd found that most people were too trusting. They would always drop their guard, assume they were safe, take for granted the world that they lived in. Rogan was different to him somehow; A man of many seasons, yet he too, took everything for granted as though the sun would always rise again tomorrow, and it would, but if Cliff Rogan ever crossed paths with him again, Rogan wouldn't be around very long. Rogan would turn, suspecting nothing, and

Phoenix would be standing there... With a .45 bullet he would snuff the light of day from the man forever!—Oh, the element of surprise! In Denver, Potts would invest in a new Colt or a Smith & Wesson; something lightweight with a hair trigger. The Schofield was a reliable gun but too heavy for him. He needed a Hog-leg. The gun that was setting the standard for gunslingers of its time. He would run out of money soon. The ranch hand he'd killed had possessed only $10 and that wouldn't get him far. Before long he would have to find money, and if that meant taking it, then that is exactly what he would do! It was becoming dark... Sounds of animals scurrying about had him on edge. He drew his Schofield from the holster and thumbed the hammer back, then rode on mumbling, out loud, as if someone nearby could hear him...

"You don't want'a mess with me... My name is Jimmy Phoenix and I'm the meanest son of a bitch you'll ever meet... Just stay out of my way... Y'a hear me..."

An owl gave hoot from a branch of an old-hollow tree. The Schofield fired and and that horse lunged into a fast gate that nearly flipped Potts out of the saddle! The Gray didn't stop until Potts regained control of the reigns which were hanging, loosely, at the side of the horse's neck flapping in the wind. Shaken, he rode on until he saw pink in the skyline on the horizon. Since leaving Tucson he'd crossed the San Pedro River; the San Simon River; and the Gila in New Mexico before turning north. He'd made camp in an ancient cave dwelling just north of Silver City, and then continued to move north the following morning. He'd just crossed over the Zuni, just south of Gallup, when he noticed a covered wagon pulled off on the side of the river. He reined up on the horse and, quietly, nudged the animal over behind some tree and shrub cover, then he dismounted and stood there and watched...

It was a family by the looks; A man, woman, and two others—younger. 'Looked like teenagers. Probably a son and a daughter around his age or maybe a little younger. He was out of provisions and he needed money. He could see that they had supplies and the smell of food cooking on a fire was drifting on the air like ribbons of smoke finding way to his flared nostrils. He staked the horse and pulled his Schofield, then crouched down and made a quick run for the back of the wagon...

Walt Parker, a man of about 60 years of age, had run out of pipe tobacco. He had another fresh pouch and was on his way to the back of the covered wagon to retrieve it when he heard a horse whinnying in the nearby tree line. He turned for a moment, viewed the area, but seeing nothing he turned back. He froze in his tracks when he saw a shadow being cast out from behind the wagon. It was a long shadow of a man holding a gun.

"Don't move mister!" came a voice from the rear of the wagon.

Desperate thoughts, quickly, ran through the man's mind of his family... he had to protect them! He, slowly, looked back over his shoulder; his wife, his son and daughter were going about their business and having no hint of what was taking place at the rear of the wagon.

"Walter..! would you bring some fresh water, please!" came a request from the distant voice of his wife. Without further hesitation Parker lunged at the man holding the gun, but his attempt was short lived. Potts pulled the trigger and shot the man through his chest killing him instantly—Walt Parker never knew what hit him.

Potts gathered the remaining family members and sat them by a tree where he could keep an eye on them while ransacking the wagon for valuables—Food; Clothing; Tobacco; Flour; Coffee; Anything he could find to make his existence more comfortable. He ate what he pleased as he filtered through their belongings, glancing at them, periodically with swollen jaws from the biscuits he was stuffing in his mouth. The woman and the younger girl were crying over the body of the dead husband, and father, lying in the dirt becoming stiff from the effects of rigor mortise. The fourteen year old boy wasn't crying though... he glared at Potts... a hatred so intense that Potts could feel the boy's stare going through his back like a double-edged dagger. Potts turned...

"You wan'na kill me don't you, boy?"

"I ain't no boy... and you sure as hell ain't no man—you ain't that much older than me!

"Who's got the gun, son?"

The boy didn't answer, just stared.

"I'd hafta say that makes me the man now—Don't it?"

"My Pa' would'a beat you anytime, mister, but you didn't even give 'im a chance! You ain't nothin' but a yella-ass coward!

The boy knew he'd gone too far. Potts jumped down from the wagon and pulled the Schofield from its holster.

"What did you say, boy..?" came Phoenix, ice in his voice. The name is Jimmy Phoenix and you'd better never forget it! I'm the fastest gun that ever lived!"

"Shut up Little Wally! He didn't mean it! He's just a boy! Please, for God's sake, don't kill my son too—Please..."

Potts had the pistol pointed right in the boy's face... Little Wally's eyes were wide and staring down the long barrel.

"Little Wally, huh? Well, y'a don't say..."

"Please!" said the woman again, standing to her feet.

"Alright... Alright! Just shut the hell up lady and sit back down damn you!"

After a moment Potts eased the hammer down on the Schofield and pinned a evil grin on the boy.

"Consider yourself lucky, boy! You keep on runnin' y'er mouth and y'er gon'na end up just like y'er Pa over there."

The boy remained silent... But, in his mind he was wishing he could get to his daddy's rifle. His Pa' had taught him well how to shoot with that rifle, often exceeding his father with precise accuracy and his ability to hit targets at great distances. His father was proud of him and had planned to buy him a rifle of his own on his fifteenth birthday the following week. Now, Little Wally Parker would never see that day with his Pa'. If he could just get to that rifle...

After Potts had taken his fill of grub and packed his bags, with plenty, he watched as the family tended to the man he'd killed in cold blood. He didn't care! He took what he needed and that was all he cared about! These people were weak, there to serve his convenience, and they were all lucky he didn't kill them right there and put them out of their misery.

He'd fared well acquiring nearly $200, the only money the family had to their name, and his saddle bags were full. Potts booted a stirrup and turned up onto the saddle. He glanced the blank-faced mourners a last time, then wheeled the Grulla around and made off to the other side of the river... up the embankment... and onto the open terrain. He was feeling a lot better now that he had provisions. And the man he'd killed earlier hadn't even crossed his mind, until...

He felt a thump of impact in his lower back... followed by the crackling report from a distant rifle. He reached around and felt warm blood. The shot was fired from the direction he'd just come. Potts turned the horse just in time to feel the ripple of a spinning round of lead streak past his face so close he could taste the lead in his mouth, then came the crackling report...

SHOOT 'EM T'A HELL!

Young Wally Parker knew of the place underneath the wagon where his father hid the Winchester. As soon as Potts crossed over that river the boy ran to it and jacked a cartridge into the receiver, then high tailed it across the shallow stream. He splashed through as he made his way to the other side. He placed the barrel in the **Y** of a tree where the branches intersected, and drew a bead on the moving target... the snake who'd killed his Pa'! He took his time... calculating the distance the way his father had taught him. He, gently, squeezed the trigger... seconds later he squeezed off another...

Potts suddenly felt light headed like he was going to pass out. Without further hesitation he kicked the horse and it bolted to the north just as a third round spun through the rear of his saddle and thumped him in his ass; 'felt like a mule had just kicked him in the seat of his pants!

Wally Parker continued to send lead flying until he could no longer see the fleeing target. He didn't know for sure if he'd killed Potts, but he knew for certain he'd put lead in him.

Yuma, Arizona

The rancid stench of death drifted into Yuma... It was a nauseating smell that turned the heads of anyone unfortunate enough to catch its drift. Compton was standing with a group of men when the raunchy smell caught his nostrils and almost turned his stomach. Coming, down the middle of the street, was a horse... A man belly down over the saddle. The dead man's shirt was torn and hanging in shreds. All of his fingers and parts of his hands were missing—evidently coyotes attempting to strip the body off of the horse's back. The buzzing of fly's wings could be heard; dozens of the green-winged maggots circled about in a feeding, and egg laying frenzy. People were stopped in the street, staring, hands cupped over nose and mouth as the death horse clomped its way through the middle of town with what was left of Ben Carter still strapped across its back. Buzzards circled overhead. The weary horse turned, then came to a stop in front of the livery stables where it stuck its long face into a watering trough at the corner of the building. From above, a vulture dropped down from the group of circling birds and flapped its way to where the horse stood, wing's wide, slowing to a stop on the horses rump. It began pecking, ripping away at the open back of Ben Carter. Nothing much remained of the man's insides; rib bones snapped away from the spine leaving only a reddened-black crater. It wouldn't have been too much longer and the body would have just separated and slid from the saddle.

Compton and several other men, hankies folded across their nostrils, attempted to approach the horse to get a hold on the reins. Compton pulled his pistol and blasted the red-faced vulture full of lead. Shards of black feathers exploded into the air with each bullet impact until the bird rolled over and lay still with its long wings spread out in the middle of the street.

The sky above cleared of the circling demons leaving nothing behind except for one of their own. Evidently they had gotten the hint and decided not to stick around to see who would be next! The horse yanked its head up from out of the trough, wide-eyed and crazy when Compton had fired his pistol. One of the men quickly ran in and grabbed a hold on the reins. The crazed animal reared back on its hind quarters and began lashing out at the men with its steel shod hooves. Carter's spine finally snapped and the body slid off in two heaps and lay in the dirt of the street. The crazed horse yanked free, then bolted out of town in the same direction it had entered, but finally free from the burden of Carter's stinking corpse. The men wasted no time, stuffing the remains into a box and getting it into the ground as quickly as possible. Compton had sent to notify the family, but not until after the body had been covered over with dirt. West Ferrell had been watching the whole of it from a chair where he sat out front of the Blacksmiths shop—his horse was being suited with a new set of shoes.

Nearly three weeks had passed since Lawson had killed West's younger brother, Trevor. Lawson had lamed West, as well, and no longer able to use his left hand. It would be, forever, concealed inside of a black-leather glove. The hand hadn't healed well since Wreck Lawson had pinned it to the top of a bar with the long blade of his Bowie knife, severing bones and tendons across the back of the hand. The hand no longer ached it just felt like a thick-slab of bacon connected to his wrist. Ferrell had been reacquainting himself with some old trail buddies of days by gone. It would be another week before he heard back from them. There was one in particular he couldn't wait to see—William Bonny—The Kid. Storm McCall and Wreck Lawson might as well start digging a hole to lie down in because they was fixin' t'a take a permanent dirt nap!

Gallup, New Mexico

Laboring to stay in the saddle Potts made it up to Gallup. The .40 bullet had exited clean hitting him low in the left side of his back. He'd lost a measure of blood from the wound which had run down his leg and onto the gray hair of the horse's side staining it. But, a good Doc' could fix him up and he'd be ready to ride again in no time at all. His legs were powerful sore from standing in the stirrups though. The thumping he'd taken on his rump from that second round that went through his saddle had rendered him incapable of sitting. One side of his rump was black and purple lookin' like he'd been kicked square by a Mule. He was lucky... that bullet had passed through a thick blanket roll, and the saddle, before finding his backside. If it hadn't who knows where that bullet would have found its entry! Potts couldn't figure out for the life him who in the hell had fired those shots! He'd searched that wagon thorough and saw no sign of a gun. Even if there had been a gun, there was no way that woman or one of those younger ones could have made a shot like that... just ain't no way! He thought about that kid... Little Wally... No! The thought, even with Potts's limited ability in thinking things through, seemed ridiculous—Impossible! Whenever he arrived in Gallup he'd take the Grulla to a livery, then he'd find a Doc' to sew him shut if he didn't die first! He found the livery. Using the saddle to hold himself up he entered the musty interior...

"Howdy! came a voice from inside of a stall. What can I do y'a for?"

Potts didn't answer, couldn't answer. He stood there swaying back and forth, eyes rolling around trying to focus in on the man speaking to him. Then, everything went black.

When he awoke he was lying in a bed. He could smell damp hay and horse dung. His wounds had been dressed. A wide wrap of white cloth encircled his waist. Everything around him was a spinning blur, but he made out the form of a person sitting near the bed.

"Where am I?" asked Potts.

"Y'er in a safe place, son. No need t'a worry y'erself."

"How long have I been out?"

"'Couple 'a days I'd guess. I'm Guss, Guss Neely. I'd be the one 'fixed you up."

When he smiled it wasn't hard to notice the man was missing his front teeth. Potts could also tell that he wasn't from those parts. He'd put him in the mind of one of those "Ozark-Mountain Hicks" you'd find somewhere in the back woods of Arkansas. Potts didn't like him from the word git. He suddenly realized his Schofield was missing...

"That's a real nice horse you got there, son. I was thinkin' maybe we could do a trade. I mean, after all I did for y'a..."

"That horse ain't for sale or trade, mister. Now, if you'll just give me back my gun I'll be on my way."

"Now hold on just a minute there, boy. After all I did for you and y'er gon'na treat me this way?"

"Like I said, the horse ain't for sale."

"Why, you ungrateful little sum bitch! I know you done stole that horse, and there's a woman and two youngsters 'just rolled into town not more'n thirty minutes ago 'said her husband was murdered by a young feller that fits y'er description; 'said he was ridin' a, real pretty, gray horse. Oh! and the boy said he put lead in'ta the killer as he was ridin' away. Now, do you want me t'a go'n tell them folks a little story about a certain feller' I heard about; what looks just like a feller I got layed up in my barn? What you got t'a say now—Boy?! I should'a went ahead 'n kilt y'a before y'a ever woke! But, I..."

Potts was trying to say something, but only grimaced as he attempted to sit up.

"Wha... Wha... What you tryin' t'a say somethin', boy?" He leaned over closer to Potts, tried to hear what he was saying...

Potts groaned, then whispered...

"I need to..."

Potts's hand swept out from under the horse blanket before Neely could flinch. In his hand was an eight inch dagger; a dagger he carried concealed down inside his left boot. Neely never took the time to take them off and check them as he should have. The blade slid smoothly into his jugular at the side of his neck silencing the scream that was choked out behind the glimmering-steel blade. Neely's eyes were bulging like cue balls trying to pop out of their Pockets! Potts withdrew the blood-streaked-blade and began to stand as the livery man backed away with his hands clutched up tightly around his throat. Blood spurted and pumped out from the deep gash that had severed his larynx. after Neely had collapsed, and rolled over onto the floor, again and again Potts sunk the blade of the dagger deep into the man's chest... liver... stomach... and his back.

...The small room at the back of the livery barn looked like a slaughter house. Blood, running, dripping down the wood-slat walls. Pott's, gun belt, shirt and hat were laying over a bail of hay just outside the room. He grabbed them and proceeded to dress himself back to proper attire, his eyes searching for the horse. He found it in a rear stall feeding on some oats in a feeding trough. He went back to where the dead man lay, searched his pockets for what money he may be holding. Finding little, he went to the trough and washed some of the blood from his hands and face. He then saddled up and led the gray out the rear doors of the barn, then slowly climbed into the saddle, rode out the livery doors and set dust to his back trail. Gallup faded behind him and he couldn't stop thinking about Neely and how stupid he was; The man had taken his life for granted and once again Potts's point was made —The element of surprise!

A wide grin came across his face and he patted himself on

the back for his own cunning.

...”'Should'a shot that little bastard, Wally, while I had the chance,” he thought to himself.

CHAPTER 13

The widow of Walter Parker gave a description of "The boy turned man" to the law office in Gallup. She told them that he'd mentioned his name as being "Phoenix" and that he would be easily identified by the majestic gray thoroughbred stallion he was riding. She was told that the name and description would be telegraphed to the nearest authorities. At that time they would print posters and begin pinning them up across the state. The posters would read:

{WANTED DEAD OR ALIVE}
FOR MURDERER AND HORSE THIEF
- JIMMY PHEONIX -
$500 BOUNTY

CONTACT LOCAL AUTHORITIES IN ARIZONA
AND NEW MEXICO UPON CAPTURE OR DISPATCH

The likeness would be etched onto paper (given the widow Parker's description of him) then taken by express mail to Albuquerque for print and distribution. Jimmy Phoenix had the heat on him now like a searing flame lashing at his backside. The long arm of the law had its way of reachin' out and touchin' y'a especially if a man stayed one place too long and got too comfortable; started thinking things were cool; then—BOOM! The slam of a hinged door dropping out from underneath his feet. And that sudden stop at the end of the rope—Its a killer!

Jimmy Potts was, now, officially known as "Phoenix". He rode the Majestic Gray onward, north, across what was once Navajo and Ute territories stopping only once at the BLANCO TRADING POST to rest the horse and step down from the saddle. He also purchased some morphine-based Laudanum to ease the throbbing pain in his side. He made short camp at the old ruins of Aztec; brewed up some of his stolen coffee grounds while chewing on a biscuit. Next morning he remounted, left the dwelling, then continued on in the direction of Durango.

Gallup, New Mexico
A short time later the same day...

A team of six horses rumbled onto the main street of Gallup. They were wide-eyed and thirsty from the long hull out of Joseph City and were racing toward the water they knew, by repeated habit, lay just ahead of them. Behind them rolled a faded-red stagecoach covered in trail dust so thick you could barely read the name of the proprietary service painted above the side door of the coach that read: {PRESTON STAGE CO.}

The driver pulled back on the reins with applied force, brought the earth pounding beasts to a slow stop.

Cliff Rogan stepped down and planted his boots in the dirt of the street. It was 12:00 noon according to his hand crafted, Dutch, time piece. 'Wasn't much to see in Gallup, just a layover for the stage route, mostly. It had the basics a town needed to sustain a small number of residents, but no real law or acting sheriff. His attention was instantly drawn to a crowd that was gathered in front of the livery. As he moved closer to the point of interest he stepped between the onlookers and tried to get a look. There, lying in the back of a freight wagon, was the bloody corpse of Guss Neely. The faces of the onlookers varied in expression from that of; shocking surprise, to plain gawking, and others—disgust! It was apparent to Rogan that the man hadn't been dead for long because some blood still oozed from the puncture wounds, and he was stiff and bent like a crooked branch on a cottonwood. Dirt and patches of dark red straw were matted to his shirt front. Rogan could see that the man had been brutally butchered. He could also see that the body had been found face down because of the unnatural position of the arms and hands; the right arm raised slightly over his head, bent at the elbow; the palm open in the gesture of a friendly wave as if saying "howdy" to the onlooking spectators... but he wasn't... If anything he was waving goodbye to his former neighbors! They chattered among themselves like a pack of curious chickens that had just discovered one of their own slaughtered by the "Big Bad Wolf." That in itself was enough to get on Rogan's nerves. He began sidestepping his way between them to find an exit out.

"Betch'a it's the same one what killed Walt down at the Zuni!" stated a man, his eyes too close together with a hawk-like face. "It's possible he's still here among us..!"

Some gasped, aloud, at the possibility of the revelation. The eyes began searching one another as a newly found suspicion swept over the town's people.

"Little Wally Parker said he's sure he hit him with at least one round from his daddy's rifle," said one man to another.

"Yeah, that boy always is dead center when he sights down a rifle barrel," replied the other gent'.

Rogan saw that it was time he step out and leave the "raised brows" to themselves. He wasn't the slightest bit interested in their personal affairs; he had more pressing issues than to waste another second of his time involved in a matter he couldn't care any less about; the man was dead—shit happens! He was a bit curious about whom Little Wally was though. He could always appreciate a young lad with sound shooting skills. Hell, he'd been one himself as a young'n' growing up in Texas.

His Pa' had been a scout for the U.S. Calvary during the Indian Wars. His ma' had been killed by the savages when he was just a sprout and he'd never gotten the time to know her before she'd died. He swore to hate all Redskins, and he did, killing as many of them as he could get in his rifle sights. Fort Griffin became his home and there he learned discipline and how to shoot with a well trained eye. While growing up among those soldiers at the military installation he'd studied the best marksmen and each of them took the time to teach him what they knew. By the time he reached age he was a highly skilled gunman. He became an enlisted man and rode with the U.S. Calvary during the Indian Wars. When the slaughtering of the red man ended he took up a badge in Carson City and thus began his career as a law man. He was young, but the leonine mustache he'd grown added some years to his face. He would keep that mustache for the rest of his days.

The stagecoach was on a two hour layover in Gallup. When it would pull out again, it would be powered by a fresh string of animals to take it into Durango. That was the final destination for the route that had started out of Joseph City, Arizona.

Rogan was going to send a communication down to Santa Fe and inform Neusome of his present location. He wasn't in the greatest of moods and he was wondering where that little shit, Phoenix, might be. He knew in his gut it wouldn't be long for the future before him and that boy was going to have it out. But, right now he had other business to tend too. At the Post office he stepped up onto the stairs and passed a woman dressed in black with a Vail concealing her face. Beside her; a young lad and what was likely the boy's younger sister. The woman was weeping, almost silently, with the young girl holding tightly to her hand. But, not the boy. He was staring at a picture nailed to the side of a post. Rogan turned back to take a look... There he was, Phoenix—wanted for murder! And would you look at that... $500 bounty on his head! Wel, now, that sure made things a heck of a lot more interesting!

A thin smile pulled across his face. At that point Rogan took the lady, and her adolescents, as the family of the man Phoenix had killed—Walter Parker.

"Is that the man that killed y'er Pa', son?"

The boy didn't turn, just said:

"'Stinkin' rat shot' im down in cold blood he did. My Pa' wasn't even carryin' a gun, and he killed 'im! I put lead in 'im though... from 200 yards out... I put lead in 'im good. If I ever see him again I'll put a lot more in 'im!"

"I'm a bounty hunter, son, said Rogan, and I know right where that man is goin'."

"He ain't no man! shouted the youth, turning to look

Rogan in the eye. I'm more a man than he is! He ain't nothin' but a side windin' snake," he said, calmly, turning back to glare the poster.

"I'll see to it he gets what he deserves son," said Rogan, but the boy paid him no attention as he stared a black hole of hate through the likeness of Jimmy Phoenix.

Rogan found the man who would send his telegraph to Santa Fe and quickly put him to work tapping out code on the machine as he listened to the irritating, mechanical, clatter of the foreign device. There was no need to wait for a response. He'd informed Judge Neusome of his location and estimated time arrival for Pueblo Colorado. 'Figured it for some time within the next week. He would make contact with the judge when he arrived there. Rogan told the judge of the wanted poster on Phoenix; 'said, after his business with McCall and Lawson he intended to restrain the kid and bring him back to New Mexico for trial; that way "The Noose" could get in on some of the action himself. It would be highly entertaining to watch that cocky greenhorn swing from the business end of a rope!

Rogan pondered the thought for a moment, then a pleasant smile came upon his face.

Two weeks later
Denver, Colorado

The ride through the Colorado High Country had been a rough one even with it being the warm season. McCall and Lawson had traveled the lowest, and most passable, areas of the mountain range staying down low in the valleys while avoiding higher elevations where the white stuff piled deep against the gray-rock of the mountain base. They came down out of the mountain range near the town of Pueblo, but they didn't stop. They made camp a last time outside of Colorado Springs near the base of Pikes Peak. The following day they arrived at some foothills near the town of Boulder drifting in along the face of the Flatiron Mountains. Their final destination lay only another nine miles ahead of them.

Denver was a growing city with plenty of action to offer for everyone from, gambling, to numerous saloons and red light districts. It was also a major railroad hub where military payrolls, and government regulated gold, intersected paths at regular intervals. It had been nearly a month since the trouble in Yuma and the long ride was over for now. The two stopped for just a moment to sit the saddle to gaze the sunset raining fire down over the Rocky Mountain Range. It would be dark soon turning the two of them, once again, into shadows of the night. It was safer for them this way; so far no one had crossed their trail, but that would change soon enough with the growing numbers of people in and around the city. The main street was fast-paced with numerous people moving about along its length. A man was lighting the evening streetlamps with a long pole, a flickering flame burning at its tip. One by one he raised the glass-globes, lit its wick, then lowered them back into place.

At the middle of the street they turned in the saddle having heard the whistle from a train making its way into town from out of the darkness. When it blew again they could see the white, ghost-like smoke spew from the stack and bellow its way up into the night sky. The chugging engine made a loud screech and the brake began to slow the smoking machine to a stop. It came to a rest in front of the depot and released a cloud of, highly, pressured steam — Ssshhh..! The blast of steam shot out across the wooden deck that fronted the train station. Passengers began exiting from the sides of the passenger cars and stepping down onto the platforms with bags in hand. The porter, dressed in black uniform, was there to assist with their baggage.

McCall and Lawson rode on in search of a hotel to stay the night. Just ahead of them was a building with a sign reading: **THE GOLDEN NUGGET HOTEL.** They pulled up to the hitch rail, stepped down, and strapped reigns over the hitching post, then entered the building. The interior was impressive; high ceilings in the Grand Entry and a split staircase that curved up the walls on opposite sides of the room... mahogany stairs rose up to the second floor. The floors were covered with red rug, lavish paintings covered the walls. The registry desk was solid maple shining in a brilliant lacquer finish that presented the dark grain and deep detail of the wood. Sounds could be heard coming from the next room. A piano that was playing a fast-paced tinkling kind of tune that you could almost tap your foot too, if you were into that kind of sound. Lawson stepped over to the counter. A thin man with an English accent came to their service.

"May I help you, S'ur?" The man asked.

"We need two rooms for a week," answered McCall.

"$15 per room, per person," stated the hotel clerk.

"Damn! exasperated Lawson.

"Must be the fight," said McCall.

"Yes, S'ur. Most of the rooms in Denver are already booked, but we still have a few available on the second level of the hotel. Would you still be interested?"

"We'll take 'em," answered Lawson shaking his head with displeasure.

"Excuse me for a moment if you wouldn't mind, said Lawson to the desk clerk. He turned to McCall, whispered something under his breath which the desk clerk couldn't quite make out.

"Sorry about that," said Lawson as he reached for a pen to sign the hotel register. They signed the registry under the names: Carson and Blaine. They were handed keys for separate rooms and up the stairs they went.

"Nice..." said McCall.

Lawson stuck the key in the door and turned it, the door opened.

"After you Mr. Blaine..."

McCall stepped into the room, then lit a flame to an oil lamp that was setting on a nightstand.

"Hey, did you notice some of the names on that register?" asked Lawson.

"Yep, I saw a couple. The event is drawing 'em in I guess."

"Well, that's probably real good for us. Maybe no one'l notice us if we just stay blended in with the crowd and lay low," said Lawson.

"I saw the name, Earp on that register, Wreck..."

"I know, and a few more... 'Have a feeling they're not going to be the only outlaws in town either."

"Yeah, I know... look at us!"

"Well, if Wyatt is here..."

"Then that means Morgan and Virgil are here too," finished McCall.

"My Colts' are already loosed," said Lawson.

"'Did mine at the edge of town," replied McCall.

They left the room and walked down the corridor to the steps. At the bottom they went to the horses and loosed the reins from the hitching post.

"After we take care of these animals we'll find Frank, said McCall. Its dark and I think we'd be better off if we stuck to the plan of moving at night—Even in town."

Lawson stood silent... he considered McCall's words,

then gave a nod of agreement. They walked the horses, crossed the street, then turned toward the livery. A large corral was attached to the side of the structure and was already holding nearly fifty horses. The stalls on the interior were reserved for the elite, and of course those with financial influence and political persuasion. Inside, a man was filling troughs, had a cart carrying 100lb. bags.

"Howdy, said the old man, sighting McCall and Lawson as they led their animals along in his direction. The names' Chappy. Well, at least that's what they call me anyway. How can I help you gents'?"

"My name's Blaine... this is my partner, Mr. Carson."
The man gave a curt nod of his head.

"We need housing for the horses for a week. Do you have the room?"

"'Got the room, said the man, nodding his head in confirmation. Seven dollars each. They'll be handled by me personally and properly, that's my guarantee!"

"'Got'ta watch my black, said Lawson. He can be mighty unfriendly when he gets a notion. 'Name is Nightmare and he's all of that—Believe me."

"Well, said the old-timer, I got a special little place for him if he gets out of hand. Oh! don't worry about it, he'll be just fine."

They paid the liveryman, bagged their personal belongings, then headed back to the hotel. Their upstairs rooms were connected. Both having an open view of the main street just below the windows.

"What y'a say we go find us a big steak dinner, Luis? I'm kind'a tired of the jerk' and bacon. I need some prime cut Angus Beef!"

"Hell yeah! exclaimed McCall. 'Sounds damn good to me!"

The restaurant in the hotel served up one hell of a 16oz. cut of prime rib. The dinner came with potatoes; rolls with butter; and a pot of coffee. They finished the meal with apple pie and another steaming pot of black coffee.

"Better go see if we can find Frank; there are bound to be more hotels in town," said McCall.

Lawson signaled for the waitress. She brought back their check and the two stood from the table.

"This one is on me, said Lawson. He put $5 down on the table. That should cover it. Let's go."

Having previously rolled a couple of quirlys, they struck fire to 'em, walking slowly as though simply discussing some sort of casual business that they may have had between them. It was late. The only sounds heard were the rattle of trace chains—a wagon from somewhere in the distance, and their boot heels gently knocking against the boards of the walkway. To the right of them was a big window casting their reflection back at them. The words on the glass read: {POST OFFICE}

Next to that window, plastered on the wall, were Wanted Posters. Among the faces were; Jesse James and his brother Frank James; Dave Rudabaugh; John Wesley Hardin; Cole Younger; And two new comers recently added to the U.S. Federal Marshals Most Wanted List—Luis (Storm) McCall, and Wreck Lawson. The list went on... All of them reading: DEAD OR ALIVE. The Bounty given for each varied in dollar amount. The Bounties set for McCall and Lawson was $10,000 reward upon positive identification to Authorities in New Mexico or Arizona, or $5000 on each.

"Man... this shit just got real scary, said Lawson, jerking his head around to look over his shoulder. I ain't about t'a get back-shot!"

"Alright... came McCall, It's probably best if you go back to the hotel and keep an eye out the window, watch for anything out of place. I'll go on and check the registers 'til I find Frank. If y'a have any problems shoot first and ask questions later."

"You do the same," said Lawson, dropping the quirly into the street and rubbing it out with the heel of his boot. He stepped off the boardwalk and down into the hard dirt of the street.

"Be careful pard'," said Lawson, over his shoulder as he walked away. He *blinked* into the darkness where the street lights ended.

CHAPTER 14

McCall found Frank McPheron's name on the guest register at the Mountain Pass Hotel. The date beside the signature showed that Frank had been in Denver for two days.

"Is Mr. McPheron an associate or friend of yours, sir?" asked the desk clerk.

"Yes... both actually, replied McCall. We were neighbors at one time."

"Oh... so you have seen the skills of his trade?"asked the clerk.

McCall's mind flashed back to Huntsville Territorial Prison where he had first met, Frank McPheron. With a vacant look in his eyes, McCall replied;

"Oh yeah... I've seen his skills. He can probably handle himself I'd hav'ta say."

"Well, as you know, said the desk clerk leaning in across the counter toward McCall, he will be fighting for a high price tomorrow. It is a winner takes all bout. Where is your money going?"he asked, McCall.

"Frank McPheron of course. Anything else would be a fool's bet."

McCall asked for pen and paper to leave a note for Mr. McPheron The note read;

Frank, we are here. Didn't want'a *hang* around Yuma for too long. We're at the GOLDEN NUGGET HOTEL under the names, Blaine, and Carson.

He folded the note and handed it back to the clerk.

"See that Mr. McPheron gets this please."

"Yes of course, sir."

"Who are the others?" asked McCall.

The clerk, with a raised brow and a look of confusion on his face, said;

"Whom, sir?" he asked.

"The fighters..." said McCall with a raised brow.

"Oh!" He reached under the desk and pulled out a promotion poster;

"Big" Jim Belcher."

"Henry "The Blacksmith" Smith."

"Monty Langford "The English Fisted Cuff."

A devilish grin pulled across McCall's face when he saw the name, Langford!

"Thanks,"said McCall, and he flipped a coin across the counter top to the clerk, then exited the building.

From the DENVER PALACE HOTEL window, Phoenix watched the stranger come out the door of the MOUNTAIN PASS HOTEL at the other end of the street... The man stepped down, from the boardwalk, into the dirt of the street to quiet his boots (smart move thought Phoenix) Phoenix studied the man closely as the stranger slipped in and out of the shadows and the dim-yellowish glow of the burning street lamps. Although Phoenix had no idea who this man was he couldn't help but notice that the stranger moved with an air of confidence. Phoenix watched the man until he entered the hotel across the street...

"I do believe I have found one of my men," said Phoenix aloud—Storm McCall in the flesh!"

Phoenix felt a tingling chill of excitement rush up his spine.

"Now all you got'ta do is lead me to Lawson, and then we'll have ourselves a proper introduction."

He let go of the curtain and stepped away from the window. He popped the cork from a whiskey bottle and tilted it up to his mouth holding it there until he swallowed. The hole in his side had been healing but it still hurt like hell. The morphine in the Laudanum made the pain a little more bearable. He put his hat on, checked his gun, and exited out the door of his room. He crossed the street to the **WICKED EYE SALOON**, his eyes searching the night for any sign that he was being watched. It was late, but Phoenix felt the need for some whiskey and some female company.

As soon as McCall entered his room there was an instant knock at the door. His Colt .44 was in his hand in a blink.

"Who's there?" asked McCall, in a low tone.

"Wreck... I mean, Carson, let me in!"

McCall opened the door, Lawson came in and locked the door behind him.

"...Right when you entered our hotel a guy came from across the street; 'came out of the hotel over there (Lawson pointed out the window) He cut across to the Wicked Eye... Right before that I saw a guy in the window upstairs. His light was burnin' 'til he saw you, then the light went out real quick like. He was watchin' you man! I think it was the same gent' that crossed the street."

"It's a big day tomorrow with the fight and all. 'Gonna draw in a lot'a faces, said McCall. Anyone looking for bounty money will, more than likely, come this way."

"Lou'..." said Lawson, looking out the window. "I think we're gonna have to shoot our way out of here..."

"Well, I think we already had that figured from the git."

"Yeah, I guess so. I'll take first watch Lou', get some rest."

"Wake me if anything happens"

"Oh, I think if anything happens you'll know about it..."

The former mining town of Denver never really slept... it just kind of slowed to a crawl. But, people still continued moving about all hours of the night. Lawson watched out the window as the same man from earlier came from the Wicked Eye, crossed the street, then entered at the DENVER PALACE HOTEL. After a moment a dim glow appeared in the room on the second floor above the balcony terrace—Yep, same gent' as before! Eventually, Lawson fell asleep in the chair beside the window. In the early morning, at pre-dawn, a knock at the door that brought both men to their feet with guns leveled, ready to throw a hail of lead down on whoever the unseen person was standing on the other side of it.

"Who is it?" asked McCall, in a low- even voice.

"Frank... Frank McPheron, boys."

"Shit!" exclaimed Lawson.

McCall went to the door, opened it. Frank entered the room and the door was closed and locked behind him.

"Dammit Frank you almost gave me a heart attack!" said Lawson, a look of relief on his face. Frank just smiled and shook both their hands as Lawson made his complaint.

"How y'a been boys'?"

"Mostly watchin' the back trail 'n ridin' at night," said Lawson.

"Yeah, it's been the ol' Hoot since Yuma" said McCall. Whats the story in Denver?"

"Lots'a people in town, mostly out'a towners here to see the fight. The other contenders are here with their fight promoters. I saw a familiar face here just this morning. He rolled his eyes toward Lawson and said:

"Wreck, ol' buddy, Langford's the one who put lead in y'a..."

"Yeah, that's what we figured,"said Lawson.
McCall gave a nod in agreement.

"I caught him between some buildings back in Yuma (A wide smile pulled across his face) "I pounded the shit out of 'im for what he done to y'a."

"Y'er not gonna believe who's here..." Frank slapped his leg—Monty Langford! How the hell do y'a like that!"

The expression on Lawson's face went blank, his jaw tightened around clenched teeth.

"I saw his name on a fight promotion poster last night, said McCall. 'Would'a told y'a, but I guess it slipped my mind."

Lawson shook his head, with a jerk, as if to dislodge an unwanted picture from his mind.

"Ain't nobody's fault, Storm, we were both worn from the trail. Besides, Id'a pro'lly killed 'im last night if you'd told me, then Frank wouldn't have had a chance t'a tenderize his brisket. No, it was best I didn't know. But after the fight I'm gonna give him back some'a what he gave to me!"

"Okay then, said Frank, the fight is tomorrow at three pm. I'll leave special invitation for both of you under the names, Blaine, and Carson. Right now I gotta go. You boys be careful and watch your backs."

"Be safe Frank, said McCall. I'm sure Langford would

enjoy repaying you for what you did to 'im."

Frank just smiled. He went to the door and opened it, then turned...

"See y'a, boys!"

He closed the door behind him. McCall pulled a slit-sized opening in the curtains and watched as McPheron made his way across the street, then up on the boardwalk and disappeared from sight.

"You know Denver has a U.S. Marshal and he knows the faces on those posters down there, stated Lawson."

"I was thinking maybe he'll turn his head for a moment, said McCall, just so's he can keep the peace. Were not the only outlaws in the town and a reasonable man would have to consider the risk of an all-out shooting war where a lot of innocents could get caught in the crossfire."

"'Makes sense, agreed Lawson. Okay... we sit. We watch for anything or anyone out of the norm. When the time comes, we move slow and keep our eyes on each others backs."

McCall went to a saddlebag he'd brought up to the room with him. He opened the flap and reached inside, pulled out a sharpening stone, then pulled the shiny blade smoothly from it's sheath...

"I think maybe it's time for a shave."

"Not a bad idea," agreed Lawson.

McCall went back to the window and looked down to the street knowing what, he sensed, was going to happen; men were going to die and he and Lawson would most likely be the reason for it. Most hadn't seen their faces and, most likely, the people coming into Denver would be from somewhere in the local area. It was unlikely that they would come from as far as Texas, New Mexico, or even Arizona Territories. It felt safe to think that most had not seen their faces; except for those who made it their business to keep an eye on such things; bounty hunters; law men; other outlaws; and who could forget all the gunmen looking to make their claim to fame.

Next Day...
Time for a fight!

Having eaten breakfast earlier in the hotel restaurant, and with clean shaven faces, the two went to the livery stables to check their horses. McCall had grabbed two apples from a basket in the hotel lobby with the intentions of feeding them to the animals. Hell, Red Horse could eat a bushel of them by himself! Nightmare hadn't killed anything or anyone, yet, but the horse was getting that wild-eyed-look, so Lawson asked ol' Chappy to put him out for a while away from the other horses so as he could wind down. Chappy did as Lawson requested. Red Horse was happy! He ate both apples without a second thought for his trail partner, Nightmare. Well, what he didn't know wouldn't hurt him anyhow...

They were in route to the fight arena when Lawson noticed a young man leaning against the side of a wagon parked in front of the mercantile and supply. He was thin, shoulder length dirt-blonde-hair, a revolver holstered at his side and tied down on his leg. He was chewing on a stem of a weed that was hanging loosely from the corner of his mouth. The kid eyed Lawson for a moment, then he dropped the twig from his fingers, turned and walked away. Lawson didn't mention it to McCall—didn't seem important. But, it looked like the kid had thoughts that were itchin' inside his head—Guess he didn't know that staring at folks could get you into trouble...

They went on about their business. Lawson glanced back over his shoulder once just to see if there was anything to be concerned about. It was only 9 am, but the town was beginning to stir about. Horse and wagon traffic was beginning to pick up on the streets. At the designated area, chosen for the fight, people were gathering in groups. They were both pretty confident that no one would recognize them with their clean-shaven faces. The wanted posters were those of men with shadowed growths of beard. This was McCall's only picture on a wanted poster. 'Couldn't say the same for Lawson though; he'd been accused of the same in the past. None of it was true, but his face was known in certain parts of the West. With nothing much to see, yet, they went back to the hotel, pulled up a couple of chairs and passed the cards across the table, and waited...

At 2:00 pm McCall, and Lawson began checking their firearms... McCall loosed his Peacemaker from its holster and thumbed the hammer back, slowly, allowing the cylinder to spin freely. He rolled the cylinder down his forearm and off the palm of his hand. The finely oiled cylinder spun, perfectly balanced, then he eased the hammer down and began a series of fancy display techniques which were very flashy to say the least— Yanking... twirling... spinning the Colt, he extended his arm out at full length, then yanked the gun to a sudden stop, then set the gun twirling on his trigger finger all the way back to his side where the revolver slid, smoothly, back into its leather housing.

"Whoa, what was that?" said Lawson, excitedly.

"Just something I picked up on along the way. 'Keeps my timing on target, and you're the only one who's ever seen me do it."

NICK L. SHANE

"Hell, I thought I taught you everything man! I sure as hell didn't teach you that! Fancy, Lou'... reeeal fancy!"

Lawson sat there for a moment shaking his head in astonishment. "Yep, pretty fancy..."

Lawson jumped to his feet and spun both .45s from their holsters, twirled them into rounded-discs of glistening steel with flashes of light reflecting off them from the vanity mirror next to where he stood. He yanked both guns to a halt, leveled, with hammers cocked back ready to spit flames. After a moment of fancy side to side and over hand twirling techniques, he eased the hammers down, then smoothly placed them both back into leather.

"That was slick, Wreck. I've never seen anything quite like it."

McCall was impressed with Lawson's gun handling abilities. He'd seen it before, but not like that.

"Nope... said Lawson with a sly smile; and you probably never will!"
Both men gave a lighthearted chuckle. McCall cleared his throat and said;

Time for the show, pard'."

"Well, then, let's not keep 'em waitin'."

A three-room-bunkhouse at the front of the horse corral was being used as last minute preparations for the fighters and their managers. On each of the three doors a fighter's name had been posted. The *fight* was a taped knuckle contest. These fights could get ugly lasting sometimes between 40-50 rounds—a meat pounding extravaganza to say the least!

Frank McPheron needed no manager; his name was well known and spoke for itself. Besides, he didn't want a third party involved when it came to the money. He'd already made that mistake, once, and wasn't going to make it

183

again!

McCall and Lawson blended in, quickly, with a group of people who were heading in the direction of the fight arena. It wasn't hard to pick out the Easterners in the crowd, dressed in their striped suits and stiff looking Derby caps. Most of the "Stripers"(as McCall and Lawson referred to them) were probably there from Kansas City or Wichita to talk horse or cattle price and were using the fight as an oversight to close in on the real markets in the Colorado territories. Standing at a corner of the fight ring they could see Frank sitting on the bed of a freight wagon near the end of the bunkhouse. Numerous men were gathered around a bookie whom was taking their bets as they placed them. McPheron saw them, 'waved his hand in a, non-attentive, manner. McPheron was shirtless, knuckles taped and wrapped to his wrists. The only other thing that McPheron had mentioned before he had left the hotel room the day before was that; he wanted Langford in the end! He wanted to take him the distance and punish him. He would make Langford repent for his sins of the past.

"Well, if it ain't my two Bueno Amigos," Frank said with a smile.

"Frank..." said McCall with a nod of his head.

"Howdy Frank, said Lawson. You ready to take the health insurance money away from these boys today?"

"It's going to be my pleasure,"said McPheron, slamming a fist into his opposite hand with a loud—SMACK!

"How much money is in the purse, Frank?"asked McCall.

"50 big ones!" said Frank.

"$5,000 "acknowledged Lawson.

McPheron gave a nod of agreement, then looked away to the fight ring.

"That'l make a man pretty hungry to win,"stated McCall.

"My appetite is pretty big today, boys!"said McPheron.

The hour of the big fight was approaching and the crowd was beginning to stir to an excited state...

"What is the lineup, Frank?" asked McCall.

"John Belcher and Henry Smith fight first. They call Smith The *Blacksmith* of pain." After that it's Langford, then I'm the last in line."

"Well, Frank, take it to 'em,"said Lawson (patted the big man on his shoulder) 'Guess me and Lou' are just gon'ta lay low and stay out of sight, in case anyone puts two and one together, if you know what I mean."

McPheron stuck out his hand, they shook it in turn, then McCall and Lawson walked away to find seats for the event. Before they'd arrived, they'd discussed splitting up when the fight took place. They thought it would be more to their advantage if they split up in case anyone recognized them, together, in the crowd. If one were to encounter trouble, the other would be there to back him. McCall took a seat at the far end of the bleacher seating where he could get a straight view of the bunkhouse where the fighters were, presently, getting ready to make their appearance. Lawson took position at the end of the bunkhouse at its furthest corner. He leaned back against the building... rolled a quirly... then struck a flame to its tip. The clock at town hall Gonged three times... At that moment two doors opened. Two fighters stepped out into the crowd of spectators. Cheers, boos and hisses, filled the air as the two men made their way toward the ring. When the two men stepped between the ropes they went to opposite corners, then turned to face one another. There was a special, unannounced, guest referee whom was scheduled to judge over the fight. Both, Belcher, and Smith stood ready... clenched fists... hands wrapped up tight in white tape. A man stepped up and entered between the ropes. He stood in place at the center of the ring.

CHAPTER 15

"Ladies and gentlemen... Would you please give a *big* welcome to our special guest referee this afternoon!"

From the other side of the ring a man reached up and grabbed a hold of the ropes, then stepped between them. He was dressed all in black, including his wide Stetson. Under the black, was a white shirt and black string-tie. He took off his black jacket and handed it to a man standing outside of the ring. With both hands, he slicked back his hair behind his ears and threw both his arms up in a V then turned in place to face the crowd from all angles.

"Please welcome, Mr. Wyatt Earp!" shouted the announcer.

This was not Earp's first attendance at a fight as referee. He was well known in the "ordered realm" of taped knuckle fighting. Earp lowered his arms and accepted the megaphone from the announcer. The cheering of the spectators had elevated to an ear ringing volume.

"Thank you! Thank you! shouted Earp through the *hand held cone*. Gentleman, and ladies, welcome to Denver for the fight of fights! Today we are proud to present to you four of the greatest fighters the world has ever known..!"

The crowd went crazy upon the revelation of Wyatt Earp being the referee. They stood at attention, hooping and hollering as the excitement grew. Earp, then introduced the men by name. The crowd booed and cheered in unison. When Frank was introduced he stood up in the bed of the wagon and raised both taped fists over his head, then he turned and pointed a finger at Monty Langford "The English Fisted Cuff." Again, the crowd went crazy! Langford went into a fitted frenzy. He was infuriated, his face turning blood-red with anger!

"C'mon McPheron! shouted Langford, I owe you one!"

"Yeah, and you'll pay up today Englishmen! If you got the sand in y'a t'a still be standin'..!"

"Okay, boys, save it for the ring!" shouted Earp through the "mega-cone."

A bell at the side of the ring was dinged, twice, to bring the gathering to order. The "Tale of the Tape" was read;

Belcher had a record of, 43-6-0.

Smith was the, more seasoned, veteran coming in with a record of 72-7-2.

They stood in their corners, backs pressed tightly up against the turn buckles.

The bell *dinged*!

With a flood of adrenalin gushing through their veins the internal instinct of the beast was loosed—The fight was on!

From outside of the ring Langford's eyes had found Lawson... Lawson returned the glare and stared a bullet hole right through the middle of Langford's forehead, and if looks could kill...

Lawson could see that Langford remembered him, it was in his eyes. Langford's attention was diverted back to the fight when the bell rang and the two fighters began to circle toward the center of the ring. With no hesitation Smith lunged in with a straight right fist to Belcher's face... He followed with a left to the head that wobbled Belchers knees, turning him, causing him to fein left just as another fist grazed across his ear. The big man found a corner and covered up in an attempt to stop the onslaught of damaging blows the Blacksmith was inflicting on him. A big right uppercut came up Smith's chest and landed like a swinging sledgehammer against the bottom of his chin— The Blacksmith went down! In stepped Earp to start the count..!

 By the count of six Smith was back on his feet and circling again...

Both men fought hard, able to take a punch as well as they could give it, but by the sixth round Smith's relentless shots to Belcher's body began to take their toll on the big man. Belcher was swinging, wildly, in an attempt to keep Smith at bay. Finally, Belcher caught Smith on the chin with a hard left hook, followed by a straight right, then a flurry of left hooks to Smith's rib cage emptying the air from his lungs like a deflated ballon. Smith fell to one knee... Belcher reached high over his head with a right that would have come down on the side of Smith's temple, taking him out, but that dream was short-lived when Smith reared back with a right and drove it straight, into Belcher's solar plexus, bending the man over at the waist. Smith stood over him and pounded Belcher with lefts and rights, splitting him on his head, his eyes, and both ears. Belcher straightened, motionless for one second, and that was it! Smith caught him with an uppercut that took him off his feet, landing him on his back, out cold and snoring on the canvas. The crowd roared with excitement as Earp, politely, pushed Smith to a neutral corner, then began to count; 1... 2... 3...

At the count of 10 the fight was over!

Smith was still in good shape; he'd taken minimal damage in the first bout, winning it in the sixth round by KO. He was now ready for Langford!

After an intermission, of 20 minutes, Langford was introduced to the ring and, once again, the "Tale of the Tape" was read:

Langford had a very impressive record of 92-3-2 with one of those losses coming by way of Frank McPheron. The bell dinged again and that is the last thing the Blacksmith remembered...

Smith woke up in a corner, on his back, in the 14th round with a broken nose, both eyes swollen to mere slits, and missing numerous teeth; Monty Langford (The English Fisted Cuff) standing over top of him, arms raised high in victory as the crowd cheered and booed.

Langford and the sky above him were spinning around in front of Smith's eyes. Then, blackness... He was hauled from the ring, unconscious. Some spectators who had placed bets on Smith in the second fight (being certain of victory by the looks of the huge man that he was the money winner) were mad as hell with some becoming, increasingly, irritated by the upset. Several groups within the crowd went into a mob-like state. Here and there small scraps began to break out. They were quickly confronted by a person of interest who was tied to big-money in the prizefighting circuit. These persons had bought the U.S. Marshal for the event to keep a "legal order" on things. Tye Brooks, U.S. Marshal in Denver, fired his Winchester Carbine into the air... the crowd grew silent. Standing with to the marshal were none other than Virgil, and Morgan Earp, both of whom had weapons drawn and pointed at certain persons within the crowd.

"This is a *legal* event and will remain so! We will keep the order! shouted the marshal. The bets are as stands! Now, get on with the next fight! Hell, I've lost the last two bets my damn self...!"

A handful of spectators chuckled. Then, gradually, everyone kind of shrugged it off and laughed for a moment, then things came back to order. Monty Langford wasn't laughing though—No! In the next 20 minutes Frank McPheron would be making his way toward the ring...

Within a few minutes a door at the bunkhouse slammed open! The people spread out allowing McPheron room as he made his way to the ring. He came into the ring bearing teeth like a ferocious flesh-eating-grizzly that had arrived just in time for dinner! For the final time the Tale of the Tape was read:

McPheron came in with a record of 107-1-4.

McPheron never discussed the one loss—Ever! The fight was said to have lasted a staggering 42 rounds before they stopped it because of a cut above McPheron's eye that his corner man couldn't stop from bleeding.

It was fight time!

A steel hammer struck the bell and the men began to circle at the center of the ring... McPheron came across the ring, quickly, rolling his shoulders from left to right. He threw a wicked right that blasted through Langford's defense. His mouth and nose caved, imploding on McPheron's wide-knuckled fist. McPheron followed with a left-right combination to Langford's stomach forcing him into a corner. Blood dripped profusely, from Langford's nose, covering the platform canvas in shiny dots and spattered-sprays of crimson red. Langford began trying to wrap McPheron up, holding him... He stomped on McPheron's foot and brought and elbow up under

190

McPheron's chin sending him back a few steps... Then, Langford was there in his "Fisted Cuff" style; jabbing and throwing straight rights into Frank's face. The bell dinged signaling the end of the first round.

Round after round the meat pounding continued. Bones cracked... blood spattered and pooled on the surface of the fighting deck. In the 15th round McPheron stumbled Langford with a foot-block (stepped on his foot) staggering him into an overhand right that split Langford's forehead open. He followed with a left to Langford's rib cage, then a right uppercut (which he dragged up through three states) then connected with Langford's jaw snapping the bone with the force of the blow. McPheron continued, with lefts and rights, pounding the man down into a corner, beating him to a battered and bloody pulp! Langford, finally, fell over onto his side half dead from the beating.

"You had better stay down, Langford, before I kill y'a..!" growled McPheron.

Wyatt Earp stepped in... the front of his white shirt covered in specs and spatters of blood particle. Pushing his hand out against McPheron's chest, holding him, he inspected Langford's injuries. Within seconds Earp waved his hand into the air signaling that the fight was over. He was stopping it before Langford could, possibly, be killed. The crowd went ballistic! A line of men instantly began to flow through the crowd to the place where they would collect their winnings. McPheron had done what he'd set out to do—punish Langford! His fists, steel mallets, solid red and swollen with blood. Crimson spatter marks covered his chest and face. He stepped out of the ring and began to walk toward the holder of bets.

Frank was told that his winnings would be placed in a deposit for him by 9 am. the following morning with the marshal giving his personal guarantee on the transaction.

Meanwhile, he would take his personal winnings from the bets that he had placed before the fight had started. McCall and Lawson did the same, coming out of it with a pretty nice stack of greenbacks for themselves. Men collected on their bets and the crowd of spectators dissipated back to their previous business in varied places. Langford was hauled away to the bunkhouse. Upon his recovery he was pulled to his feet and taken to the Doc for repairs, Belcher had already left earlier. Smith was walking out just as Langford was approaching the front door to the doctor's office. He went on inside where he would soon be sewn and wired back together. McCall, Lawson, and McPheron walked down the street headed for the WICKED EYE SALOON for a celebration drink. The way they figured it; with all the people in town for the fight things would probably be pretty calm for them during the daylight hours. But, after the sun went down, anyone looking for bounty money, or just to make a name for themselves, that would be when the trouble would begin. They entered in through the bat wings and stepped over to the bar. The place was packed, ribbons of gray-white smoke floating on the air and the smell of whiskey and cheap perfume heightened their senses. They spotted an empty table and made their way toward the chairs, sat down. A pretty little gal with shoulder-length Auburn hair, and a split-side dress that showed plenty of leg, was making her way toward them from across the room. She was pounding out a beat with her hips and revealing plenty of cleavage as she approached their table...

"What your poison, boys?"

"Well now, what crosses my mind is; whiskey and you darlin'," said Lawson.

"You can kill yourself slow on whiskey, cowboy, but you couldn't handle my kind'a poison."

She smiled, winked at McCall and McPheron.

"Whiskey, a bottle and three glasses," said McCall.

"My, she is mighty pretty... Funny too," said Frank.

"Mister, she said, looking at McCall, don't go gettin' these boys too drunk, I kinda' like what they're sayin'!"

McCall just smiled and leaned back watching her as she worked the two of them.

"The names' Lottie Dino—Be right back..."

She turned and walked, In a way that had all three of them bending their necks to gaze at her backside.

"Damn!" said McCall.

"Uh huh..."said Lawson, nodding his head in agreement.

"'Ain't no doubt about it," said Frank, a huge smile plastered across his face.

She brought the whiskey and glasses back and sat them down. She looked at Frank and said;

"Hell of a fight today, I watched the whole thing!" She smiled, then turned—"Thanks boys!"

She walked away leaving them with big smiles smacked across their faces. Especially Frank; It would have been hard to imagine a smile that could get any bigger.., 'seemed it was stretching his face apart! He finally had to drop the smiling because the pain in his bruised cheeks had become a little too unbearable.

"I'll be right back, boys," said Frank. He went to the bar and came back with three cigars. "Let's celebrate boys, I'm a semi-rich man!"

"Good fight today Frank, said McCall. Never seen y'a look'n better in the ring."

Lawson grabbed the whiskey bottle, popped the cork from its top and poured three glasses half full of the amber colored liquid.

"Here's to you Frank," said Lawson.

They raised their drinks up high then threw 'em back and

whacked the glasses down on the table.

"Hey boy's, said Frank, don't look now but over yonder in the back... that's Wyatt Earp and probably one of his brother's, Virgil or Morgan. You already know the story on them, so I won't waste my air tellin' you about 'em. But, if they're around you can bet your last double eagle that Holliday is nearby."

"Well, I never met 'em and I think I would like to keep it that way, said McCall. That's all we need is to be accused of killing one of the damn Earp's and gaining that reputation."

"Doc would be the one t'a give trouble, said Lawson. I hear he's a hard man and even harder t'a kill."

"We'll just leave 'em be, said McCall. Hopefully they'll do the same for us."

Wyatt Earp had just looked their way. He was leaning in and making a comment to the man seated beside him. The other man turned and looked over his shoulder, Earp threw an accusing glare.

A group of people had gathered around Frank, recognizing him as the winner of the fight. Frank McPheron really was quite the celebrity and was gaining a reputation in the West, not only as a champion fighter, but also as a gentleman of education and standards that most good folk could relate too. When Frank McPheron spoke people listened.

"Damn, you'd think he was runnin' for Congress or somethin'!" said Lawson.

The two caught each other's eyes, same expression with a raised brow. McCall lit a cigar, Lawson followed suit. Frank had excused himself from his growing number of admirers and was making his way back to his seat at the table when he was approached by a man wearing a confederate style hat, and long coat. Frank leaned in toward the man as he introduced himself, then he gave a nod and pointed to the table where Lawson and McCall sat, casually puffing away on their cigars. Frank came back to the table with the gent' following closely behind him.

"Boys, I would like you to meet mister..."

"James... Jesse James..."

"Your reputation exceeds you" interrupted, McCall.

"'Saw my face on a wanted poster, maybe?" asked James.

"Likewise I'm sure," stated Lawson with an intent glare.

"'Mind if I sit?"

McCall gave a nod, never loosing eye contact with James.

"Your friend here is a hell of a fighter," said James. "Tough man!"

"The toughest,"said McCall, mildly.

"How can we help y'a'?" asked Lawson.

"Well, said James, looking down at the table with a smile. You two are making quite a name for yourselves out here. I've seen your faces, 'heard the stories about some of your troubles. I've got this job I'm thinking about and maybe you could... help me?"

"What kind'a job? asked Lawson."

"I only do one kind of job, he said," narrowing his eyes.

"We got enough troubles of our own Mr. James," stated McCall. "I think our plate is already full, but thanks just the same."

James continued on...

"Maybe, just think it over and..."

"Nothin' t'a think about, said Lawson, leaning in, he gave James his most serious look. "We don't rob people, and we don't really care for those who do."

"And is that how you feel, Mr. McCall?"

A couple heads turned in the saloon when they heard the name, McCall.

"Y'ep, he speaks for both of us."

"Well, maybe you're just scared," said James.

The words came through a tightened jaw and his right hand began to slip, slowly, from the table. Suddenly, James heard the steel-ratchet sound of a hammer locking back. Lawson's .45 was leveled at him from underneath the table.

"'Wouldn't do that if I were you... remember, you are still breathing, but y'er about one second from not. Keep y'er hands where I can see 'em..."

"Okay fellas, said James. If that's the way you want it" He stood, slowly, showing his hands with his palms facing out.

"If we meet again, he said, don't expect me to extend my hospitality's..."

"Oh, we won't! said McCall. But, if we do meet again, James, you won't be around to know the difference!"

Jesse James backed away, smiling, hands raised. Then, he casually turned and walked out through the bat wing doors and set them swinging until the springs caught hold.

McCall looked at Lawson...

"How in the hell did you get your Colt out so quick? I didn't even see you move."

Lawson smiled a sly smile.

"Did it when he first walked over. 'Had a feeling about him I didn't like, so I went ahead and brought it out when nobody was lookin'."

"Hell, said Frank, I thought for a minute you'd gotten as fast as ol' Storm!"

Lawson just kind of chuckled, looked at McCall with a tilt of his head and a smile, and said, "Whatever man..."

McPheron lit his cigar, blew out a cloud that drifted up, then settled in long-curved-ribbons of flat smoke. It encircled them, intertwining around them like a Wrangler's rope thrown from some *unseen* apparition.

Wyatt, and Virgil Earp had been watching from their table

across the room.. They'd also heard the name, McCall.

The bat-wing doors swung open. A tall-slender man, dressed in black with shoulder length hair, preceded across the room. He took a seat at the table with Wyatt, Virgil and Morgan Earp! After a moment Morgan cut eyes over to McCall, and the two men seated with him. He gave a narrow-eyed stare.

"Maybe, they saw me when I pulled my Colt," said Lawson.

"That's good! said McCall, now they know we ain't playin'! Besides, we already got one gun pointed at 'em—right?"

Lawson shifted the .45s muzzle in their direction...

"Right!"

Wyatt Earp's blood began to boil at the realization that he was staring down the nickel-plated muzzle of Lawson's Colt .45

"That son of a bitch is pointing a gun at me!" said Earp in a whispered growl. Virgil Earp clinched jaw showing his grill of straight teeth, stood up and took a step, but he was stopped abruptly as Wyatt's arm came up across his chest.

"No, Virg', just let it go! That man is a Professional Shootist, so is the one sitting next to him. Both of 'em are said to be deadly fast."

"I don't care!" said Virgil Earp, his eyes all wide 'n crazy. "No man points a gun in my direction, nor toward my brother, dammit!"

McCall touched the brim of his Stetson and gave a curt nod towards the three Earp's. Lawson holstered his .45, Virgil Earp sat back down. McCall turned to Frank...

"Frank, things are getting pretty heated up, and you're not wearing a gun. Maybe you had better stay clear of us for a spell."

"I'll be damned if I will! said McPheron. And I am totin'

iron!"

He opened his big hand revealing the twin-barrel .41 Smith & Wesson Derringer hiding there, his finger wrapped around its trigger. He smiled with intent in his eyes.

"I stay!"

McPheron leaned back and puffed on his cigar, blew out a thick cloud of smoke.

"This ain't such a bad idea, really" said Lawson.

"What do you mean?" asked McCall.

"Well, as long as we sit here nobody can shoot us in the back. I say we just sit here a spell and see who comes wondering in through those doors."

"Yeah, you're right," said McCall, and Frank agreed.

CHAPTER 16

Cliff Rogan had tired quickly of the stage route. At Farmington he ditched the coach and took the train from there, to Raton, and from Raton to Pueblo. At Pueblo he stepped down from the steam-breathing machine and stood for moment to examine the terrain. He reached in his shirt and pulled out a pouch containing a slab of uncut tobacco. With a knife that hung from a lanyard underneath his arm he sliced off a thick chunk, then poked it into his mouth, back to his jaw. He chewed on the plug of moist leaf until it produced the taste he was working on then turned his head and spit a dark-brown puddle of the stuff on a flat rock at the side of the platform boards. He wiped his mouth on his sleeve, carefully checking his mustache. He stretched his arms out high over his head, then went to the livery car to retrieve his horse and find a rental room. Not much in Pueblo, but he did find a room. He lay back on the bed of the hotel room and looked over the posters of McCall and Lawson. The room was small, and musty smelling, but for now it would have to do. Something in his gut told him he was in the right place; If Lawson and McCall were in Denver, eventually, they would move south. They would come to the town of Pueblo and he would be there waiting...

Jimmy Phoenix left his room, closed the door behind him, and stepped onto the red carpet that lined the hallway. The giggles of the saloon gals faded behind as he strolled down the length of the hallway. He came to its end and turned toward the stairs sliding his left hand along the wooden railing as he eyed the smoky bar room of the WICKED EYE SALOON, below. Suddenly, through the smoke and many faces in the lower room, the faces of two men jumped out at him like a striking rattler! His heart skipped beat and he froze with his hand on the rail. Then, he remembered...

"They don't know me!"

He relaxed... placed both hands down on the rail and stared down at McCall and Lawson. He gazed on them with amazement! The men he had traveled so far to find were now within range of his deadly bullets. No... he wanted it to be face to face... dragging iron in a true life or death showdown. Phoenix had something to prove not only to himself but to anyone who thought they were faster at the art of the Quick Draw. No... he would take the time to study them, maybe even meet them and befriend them. Then, when the time was right, he would kill both of them and earn his claim as the fastest gun that ever lived!

...Jimmy Potts had read the dime store novels of famous men and their guns in the Wild West since he was 10 years old. All his life he'd wanted to be a gunfighter. By age 12 he was faster than most, practicing with an old Colt Walker

.44 that his father had left him. At age 15 he killed a man in a shoot out in Abilene after the man had told him his mama needed to change his diaper 'cause he was full of shit! When the man blinked, Potts put a .44 bullet through his face entering at his cheek bone just below his right eye, then another through his heart.

He reached for a smoke he'd rolled earlier on and put fire to the end of it. He drew on it making the tip glow brightly, then exhaled the smoke down toward the open room of the saloon below. He unhooked the thong from the hammer of the new .45 Peacemaker he'd paid for with his blood money, then turned and walked to the stairs. His spurs jingled a metallic chime as he began his dissent down into the saloon where halos' and horns would lock up in a confrontation of; Who's who...

The piano man, black derby, white shirt and fancy cuff links, sat at the piano plinking out a rickety tune on the old music box that sounded like it had been wound too tight and could no longer hold a tune. The steel strings inside whined and bellowed its, almost irritating, sound. Phoenix made the last stair and hit the floor, began cutting a path across it to the big bar. He placed his steps, slowly, each spur producing a chime when his heel hit the floor. He made no eye contact with the patrons who were raising and turning their heads in his direction as he moved past them. His soul gaze was fixed on the table where Storm McCall and Wreck Lawson were seated.

McCall looked up, 'caught a hard glare from a kid with thick-yellow, shoulder length hair. McCall noticed the new shooting rig he was flashing and how it was tied down on his leg, thong loosed from the hammer. McCall saw the kid's eyes cut to Lawson, for only a split-second, but he did it just the same. McCall knew that look! The stranger then put a finger to the brim of his hat and gave a curt nod.

McCall's expression stayed blank and his eyes didn't move from Phoenix's nor did he blink. In that exact moment time and space stopped... frozen... as the two men remained locked in gaze. Phoenix turned his gaze as he made the bar, then time resumed it's normal pace. Lawson and Frank had been talking between themselves and had missed the moment.

"Wreck," said McCall.

"What pard'?"

"We've got a player... I think he wants to get in on the game if you know what I mean. He's the yell'a haired one totin' the fancy rig standing at the bar. He's tied down and his eyes are sayin' he's lookin' for action."

"He's young, Lou', said Lawson as he eyed the kid standing at the bar.

"So were you, and you know it don't make no damn difference!"

Lawson turned and caught McCall's eyes...

"Does it!?" exacted McCall.

Lawson's memory drifted back to a place in time where a young boy stood... six-shooter tied down against his leg... bitterness in his gut like he'd swallowed a wild berry infested with hate!

"No... said Lawson, in a low tone, It doesn't."

"Alright then," said McCall.

Wyatt Earp, and his kin stood, then began to move toward the bat wings, Wyatt leading, Morgan and Virgil trailing the back. They moved like one, together, in their black Stetson hats, black pants, black boots and black Mackinaws. Hell, even their hair was black! The final touch was the black-ribbon ties. The only thing that was not black was their white shirts. Morgan and Virgil eyed Phoenix at the bar as they strolled by. Wyatt's eyes stayed on the table where McCall and Lawson were seated. The "ching" of boot spurs faded when the men exited the saloon.

After another hour of drinks and chatting with the patrons, McPheron was beginning to tire.

"Well, boys, said Frank, I find I am in need of some rest. It has been a long afternoon and I am damned tired from beatin' on Langford's head!" He chuckled at the thought and some others joined in on the humor of it. He turned and spoke directly to McCall and Lawson.

"'Gonna' get some rest. I'll take a hot bath and catch up later. If I hear shots I'll be right there...'Got me a carbine up in the room with one already chambered."

"Get some rest, Frank, said Lawson. Me 'n Lou' can handle it. We'll see you come morning, then we'll collect your money."

"Alright, said Frank, be safe boys."

He reached for the bottle and poured one more round for the three of them. They raised them together, then smacked 'em down on the table.

"You know what... A little rest don't sound too bad," said Lawson.

"I think I'm ready to mosey on back to the hotel myself," said McCall, following with a yawn.

"Alright then, let's get out'a here," said Lawson.

McCall and Lawson stood and the three of them walked toward the bat wing doors. Lottie Dino gave a smile and a wink.

"Behave yourselves, boys..."

Lawson was the first to exit the doors; Frank was following, closely behind, with McCall trailing them. Immediately, Lawson saw a man walking, quickly, crossing a side street from one boardwalk, then he stepped up onto another on the other side. Lawson had just pushed his way out the swinging doors, when...

"Hey you son of a bitch!"

Lawson turned and saw a man racing toward him with a sawed-off shotgun pressed tightly against his shoulder and looking wild-eyed at him down the length of both barrels! Lawson was already spinning to knock Frank out of the way when fire erupted from one of the barrels blasting eight .38 balls of lead into a six inch wooden post right in front of Lawson. Pieces of the post exploded into chunks and splinter shrapnel right where Lawson's next step would have placed him! The man continued coming, quickly with the stock of the gun still pressed hard to his shoulder. McCall had jumped back when he heard the shotgun blast. He waited for a split second, then ran forward slamming through the doors and quickly dove across the stairs. Landing in the street, he came up on one knee...

"You're dead McPheron!"screamed the shotgun toter.

The steel-barrels were so close to Frank's face he could smell the fresh blast of gunpowder oozing from the hollow tubes. McCall's hand had just touched the side of his holster when—Boom! McCall watched as a large hole appeared in the side of the shotgun toter's neck. Part of an earlobe and jawbone disappeared instantly in an explosion of bloody tissue.

—Boom!

Again, a gun roared and a bullet drilled deep into the man's rib cage going through his lung, then searing a hole straight through his heart! The man fell back... both shotgun barrels tilted up... he fired through the overhanging roof exploding wood, and cedar shingle, high into the air. The man fell to his side and dropped the shotgun. Dark crimson cascaded from his nose and mouth and a tendril of smoke was curling out from the blackened-hole in his side...

Monty Langford lay still... his eyes staring blank and lifeless into nowhere. One of his arms was pinned beneath him, bent at the elbow with a hand in the middle of his back as a thick pool of blood was forming around him. Lawson and Frank had gotten to their feet with guns in hand.

McCall stared intently at the dark figure standing in between the bat wing doors of the Wicked Eye... a smoking Colt in his hand. McCall's .44 was leveled on him with the hammer ready to drop!

"I'm not looking for trouble... just trying to right what looked wrong," said the person stepping out from between the bat wing doors.

"'Names, Phoenix..."

He twirled the gun back several times on his finger and, smoothly, eased it back into its stiff leather holster. His gloved hand fell away, but stayed near the butt of the gun.

"Don't shoot me fellas... 'just looked like you could use a hand there for a minute. Ol' boy came up on y'a kind'a sudden like." He turned, gave a nod in the direction of Lawson and Frank.

"Son of a bitch, thought McCall—Its that kid!

"Mister, said McCall with pure intent, you had better not even breathe 'til I know who you are!"

McCall was staring down the muzzle of his Peacemaker pointed straight between the stranger's eyes. A crowd had gathered nearby and were watching the whole of it. In the distance they could see the marshal running down the boardwalk, the sound of his boots growing louder as he approached. He jumped off into the dirt of the street and levered a round into a Henry rifle, then threw it up tight to his shoulder. He stopped,then locked the barrel down against the side of a post and placed the sights on the side of McCall's head.

"Mister, you'd better drop that there iron in your hand real slow..."

Just then the marshal heard the ratcheting sound of a cylinder and a hammer locking back...

"Hey marshal... drop that Yellow-Boy y'er pointin' at my partner or this could get real ugly—Real fast!"

The lawman lowered the rifle.

"I know who you boys are, and I don't care for no trouble with y'uins, but murder is still against the law. And,well... I am a man of law! He said it as if unsure of the fact for a moment.

"That's Monty Langford!" shouted someone from the gathering crowd. "He was one of the fighters today."

"Yep, said another person. And that man there (pointing to McPheron) is the one who whooped 'im."

"Sure is, whooped 'im good too!" said the other gent'

"Did anyone see what happened?" Asked the marshal.

"I did, said Phoenix, in a cool voice. "'Saw the whole thing. 'Matter of fact I would have to say I'm the one who killed 'im... Mister Langford there ran in out of nowhere pointin' and firin' that scatter gun at these fellas, and he would have killed 'em, 'til I drilled 'im! I'd haf'ta say that put a real change in his plan real quick..."

"That's what we saw! said a couple of older folks. That man there (pointing to Langford) just came runnin' and hollerin' and shootin' at these here fellows from out of nowhere."

"That's what happened marshal," said McCall, lowering his Colt as he began to ease up a little bit, but still not taking his eyes off of Phoenix.

"Thanks mister," said Frank, to Phoenix. We're much obliged to y'a, he said, looking down on the lifeless body of Monte Langford.

"Dammit! Poor son of the bitch just couldn't take it. He'd have rather killed me than say I beat him. And just looked at him now..."

Frank just stood there shaking his head.

"'Suits him fine, said Lawson. 'Bastard put lead in me a little while back" (Lawson hadn't forgotten about it) "One of those barrels was meant for me!"

"I'm satisfied with what I heard here. Plenty of witnesses to account for the fact that it was self-defense. I may need to take statements from you gentlemen later on. Nothing left to see here folks, said the marshal. Go on about your business now!"

"We'll be around, marshal, if you need to find us," said McCall.

McCall holstered his .44, then turned to Phoenix;

"'Reckon me 'n my friends here owe you a thanks, mister.."

"Phoenix... as I stated before, the name is Phoenix."

The marshal left walking up the middle of the street. Most likely heading back to his office at the jail. McCall's eyes shifted from the marshal, back to Phoenix, then to the crowd (most of whom were standing and gazing over the lifeless body of Monty Langford) Lawson and Frank were talking amongst themselves when a group of men on the opposite side of the street caught their attention. McCall recognized them immediately; 'may have had something to do with the fact that they were all dressed in black and staring in his direction. Approaching the group of men from the street was a man McCall didn't recognize. The newcomer stepped up onto the boardwalk and joined ranks with the other men. It was apparent that the men in black had been previously acquainted with him. The newcomer was an older gent, slim with a thick-Leonine mustache and graying hair. Although it was apparent he was not a brother, one could only see that the bond between the men was thick as blood. Lawson came over and moved in to stand at McCall's side. He too had noticed the group of men. Frank came up from behind and took a stand joining McCall and Lawson as they returned the new comers *speculative* gaze. There was no doubt in their minds who he was—Doc Holliday!

The foreign looking vehicle turned onto the main street; 'wasn't no ordinary wagon though; It was black, shiny. Glass panels revealed its interior of dark curtains and lace. The fancy wagon was being led by an old Bay with a broke down back that no doubt had seen its better days of previous pony life. Holding the reins was a man, a white-haired apparition of a man dressed in black. Seated beside him, on the perch, was a midget-of-a-man. He looked anxious about something, couldn't seem to sit still. The ghoulish looking mortician sat, silent, staring ahead with his sunken eyes as though some great unknown destination lay on the horizon just ahead of them. The rig came to a stop and the mortician stepped down from the perch, adjusted the split on the back of his long jacket that hung down past his knees near his black shoes. The *freaks* hair was shoulder length hanging in thin strands blending with his creepy-pale colored skin. He stepped (seemed more like floated) toward the body of Langford with a long-bony finger pointing out from his extended hand. Slowly, the apparition turned... his ghostly head came to rest with his chin propped on the curve of his shoulder. His sunken eye sockets were deep-black holes, seemingly void of any life within them. Then, he blinked and smiled a wide-crooked smile revealing both rows of tall yellow front teeth that instantly transformed his features into that of a wicked looking skull. The hair on the back of McCall's neck stood on end. His hand jerked toward his side as he began backing away from whomever, or whatever it was grinning at him. Lawson instantly had McCall's hand gripped at the wrist.

"Luis!" exclaimed Lawson, with an urgent tone.

McCall yanked away.

"Let's get the hell out'a here" said McCall.

The train whistle blew from the 8:45 out of Cheyenne. The chugging sound of the train could be heard as it steamed it's way into the station, then expelled it's hot-cloudy breath as the mega-steel wheels came to a stop. Three men stepped down at the rear of the train and stood along side of the caboose. Two carried rifles, the other a shotgun. The train would stay until morning and then transport the $20,000 payroll to Fort Union Texas. The Union Pacific Railroad had contracted with the U.S. Military to run to Cheyenne, back to Denver, then south to Fort Union once a month. The railroad had hired the men to ride shotgun until payroll was delivered. The conductor, a gray-haired man with a fine trimmed beard and black uniform with matching short-brimmed cap, stepped off, then turned and shouted—Denver! He reached in his vest pocket and pulled out a watch with gold chain attached. He flipped it open, checked the time, and gave a nod of approval—Right on time!

CHAPTER 17

The *gonging* sound of the bell faded behind them...

McCall and Lawson were going to stop in one more time and check the livery to see how the horses were doing. When they entered a young man was sweeping out an empty stall and had several fresh bales of hay stacked up against a wall. The air inside the livery barn smelled strongly of fresh hay and trail apples. Lawson's horse, Nightmare, had been brought back inside and placed in a stall at the far end of the building. Horses whinnied and snorted as the two men walked by the stalls that were lined along both sides of the building's length. As they approach the far stalls Lawson could see that Nightmares' neck was stretched out over top of the stall gate. A man was standing there with his hand stretched out. The black stallion had it's lips stretched out *fingering* through whatever it was the man was holding in his hand.

"Can I help you mister?"said Lawson. "That's my horse y'er messin' with. I don't take kindly to people who can't mind their own business, and that had better be just oats y'er feeding to my horse!"

"Easy son," said the man. "Just admiring this beautiful animal of yours. Hell, we just became friends! Laughing, the man continued... Well, that is after he tried to take a piece of my shoulder off when I was walking by."

He dusted his hand off on the leg of his pants, then threw it out to Lawson... "Murdocks' the name—Sal Murdock, and thoroughbred horses are my line of business. Well, that and some Texas White Face here and there. I will give you $500 for this horse right now!"

"Mister, that horse ain't for sale at any price," said Lawson.

"I will give you $1,000!"

"Like I said... my horse ain't for sale."

"Damn, young fella, I like that horse! I'll tell you what... You boys ever do any work with horses? I mean as far as making money off of 'em?"

"Never really done it for any business, said McCall, but we have broken our share of broncs'."

"I thought the likes," said Murdoch with a hint of excitement in his voice. You fellas got any money?"

"We got enough," said Lawson.

"Well, you need more like I always say!"

Murdock reached in his suit pocket and retrieved a business card and handed it to Lawson.

"'Got horses back in Kentucky, and White Face Cattle spread from Wichita clear down through San Anton'. You boys every get the notion, look me up. I'll give you top dollar for Colorado wild Mustangs—Delivered of course. If you can handle cattle I'll give you the same offer. That is, if I can get me an offspring from that beautiful animal you got there—What an animal!" exclaimed the man as he gazed upon the black stallion in an, almost mesmerized state.

After a moment he shook it off and said; "Gotta go

fella's. Nice meeting you boys!"

Sal Murdock walked away. McCall and Lawson examined the card that he had handed them. It read;

{AMERICAN THOROUGHBREDS}
BREEDING AND STUD SERVICES OF THE FINEST
HORSE STOCK FROM EAST TO WEST.
-SAL MURDOCK-
PRESIDENT, SOLE PROPRIETOR.
DODGE CITY, KANSAS.

The men checked their animals, then started on their way back to the hotel. McCall was kicked back enjoying the tub of hot water (a rarity when riding the trail) Next to him a glass (half empty) and a bottle of Bourbon Whiskey. From outside the open window of his room he heard several shouts in the distance followed by gunfire, then silence. Just as they had figured earlier; the snakes crawl at night! McCall had placed a chair beside the tub to use as a table. His Colt was in it's holster, next to him, hanging from the back of the chair. He lay back in the comfort, sipping of the whiskey and lightly puffing on a sweet cheroot cigar. From the open window he could hear a piano whining out it's tune from the WICKED EYE SALOON. Suddenly, a knock came at the door, a subtle knock. The .44 was in McCall's hand, hammer locked back before the knock ended.

"Who's there?" he asked in a low-even voice.

"A friend..." came the voice of a man.

"You'd better be," said McCall, because If you come through that door, and you're not, I'll blow you right back out of it!   Now, come on in..."

The door opened, slowly, and a man stepped into the room. From the vanity mirror McCall could see the man's reflection. He could also see out the door and into the

212

hallway... the man was alone.

"If you would be so kind as to close the door," said McCall.

"Mr. McCall, said the stranger (showing that he already knew who McCall was) we should probably talk, sir."

"Well, mister, step into the light a little better and tell me y'er name."

The man did as he was asked. His shadow came to light revealing his features.

He stood eye to eye with McCall and said;

"'Names, John Henry... most know me as Doc' Holliday."

"Well, Doc', nice t'a meet y'a. You wouldn't mind keeping your hands where I can see them would you?"

"Of course not, Mr. McCall. I didn't come here to do battle against you, sir. I come to... mend a fence you might say, before things get out of hand."

"'Sounds like the gentlemanly thing t'a do," said McCall.

Holliday pointed to a vacant chair...

"Do you mind?"

He grabbed the chair by its back rest and spun it around in one hand, then came around it and sat down.

"My associates have come to the conclusion that... to have any further business with you and your colleagues would tend to be of "non beneficial" importance to either party involved. They feel it more beneficial to let bygones be bygones."

"Real glad ta hear that because that's the same way we feel, said McCall. Tell the Earp's' that we respect their good judgment and from this point forward we have only good intentions toward them. They can count on our full cooperation in honoring their request."

McCall eased the hammer down on the Colt, redirected the muzzle.

"Whiskey?" asked McCall.

"If you please..." I would be more than willing to join you in your venture of a toast to... say, friends..?"

"Friends it is then Doc'! said McCall, pouring Bourbon Whiskey into Holliday's glass. Oh! Is it all right if I call you Doc'?"

"By all means do, Storm. May I call you, Storm?"

"By all means Doc'! said McCall with a wide smile, by all means..."

He handed the half glass of whiskey to Holliday.

To, friends..."

They threw back the whiskey. Holliday held out his glass.

"Another?"

"Don't mind if I do, thank you kindly. I feel inclined to tell you that upon my return to Denver I have acquired the name of Tom Mackey. Reason being... a man named Budd Ryan chose to step on my toes a while back and the only way to get him off of them was to grant him a nasty wound to his neck. 'Thought I'd killed him, but he lived to tell my name to the officials—Anyway..."

Holliday drew a deep breath...

"Hell Doc'the dumb bastard prolly had it comin' anyway."

"My sentiments exactly!" said Holliday.

"They both laughed, mildly, at the comment, then...

McCall couldn't help but notice, Holliday had a gun in a holster facing butt foreword.

"That is a hell of a six shooter you got holstered there Doc'... Smith & Wesson, Russian. Is it .44 caliber?

"Why, yes it is! You have a keen eye for custom weaponry."

"I only ask because it was rumored that normally the .36 Colt was your preferred weapon of choice."

"True, but being of cartridge conversion in 1871, the Colt now takes .38 caliber cartridges. I rarely exhibited this pistol. The grips are of ivory taken from elephant tusk. A stately gentleman whom I befriended back East gave me the gun as a gift made special for me. He probably would not have been so kind had he known that his wife had had a special attraction to my overwhelming charm, but a great gift nonetheless."

Both men laughed at the humor in it

they raised glasses and threw back the shot of Bourbon.

"There is nothing quite like a good quality Bourbon, said Doc'. Now, if you don't mind, I'll be on my way. Thank you kindly Storm for your hospitality."

"I'll see y'a around Doc'... Thanks."

"I am certain you will... friend."

Holliday went to the door, opened it, and left without looking back. His boot steps faded as he turned out of the narrow hallway. A few minutes later McCall got dressed. He retrieved some fresh Levi's from his bag and pulled them on. He blew out the lamp on the table and then sat down in a chair he had placed beside the window off to the side where he couldn't be seen. He watched out the window, Colt in hand. He watched the streets below until the town grew silent, except for a couple of men talking at the train depot, their voices being carried to his window on the cool night air. The, otherwise, calm evening was filled with the sounds that were pouring out from inside the WICKED EYE SALOON.

Lawson had heard a man talking with McCall through the thin wall of his adjoining room. He had, quietly, opened his window and listened to the conversation with Colt in hand. He heard McCall's door close and he listened as the footsteps faded out down the hall. He holstered his .45 and went to McCall's room, knocked on the door and went in.

"So... what was it like talkin' t'a Holliday?"

"He's a likable character. I think he's trustable

"Well, what do you think we should do?" asked Lawson.

"I think trouble is in the air tonight if we leave this hotel."

"I think you're right."

"That train... 'somethin' goin' on with that" said McCall.

"Armed security guardin' somethin'," replied Lawson. You remember what James said today about a job he needed help with? I'm thinkin' that's the job."

"Me too. I say in the morning, after Frank collects his prize money, we saddle them grain burners of ours and get the hell out of Denver before someone finds us parkin' our asses in one spot for too long!" replied McCall.

"I got no problems with that, I'm ready to ride."

"We can't run forever, Wreck. I've been thinkin' about this shit. Somebody wants us dead and it started when we got tangled up in the web with that little black widow named, Marla Carlson. 'Just got a feeling, somethin' in my gut telling me this whole damned situation started with pissin' somebody off—The wrong somebody!"

"Well partner, if it started in Santa Fe, then that sounds like the place t'a start" said Lawson.

"Gonna be a lot more killing before this thing is over, 'gonna' be a lot of people shootin' at us."

"Then we'll just shoot back... Matters of fact, we'll shoot 'em all t'a Hell if that's what they really want!

From out of the inky-gloom of night approached riders. They rode in, slowly, quietly, down the middle of main street. McCall watched as the riders approached. He had eased down to one knee and was watching from a corner of the window while keeping an ear close as to hear any conversation.

"You see that..?" came Lawson's whisper from the next window over.

"Yeah, I see it."

McCall thought of Lawson... The man's ability to stay with the situation, always poised and ready to strike. His instincts were sharp. His senses always alert. There was no wonder as to how Lawson had stayed alive for as long as he had. The man could turn from prey into hunter in a blink! And his skills for survival matched his cunning.

"'Knew you was there, whispered McCall; here they come —Shhh..."

The riders crept their horses on past McCall's window and the WICKED EYE SALOON. At the DRAGON'S BREATH SALOON they dismounted and tied reins to the hitching post. One of the men was talking, but neither McCall nor Lawson could quite make out what was being said.

"Alright, keep it quiet boys. We'll have a couple of drinks and then we'll bed down for the night. The boss should be around somewhere."

Spurs chimed in rhythm as boot-heels clomped against the lumber of the boardwalk. The four horses reigned at the post were looking around, wild-eyed, yanking, jerking, and apparently thirsty. They could smell the cool-wet vapors of water on the air from a nearby trough. One thing Lawson hated was mistreatment or cruelty toward a horse.

"They didn't even water them horses..." whispered Lawson through clenched teeth. I wonder how they would like to be hitched to a rail and left without water... Damn them!"

Lightning flashed across the sky in the distance revealing the massive thunderheads that were rising to incredible heights. McCall expected the worst of it. Lightning flashed in his pupils from where he stood looking out the window.

He unbuckled his spurs, left them on the floor...

"I'll be back," he said.

Lawson was keeping watch from the window. His Henry rifle had a live round already jacked into the chamber ready to bang at the first sign of trouble. Quietly, McCall closed the door behind him and crept down the hallway with Colt in hand. At the end of the narrow hallway a door opened. A cowboy was backing out of a room followed by one of the saloon gals. They closed the door behind them and walked away down the hall. Quickly, McCall dashed across the hall towards that room! He turned the door handle and went in. The room was dark, but he could see bright flashes of lightning through the thin curtains. He went to a window and yanked it up. He was now at the back of the building. The rushing winds whooshed the curtains, whirling them about inside the room. Just below, where he stood, was the roof of a storage building. He lowered himself out the window until his boots touched the roof. A few seconds later he was on the ground with his back pressed into a corner where the blackened shadows swallowed him. He loosed the thong from the hammer of his Colt and turned moving, slowly, along the back of the building until he came to it's corner. Thunder rumbled in the deep-depths of the night sky... the musty smell of rain was thick on the cool-damp air. He pulled his Stetson from atop his head. Slowly, he peeked one eye around where he could look between the lengths of two buildings that formed a narrow alleyway. Seeing nothing he cut across to the back of the next building. Reaching it's far corner he turned one eye into another narrow alley. The view could not have been any better. Straight ahead of him were the bat wing doors of the **DRAGON'S BREATH SALOON**. He slithered into the alleyway moving along the wall of the building, staying within the shadows. Thunder rumbled off in the near distance and strong gust of wind came whipping in between the two buildings almost blowing his Stetson off, but he caught it with both hands before it was carried away. The swirling winds continued up the alleyway and into the main street. A bellowing cloud of dust plowed into the horses hitched outside of the **DRAGON'S BREATH SALOON** causing them to jerk and whinny, eyes bulging with excitement like, shiny black, eight balls. The bat wing doors of the saloon slammed open with a loud bang as the devil of swirling wind punched through the entrance way. Two men came running out, grabbed at the horses reins trying to calm the animals. A couple of them reared up trying to free themselves from the hitch.

"Whoa... Whoooa!" shouted the men until, finally, settling the frightened animals. Watching the men, McCall recalled the way they'd came winding into town like snakes slithering in from the dark of night on their scale covered bellies... forked-tongued-reptiles planning to sink their fangs into some unsuspecting prey! He knew their type; thieves; back-shooters; rapists; murderers; and sadistically cruel to animals.

Suddenly, the wind grabbed hold of a thin door where McCall stood swinging it open and slamming it hard against the back wall with a loud—Whack!

McCall yanked the Colt from its holster and spun around to see the door hanging half open and returning back to it's frame. The two men outside the Dragon's Breath were returning to the interior. One of the men had already entered while the second man stopped, dead track, when he heard a loud bang from across the street. He turned, quickly, cutting his eyes to the narrow alley where McCall was standing in the shadows, his stomach muscles tightening at the thought of being discovered. The man turned and walked back to the edge of the boards, then drew his pistol. He stepped out into the middle of the dust blown street and yelled out...

"Who's there!"

McCall heard a steel hammer locking back as the man stepped down and made his way to the middle of the street. The stranger began sidestepping, coming in line with the dark alley. McCall bolted, quickly, to a dark corner where a part of the building was bumped out about two feet. He pushed his back into it and became shadow. The stranger stood at the edge of the dark alley. In a deep-gritty voice, he growled...

"'Know y'er there! If I find y'a—I'll kill y'a..."

McCall stood, silent, trying to control his breathing as the man entered into the blackness of the alleyway. Lightning flashed straight overhead followed by an instantaneous boom of thunder. McCall was pressed back into the corner facing the rear of the building where earthy hills climbed up at steep angles. Spruce and pines lined the face of an eroding bluff where large rocks and dirt boulders lay at its base, compiling from years of slide and run off. Trees were bending... the ripping winds grabbing hold of them, shaking them, violently! Leaves swooshed about in the air like debris caught in the swirling funnel of a twister!

CHAPTER 18

lightening flashed revealing the long shadow of a man creeping along... moving between the two buildings... In his hand was a gun.

Again, the wind slammed the screen door against the back of the building with a loud—Bang! The man jumped into the air, both feet leaving the ground, and almost squeezing off a round from his revolver! McCall stood silent...

"Ahhh... shit! Just the damn wind," he said, out loud, as he watched the thin door swinging back to its frame. He chuckled lightly to himself, shook his head, then turned and holstered his guy when he heard a man speak from behind him...

"Wasn't just the wind, mister... and if your hand drops any closer to that iron I'm gonna' blow it off at the wrist!"

"I... I... I'm not movin,' mister!" said the trembling man, his voice shaking.

"That's real good. Now, who the hell are y'a'?"

"I ain't nobody, mister! 'Just passing through!"

"Don't lie t'a me! I saw you ride in earlier. Now, I'm gonna ask you one more time... I won't ask again..."

"Okay... Okay! 'Names, Wic Farley. I rode in with some trail buddies lookin' for work."

"Sure y'a are, said McCall. Ain't any of you lookin' for work! Not trail dirt like you. But, I would be willing to make a bet y'er lookin' t'a do a job; one that pays real good for just a little *killing* of innocent people, perhaps..?"

"No, now! That's not the way it is with me, mister... I ain't 'a killin' nobody!"

"Turn around..."

"Wha... What?"

"Turn, and I mean real slow..."

Wic Farley turned to see the tall shadow that was standing in front of him.

"Tell James to forget about it and move on or he may end up losing more than he bargained for. He's been warned— You got it!"

"What? What?"

"Shut up! Look mister... you got a lot to learn and a lot of space between your ears, It's not a good combination. Tell James what I said... you got it!"

"Yeah, sure! Got it! You ain't gonna' kill me are you..?"

"Like I said... lots of space between the ears. I'm not gonna' kill y'a right now...

McCall cocked the .44 and leveled it right between Farley's eyes just as a flash of brilliant lightening webbed over the skies with a crackle of electrical charge so intense it raised the hairs on top of the man's head. McCall could see the fear in Farley's bulging eyes... shiny-silver-dollars jammed into his sockets.

"But, if you ever cross my trail again I'll send y'a t'a Hell so fast it'll take a week for your screams to catch up to y'a —You hearin' me boy!"

"Mister... I'm pissin' down my leg right now!"

"Tell James—Now move!"

Farley turned and began to walk away. Just then the thin door slammed against the building. Farley jumped into the air, both feet leaving the ground thinking he'd been shot in the back. He spun around, McCall was gone. In a fit of panic Farley ran up the alley and into the street falling down once due to weakness of his knees from having just flirted with death. He struggled back to his feet, looked back over his shoulder. The horses (tied to a hitching post) stared at him with black liquid eyes as he struggled to reach the steps at the edge of the boardwalk. He ran up the steps and threw the bat wing doors open, staggered in, then stopped and placed his hands on his knees as he tried to catch his breath. One of his trail buddies was standing at the corner of the bar; he was raising a glass of whiskey to his mouth when he saw Farley come bursting into the room out of breath and shaking.

"What the hell... What are you doin', Farley?" asked his trail buddy. "Look fellas he's whiter than a ghost and he's pissed down his britches! What'sa matter boy? You look like you've seen the devil himself!"

All the men in the room busted into hilarious laughter, slapping knees and wiping tears from their bloodshot eyes. The room was spinning around Farley like a silent carousel of ugly-laughing faces. He moved swiftly to the bar and pounded a fist down on the wood counter top.

"Whiskey!" He yelled to the bar keep. With a shaking hand he threw back the drink. "More!" He yelled again, his voice cracking. He caught his reflection in the mirror behind the bar and his surroundings faded to black...

...Who was that? he thought to himself... Haunting pictures came to his mind... Monstrous looking faces, ghostly images and—Lucifer! His eyes welled up and his lower lip began to tremble.

Irv Kimble, the man who had started the laughter, came from behind Farley and threw his hand down hard on the shaking man's shoulder.

"What has gotten int'a you boy?"asked Kimble.
Farley jumped, fumbled for the butt of his revolver, then spun, clumsily, around with weapon in hand. His eyes were crazy... Kimble saw it and began to back away...

"I saw 'im!" said Farley, all crazy eyed, the revolver shaking in his hand.

"Who?" asked Kimble, still backing away.

"I saw him I tell you!"

Kimble was staring down the barrel of Farley's Remington revolver, feigning from side to side while fearing Farley's jerking finger might accidentally squeeze the trigger.

"Who, Wic!?"

"The Devil, I done seen the Devil himself!"

"Whoa there boy. You ain't talkin' right. I think you might have been in the saddle a little too long partner. Yeah— That's it! Now put down that gun..."

"He said to tell James to forget the job."

"Who did? asked Kimble, who said it?"

"McCall" is all he said!"

"McCall! Shit man, he ain't the damn Devil boy! He's just a man!"

"I don't know..." came another voice from further up the bar. Ned Drake pulled his glasses off and commenced to shining the lenses with the corner of his shirt. Some are startin' t'a say the man can't be killed. They say he's madder than hell over the death of his gal. 'Guess she was killed a few years ago down Texas way. Murdered by an Ohioan, but it was rumored that McCall may have killed her himself."

Farley had lowered the gun as he listened, intently, a

lump caught in his throat.   Drake continued...

"Some say he's ridin' with Death, the one they call Wreck Lawson. Some say McCall may even be Death himself"

"Where in hell did you hear that shit from Ned!" yelled Kimble.

"From this here dime novel, he said reaching into his back pocket. I done been readin' about that Lawson fella too... 'say he's plumb crazier than shit! They say he's done killed about a hundred men between here and California... A bunch, down way, in Texas too!."

Farley's gun hit the floor with a loud—Whack! He bent over fumbling at it with his fingers. When he grabbed hold of it he, awkwardly, put it back in its holster.

"Well, I'll tell y'a what, started Kimble, we're goin' t'a do do that job with James... And there ain't nobody gonna' stop us from it! Not McCall... Not Lawson... And not even the Devil himself!"

Kimble looked around the room staring at the men who had ridden into town with him.

"Ned, put that damn book away—NOW!"

At that moment a man stepped through the swinging doors. He wore a black army issue confederates coat with black boots, narrow brimmed hat, and thick leonine mustache.

"I'm looking for a man named, Kimble."

"I'm Kimble, mister."

The man gazed the other faces in the room...

"Are these, others, your men?"

"Y'ep, they're with me."

"I'm Frank James. My brother wishes to speak with you. Take your horses to the corral at the edge of town—We'll meet there. You and my brother can discuss things then. Be there in 30 minutes, and don't be late."

The bartender stood, towel in hand, drying and polishing

glasses, his ears taking it all in. Just as Frank James exited the bat wing doors, Kimble turned and caught the barkeep's eyes.

"What are you lookin' at, mister... 'Hear something did y'a?"

"No sir, didn't hear a thing..." said the bar keep.
Kimble signaled Drake to go around behind the bar. Drake hurled himself across the counter top.

"You don't need t'a be stick'n your nose where it don't belong there whiskey peddler!"

An arm, suddenly, came up from behind and went around the bartender's forehead yanking it back exposing his throat to the honed edge of a barber's razor. Drake pulled the chromed blade tightly up against the man's neck...

"Please... the bartender whispered; I have a wife and child —I won't say anything—I swear it!"
Kimble pressed his nose against the side of the man's face. The smell of whiskey, mixed with the stench of his soured breath, turned the bar keep's stomach.

"You'd better not, whispered Kimble, or I'll have ol' Drake here give you a shave from ear to ear—Got it!"

The razor fell from the barkeeps neck. Drake pushed the man away making him stumble, clumsily, into the bar.

"Now, pour whiskey and keep your business to y'erself!" growled Kimble.

Drake folded the razor back into its handle, then hurdled himself back across to the other side of the bar.

Lawson had seen a man (from the hotel window) standing in the street with a gun in his hand. He figured it might have something to do with McCall. He put the stock of his Henry rifle against his shoulder and laid down a bead on the cowboy. He pressed his finger lightly against the trigger ready to place the shot in the man's torso if given a reason to do so. He watched as the man stepped across to the other side of the street and faded from his site. A few minutes later the same man came running out into the middle of the street, fell down on his face beside the horses tethered at the post. The cowboy seemed to be in a hurry. He got to his feet after a momentary struggle, then stumbled to the front doors of the DRAGON'S BREATH SALOON. A couple of minutes later, Lawson could hear laughter from inside the saloon. Then came a knock at the door of his room...

"It's me," said McCall.

A door opened at the end of the hallway and a real pretty gal stuck her head out and gave McCall "the once over" from the top of his Stetson to the tips of his boots. A smile crossed her face and she licked her lips, seductively, at him.

"Ma'am..." said McCall, smiling as he touched a finger to the brim of his Stetson.

Lawson opened the door, McCall stepped in and closed it behind him.

"So, what happened? I saw a guy standing in the street wielding an iron. I had my sights on 'im..." said Lawson, patting the wood stock of the Henry rifle he was cradling in his arms.

"Yeah, I met 'im between a couple of buildings down there... Scared the piss out of 'im when he realized he was starin' into the barrel of my Colt. Anyway... I accused him of being here to do a job with James and his boys. He didn't admit to it, but his eyes gave it away."

Lawson stepped back over to the window and spread the thin curtains apart, then gave a glimpse down onto the street.

"Right before you knocked on the door I saw another

gent' enter the Dragon's Breath. He was only in there for a minute, then he left. He walked in the direction of the livery stables. 'Could'a been one of the James's I guess?"

"Yeah, those two rarely separate. Especially if there's a large count of bank notes or gold to be acquired."

"'Sounds like *brother* Frank is here too, stated Lawson."

The storm that had been brewing in the distance was now overflowing from its rim. The rains were coming down in ripping sheets, high winds whipped it around, violently, like something (or maybe someone) had a hand in it. At times it *scattered* across the windows like buckshot fired from a distant gun.

It was dark in the room where they sat at opposite sides of the window, backs pressed against the wall with rifles in hand. Every few seconds a flash of lightning would light the room, then darkness again. Electrically charged currents webbed the churning skies with roaring canons of thunder firing across the Rockies; their steel-balls thundering across the heavens overhead, the rumble fading away to the distance.

"'Wonder what James and his boys are up to right now" said Lawson.

"If they got any sense they'd be someplace dry, replied McCall (lightening flashed) I wonder if it was a mistake for me to give James a heads up (lightening flashed) that he was being watched, said McCall. I warned him. 'Don't think he'll listen though."

"Well, Storm... When a man does wrong, often enough, other men will follow him. So, that's why these Colts' carry six cartridges. When a man needs killin' his followers usually need the same.

McCall gave a nod in agreement.

"Well stated, Wreck. That's about the swell of it I guess. If need be, we'll take 'em all down."

"I like the way you think partner. I knew there had to be some reason why I liked y'a," said Lawson.

"Hell, 'thought it was just my fun-loving and friendly disposition," replied McCall.

Both men chuckled, silently, (lightening flashed) stomach muscles tightened, heads bobbling around. It finally escalated into gut busting laughter as they tried to remain quiet wiping tears from their eyes.

The Ferrel Gang; Kimble, Farley (and three others) had left the saloon staying on schedule with meeting James at the nearby stables. The last to leave was Jimmy Phoenix. He'd stood at the far end of the bar where it turned in a rounded curve and stopped dead against the wall. He'd stood, leaning, in the dimly lit corner while sipping on his suds 'n whiskey and taking it all in.

"I'm closing, mister, said the bar keep. If I was you, I'd..."

"Y'er not!" snapped Phoenix with a "*how dare you*" sort of tone.

"I apologize, sir. It's just that I am highly shaken over what those men did to me, and I..."

"Hey... Hey! Y'er still alive ain't y'a?"

"Yes, I just..."

"Then shut up while luck is still in your favor! I'll leave when I'm damn good and ready—You got that?!"

"Yes, sir, I got it."

"That's real smart of you. Now hand me a bottle of whiskey, and maybe, after while, I'll think about lettin' your chicken-liver-ass go home!"

Phoenix said "*Your chicken liver ass*" with a sniveling expression and tone.

After about twenty minutes of staring down the, unnerved man, Phoenix flipped some coins onto the bar;

they hit, rolled, and spun with a few of them sliding off onto the floor. He snatched the bottle up in his hand and made his way toward the bat wings...

"Y'er pathetic," he said to the man, locking eyes with him. The pride-beaten man just dropped his head and turned his eyes to the floor as the mean little bastard punched his way out the saloon doors, then disappeared into the cold wetness of the night.

Outside, on the boardwalk, Phoenix stopped. He flipped up his coat collar and pulled the front of his hat down over his brow. The rain was really coming down cascading off the edge of the overhanging roof in front of him.

So... he thought to himself; "Them boys got somethin' up their sleeves... bet its got something to do with that train sittin' at the rail station. Them's Wells Fargo's men guardin' that car... 'Lookin' like a job in the makin' t'a me."

The whiskey lubricated gears inside Phoenix's mind were beginning to turn...

The rain was hammering the overhang above him as he walked along the length of the boardwalk. At the end of it he stepped down into the mud of a side street. He turned his head over his shoulder and eye'd the foggy corridor that spanned the length between two buildings. Squinting his eyes, as the wind smacked the rain across his face, he saw nothing. A few more steps through the mud and he was on a boardwalk again. He walked, quietly, along its length. The roof above him angled the rushing rain downward where it cascaded off of the edge like a wide falls splashing into puddles along the lengthy span of ground ('sounded like a cow pissin' on a flat rock) He shuttered once when the cold air rushed up into his face and down his neck. He grasped the open collar of his flannel shirt and pinched it together further blocking the icy assault from his body. A few more steps and he found himself standing at the door to the PALACE HOTEL.

He pushed the door opened, closed it behind him, then made the stairs up to his room. When he entered his room he lit a lamp and went to the window to pull the curtains closed. In a moment of drunken carelessness he'd made a mistake—He was being watched!

"Well, I guess that ends that mystery" said Lawson.

He'd been watching from a window when Phoenix had entered the hotel across the street. McCall and Lawson were both hold up in the darkness in Lawson's room and were using McCall's room as a decoy (where an oil lamp was dimly burning) If anyone were watching, or planning to rush into McCall's room, well, that thin wall that separated the two rooms would not be enough to hold back the barrage of .44 and .45 lead that would be blasting holes through it! And whoever stood on the other side of that wall, well...

"'Wonder what the hell is up his sleeve..." continued Lawson.

"'Don't know... 'been thinkin' about it though and keep gettin' an uneasy feeling in my gut. He's young, but we know he's killed before by the way he took out Langford. It was almost like he enjoyed it."

"He did have a look of grim satisfaction on his face, and I've seen that look before—a cold-blooded killer! He's dangerous," said Lawson.

"After the way he looked at me in the saloon I would say he's lookin' for a reputation, and who knows what he'd do t'a get it," replied McCall.

"'Think he'd shoot y'a in the back?"

"'Don't know, but I wouldn't trust him far enough to find out."

"Me either."

"If he comes callin', again, just keep your eyes open and

try to keep your back to a wall."

"No shit!" replied Lawson.

Across the street, at the **PALACE HOTEL,** young Phoenix poured a glass of whiskey and swallowed about half of it down. He put the glass down on the stand beside the bed where he sat. He pulled the dagger from his boot and commenced to carving a notch in the dark-maple-wood hand grip of his new Colt .45 Peacemaker. As he notched the first V into the grain of the wooden grip, his imagination took him over...

"...As the fastest gun he will have made a name for himself across the entire West, even as far as to the east. Men would envy him and woman would fantasize about him and long for him. But most of all; men would fear him!"

He threw back the rest of the glass of remaining whiskey and admired his work. He began to carve a second notch for the posse man (Ned Bartley) he killed in Phoenix. Then a third for the man he had killed in Abilene back in "73". He carved another for Walt Parker and another for the ranch hand he'd killed over by the Gila River. When he'd finished he felt a sense of completion like "he'd found his reason." He lay back on the bed and closed his eyes and brought Storm McCall into his mind's eye. McCall was his ticket to fame, and he would kill him soon. Phoenix soon drifted off in his mind to a dense, smoky haze...

...He stood in an ominous fog—Smoke-like tendrils rose up from the gritty sand-like dirt and intertwined at the soles of his boots. Before him a mound of fresh dirt with a grave marker bearing no name. There was no sun, but it was hot. Sweat was running down his forehead and onto his brow. For some reason, he couldn't quite understand why, he felt a sudden sense of panic. The winds began to whirl about around him. Stronger... then stronger... it began blasting the desert sand across the surface of the headstone! Suddenly, it turned into a raging sandstorm! Small pieces of the headstone began to chip away from its corners being blown away with the dust. Something began to appear on the sandblasted surface of the headstone... grooves... lines... something... letters! He bent closer to read it. Slowly, words began to appear on the stone...

{HERE LIES NOBODY}
JIMMY POTTS
-PHOENIX-
1860-1877
AGED-17 YRS.
HANGED FOR MURDER
AND HORSE THEFT

Phoenix gasped for air, but he couldn't breathe. Run! But he couldn't move. Suddenly, he realized something had a tight grasp around both of his ankles ('felt like hard-bony fingers pulling him down into the sandy dirt) He screamed, but made no sound. His heart pounded inside his chest. He struggled to stay atop the ground, his fingers scraping and digging along the surface until only his face and hands were visible. He screamed a last terrifying scream and was yanked under...

...At the edge of the bed stood Phoenix, bug eyed and

soaked in sweat, chest heaving, fighting to catch his breath. The room was spinning and he was dizzy. Then, slowly, it stopped and he realized he wasn't dead. In the mirror he caught his reflection. He grabbed a chair next to him and slung it viciously into the glass shattering it into a thousand fragmented pieces scattered about the floor. And there he was... A thousand Jimmy Phoenix's shattered on the floor. Each broken piece of his reflection looking to the other to put himself back together again.

CHAPTER 19

The metallic-rattling of trace chains (from a nearby wagon sloshing through the mud) woke McCall from his sleep. He saw that Lawson was asleep in a chair by the window, his Henry rifle lying across his lap. McCall put his boots on and planted both on the floor, then walked over to the window for a look. The dawning of the sun gave a smoky orange tent to the mist that was floating above the streets below. He saw the freight wagon being pulled along by two horses, team and wagon fading in, from out of the cloud, like ghosts on an icy mist. The bed of the freighter was stacked with wooden crates; keg barrels and the likes, most likely an order arriving in town for delivery to the local retailers and merchants. The man who sat the buckboard of the freighter turned the team south onto a side street. McCall watched as the wagon began to fade, then disappeared into the orange-tinted-fog. McCall's stomach was touching his spine and he realized he had not eaten anything for quite a while. He stood and went to a can sitting in a corner to relieve himself of the beers and whiskey he'd had the day prior. A few minutes later

Lawson began to stir about.

"Hey pard'," said Lawson, rubbing his eyes.

"Mornin', replied McCall. I think it's time we find some grub... What'a y'a say?"

"'Sounds real good t'a me, said Lawson. I'm about t'a fall out if I don't find somethin' t'a eat soon!"

They left the room in search of a diner that served a decent breakfast to fill their empty stomachs. Just as they started to exit out the hotel door, Lawson said...

"Remember... shoot first and ask questions later!"

He patted the stock of his Henry and gave a nod to confirm his intentions. When they stepped out, McCall looked across the muddy street and gave a disapproving sigh—The boots!

They searched for higher ground in the midst where they could cross the mud and puddle covered street. The streets were already busy with men, horses, and wagons moving about with their spoked wheels sloshing through the thick of it. Across the street, in the opposite direction of the **DRAGON'S BREATH SALOON**, they stumbled across **RUSTY'S MORNING CUP**. They entered and a bell on the door gave a loud jingle. They found a table on the wall near a corner. Lawson pulled out a chair and leaned his Henry .44 .40 in the corner, then sat down, his eyes searching the room. McCall sat opposite of him in a chair against the wall. He took his Stetson off and ran his hand through his thick dark hair, then placed it back on his head and eyed the balding red haired man who was approaching their table; he was wearing a white apron.

"G'morning boys! said the man, with a bearish voice. What can I get for y'a?"

"G'morning," said McCall.

"Mornin'," followed Lawson.

"Coffee fellas?" asked the big man wearing the apron.

Both men gave a nod to confirm.

"I'm Rusty and this is my place. My regular cook is off today, but I'm gon'na see what I can do for y'a! He wiped his hands on the front of his clean-white apron. How's about I just give you fellas the workings of what I am callin'—The Big Breakfast! I got a fresh smoke-cured ham back there that is just dying to be dipped in my world-famous red-eye gravy! It'l help cure y'a from the night before if y'a know what I mean?"

He leaned over and nudged Lawson slightly with his elbow and winked.

"Red eye... get it? Damndist thing you ever seen! Made with fresh coffee and ham grease. Guaranteed t'a put the whites back in your eyes!"

He smiled a friendly smile and put his thumb and index finger to his chin and rubbed. With one brow raised, he finished with;

"So, what's it gon'na be boys..?"

"Well, Rusty, said McCall, I think were sold on the big breakfast!"

"But, can we go ahead 'n get the coffee now?" asked Lawson with a nod of his head.

"Oh, by all means young fella. You boys just relax and I'll be back in a jiff'' with somthin' t'a warm up y'er insides!"

He gave a wink, then turned and went to the kitchen. A young couple entered and a bell on the door jingled signaling to Rusty that he had new patrons. He came from the back and smiled at them as they seated themselves, then he sat a pot of fresh coffee down on the table in front of Lawson and McCall with two cups and a small server of fresh dairy cream. They filled their cups and enjoyed the smells of ham and eggs drifting on the air.

"Good coffee," stated Lawson after taking a sip from his cup. McCall gave a nod in agreement as he sipped from his.

"I'm so damn hungry I'm about t'a chew one'a my boots off 'a my foot."

McCall about choked on his coffee, then smiled and shook his head at Lawson's never ending depth of humorous expression.

The door-bell jingled and a gent' in a striped suit came in. He had a newspaper folded underneath his arm. He made his way to a table at the other end of the room, pulled a chair out and sat down right next to the big window where the words "RUSTY'S MORNING CUP" was painted on the glass front. He reached inside his vest pocket and retrieved a pair of wire spectacles which he spread and attached behind each of his ears, then opened the newspaper and began browsing over its contents. The front page read *"Denver Daily."* He gave an occasional glance out the window as if waiting for someone, or something.

The Big breakfast came a few minutes late, but it was a lot of food so the two made no complaints. The red-eye gravy was excellent with the ham. There were also flap jacks, Maple syrup, eggs, and biscuits with butter and a bowl of fried-crispy potatoes. When they had their fill of the grub Lawson leaned back and put his hands on his stomach and patted it a couple of times. Then, drawing in a deep breath, he exhaled.

"Wheeew! That was good."

McCall wiped his mouth on the red and white checkered cloth napkin that was provided and tossed it down on the table. He slumped in his chair and stretched his legs out to take the strain off of his stomach so he could breathe. McCall looked around the place checking out a few of the new faces that had filled the room while he and Lawson had been partaking of their grub. Something caught his attention; the man in the striped suit was turned to the side, his long jacket had parted open revealing a holstered pistol. Something about it just didn't look right to him. He nudged Lawson with the side of his boot and, nonchalantly, signaled him with his eyes. The man lowered the newspaper, looked over its top edge just as Lawson was eyeing his exposed gun and holster. The man's hand dropped down and pulled the jacket across concealing the weapon from their site, then his eyes disappeared behind the newspaper again.

Rusty came back to their table. In his hand was a booklet of white tickets.

"'Everything suit you fellas okay?"

"Oh yeah, said Lawson, best breakfast we have had in a while I think, thank y'a!"

"That red-eye thing you got goin' there, that is really something else," said McCall.

"Thank y'a! You boys need anything else t'a finish?"
They both declined with a shaking of the head.

"Alrighty then."
He tore the paper from the pad, then said:

"Here's your check. Just leave payment on the table and feel free to come back anytime!"
They both thanked him and gave their appreciation.

With a grateful nod he turned and walked to another table, pulled out his pad and pencil...

Over in a corner were two keg barrels, one on top of the other. Above them was a regulator clock that read a time of 8:am.

"Wells Fargo probably won't open for business until around nine, stated Lawson. So, we got about an hour to kill. What do you say we get a jump on supplies so we'll be ready to ride when all Hell breaks loose?"

"Y'ep, we need to light a shuck and get them horses into the wind, replied McCall. You're right though, all Hell is getting ready to break loose!

"I'm beginning to think that's the way they want it, said Lawson."

"They all know we're here. What better cover does James need? They do the job, take the lute..."

"And we take the heat by association,"finished McCall.

"Yep, looks like a nice little set up don't it?"

"Maybe. If James get us involved in it they'll be lucky if any of 'em survive to tell about it though."

"They're not real smart are they?"

"Smart, or stupid, it don't really matter. Smart people die every day—Let's go!"

They laid the notes on the table for payment, then grabbed their rifles and walked to the door. Lawson levered a live one into the chamber drawing the attention of the gun toting "stripy." The man just about jumped out of his skin!

When the door closed behind them they took a moment to study the street. McCall looked back over his shoulder; the man seated on the other side of the glass was eyeballing him. Lawson threw up a finger and a hateful sneer which made the man quickly turn his eyes in another direction. Seeing nothing of a threat McCall looked up the length of the street.

"Damn mud!" he said, then he stepped down into the *brown shit* which is just how it felt under his feet. No doubt about it he was definitely going to have to clean those boots!

It was cold and the mercury was dropping fast... It wouldn't be long before the mist-like rain would turn to icy-pellets, then the white stuff. The brief window of early sunshine had been showing some hope for the day but it was looking as if that hope was about to disappear with the ash-blue clouds that were creeping in over the Northern Rockies. After dredging through it they made the other side of the street and stepped up onto the boards of the walk. They used the edge of the boards to clean their boots off, then headed down toward the TRADING POST AND SUPPLY. The thick oak door at the entrance opened as they approached; A fair-skinned lady with dark hair and wearing a red dress came out of it—she was smiling. She was joined at the elbow with a gentleman, his head down as he was closing the door behind them. In his free hand he carried a brown paper sack. When he turned he was staring McCall square in his eyes.

"Why... Storm!" he said, in his *gentlemanly* Southern drawl.

"Doc," said McCall with a nod and a finger put to the brim of his Stetson. "Ma'am," he said to the lady.

Lawson gave a nod and touched the brim of his hat.
Doc' looked the two of them over.

"My dear... I would love for you to meet my *dear* friends; Storm McCall and Mr. Lawson."

"You can call me Wreck, Doc'" said Lawson.

"Very well, then... My dear, meet Mr. Wreck Lawson."

"Ma'am, said Lawson."

"The pleasure is mine" said the lady.

"This is my lovely companion, Kate."

Her eyes had already traveled McCall's length and he could see there was a twinkle of interest in them. She held out her hand and McCall lightly placed his hand under her palm, she instinctively batted her eyes at him.

"Nice t'a meet y'a, Miss Kate," said McCall.

"Likewise I'm sure," she said, her eyes still running his length.

"Wreck Lawson, sir, your reputation exceeds you. Mostly to an elite group, in farther points west, who can no longer speak for themselves due to their... untimely demise I should guess?"

Doc' smiled and held out his hand, Lawson took it.

"Ahh... 'Pleasures all mine Doc', said Lawson. 'Saw you once in Texas; you were high tailin' it out of Jacksborough. 'Didn't look like you was gonna slow down anytime soon."

"Yes, I do seem to recall a moment similar to the one which you have just described. My... my... ain't it funny how time seems to slip away. Needless to say I won't be going back to Jacksborough for some time!"

"No time like the present!" said the lady in red—Kate Elder.

She pulled a bottle from the brown bag and popped the cork with her teeth, then tipped the bottle up to her lips and rolled two bubbles up to the bottom of the bottle. Her eyes cut from side to side as she lowered the bourbon bottle. No one had seen her. She pushed the cork back into its top.

"A bit early isn't it dear?" said Holliday, with a raised brow.

"Don't worry about it Doc', she said, with a glint of irritation in her voice."

"And attitude with which I'm sure there may be plenty more of just below the surface. This may prove to be a most interesting day," he said, breaking eye contact with her. She turned facing the street and her arm dropped away from his. All the sudden the Doc' didn't look too good. He was perspiring and seemed a bit pale.

"That man over there... (Doc' was cut short in mid sentence by a cough, then another) After a moment he continued...

"Excuse me, men. My position on health is not what it used to be."

Kate, patted his back. Suddenly, his female companion

242

seemed to be genuinely concerned.

"It's alright, Doc', let's get you back inside where its warm..." said Kate.

"Yes, dear... just let me finish for a moment. As I was saying... That man in the window across the street has not taken his eyes from us since we have stood here. Your friend?"

"No, said McCall, we just left there. He's carry'n a gun underneath that fancy striped suit he's wearin'. Funny thing, 'just didn't look right to me."

"Me neither," said Lawson.

"Hey Doc', I got an idea, said Kate. Let's go over there and grab some coffee and put a ear to the floor."

"Grand idea!"said Doc', with a wide grin. He turned from Kate.

"Be careful, men... There is danger on the prowl today. Keep your eyes open. I will be in touch."

Both took heed to his warning. Holliday and his companion, Kate, walked away.

The two came to the entrance at the *BIG BEAR TRADE AND SUPPLY*. The solid Oak door in front of them had to have weighed nearly 200 pounds. It was heavy. Three men were coming out the door, each in possession of supplies and saddle gear they'd just purchased. Lawson pulled the heavy door open and they stepped inside...

In the nearby timber line someone was watching McCall and Lawson as they'd traveled the length of the boardwalk. The stalker stepped down from the saddle and tethered his horse to a tree branch. When the two entered the Trading Post the man pulled his Remington Frontier .44 and checked the cylinder for loads...

The lumber of the interior was rough frame and was exposed to an open ceiling which added even greater dimensions to the already remarkable interior of the place. Positioned in a corner was the "Grandfather" of Grandfather clocks being nearly four feet wide and nine feet tall. In the fancy etching design of its glass front was the word—REGULATOR. The hands were pointing to a time of 8:14 am. The place smelled rich of Cedar-Wood; Pine; Grains; Candle Wax; Spices, Gun Oil, and Tobacco. Firs and animal pelts hung from the walls. A life-size Grizzly, and Bull Elk were positioned in the opposite corner. The taxidermist (whoever he was) had done a fine job at restoring the true nature of the life-like features on both beasts. The definition and natural positioning showed that someone had taken careful consideration when attempting to re-create the inanimate beasts. The wall in between the clock, and the Bear, and Elk was a very large glass window. The antlers of Rocky Mountain Bighorn Sheep; Mule Deer, and Elk were hung about on the wall covering most of the surface. Leather goods; Saddles; Boots; Belts; Holsters; Rope; Saddle-Soap, and other fine leathers were shelved along the back wall. Three middle aisles contained dry goods such as; Coffee; Flour; Cornmeal; Clothing; Blankets; Cooking Utensils, etc. All firearms were under lock and key on display behind the counter located in the furthest corner of the room. A big man with long brown hair, and beard, was standing behind the counter and was looking over the top of his wire rimmed glasses. He resembled a brown bear wearing spectacles.

"Good morning... I'm Colorado Charley! Can I help you with anything in particular gentlemen?"

"We could use some coffee and some flour to start," said

Lawson.

"Yes sir, said the clerk, we have standard two pound bags of each—How many for you today?"

"Two bags of each should be fine," stated Lawson.

McCall gave a nod in agreement, then disappeared around a corner. When Lawson caught up with him he was searching a stand looking for his favorite Cheroot Cigars (Havana Honeys) and it appeared he had found them. He grabbed two packs of 10, smiled, then disappeared around another corner like a kid in a candy store with Lawson following closely behind. The final list of inventory ended with; Sugar; Flour; Coffee; Beans; and a 10 lb. slab of bacon. Two pair of Levi's; Cigars, and Tobacco. Three boxes of .44 shells; Three boxes of .45 shells and a case of dynamite—just in case! The last item they grabbed was a bag of assorted candies Lawson had handpicked from the glass jars on display atop the wooden counter. The smell of gun oil and steel was overwhelming. They were suddenly locked, deep gaze, on the display of fire arms behind the counter;

"1873 Winchesters" and "Yellow boys"

"Sharps rifles."

"Spencer Carbines" of assorted calibers.

"Springfields'".45 and .50"

"Henrys'".44"

"Two Hawken Muzzle Loaders" Both in .50"

"Just to mention a few..."

The selection of handguns on display behind the glass was impressive, most of which were exceptional choice weaponry for their time;

"1858-1875 Remingtons" in .44 (The 1858   Remington being gun of choice by Frank James)

"1860 Colt Army with ivory grips" (The gun of choice by Bill Hickok)

"1851 Colt Navy" .36 and .38"(Usual choice of Doc' Holliday)

"1873 Colt Peacemaker"(Hog Leg) in .44 and .45 (The choice of most, including the Earp's' and Masterson)

"1875 Smith & Wesson Schofield" Top Break (Choice of "Buffalo" Bill Cody and Jesse James (Cody had two, both nickel plated with scroll engravings)

"1860 Starr Double Action" Army .44

Just to mention a few... But there were well over one hundred firearms on display there. Most of the hand guns had been re-suited with a cartridge conversion cylinder in the year of 1871 from the previous cap and ball method.

Colorado Charley stood behind the counter while his two employees (men in brown clerk's aprons) tended to other patrons. Charley had already spoken once, trying to gain McCall's and Lawson's attention. Now he would try again...

"Excuse me, gentleman, is this going to be all this morning..? he asked."

Both gave a nod, but said nothing, mesmerized by the smells of gun stock, oil, steel, and the rancid smell of previously fired gun powder residue.

The cash drawer opened with a loud—Bang!
Like a voice coming from somewhere off in the distance, slowly, they turned their attention toward the sound.

"Like the guns, huh?" Charley asked with a thin smile.

"Thems' some mighty fine shootin' irons," said Lawson.

"You've really got one heck of a place here, mister," stated McCall.

"Biggest in the West as far as I'm concerned," replied the *grizzly* looking clerk.

"I think you're right, said Lawson, I haven't seen anything like this in Texas, California, or anywhere to that matter!"

"Nothin' like it where I come from" stated McCall.

"'Ain't likely you'll see somethin' like this anywhere else, said Charley. I partnered up with a guy who had a big dream of becoming the world's greatest outdoor supply and outfitter; 'Man by the name of Cabella. His idea sparked my curiosity y'a might say. Well, here we are, our first supply warehouse and in the makings of another in San Francisco. Big trade and supply demand out there! 'Don't know what were gon'ta name it, but don't be surprised to see my partners name on the next one. And I don't mind, he's the man with the plan so to say! Besides, I got what I wanted for my investment capitol, but Cabella has plans t'a go all the way with this thing; and believe you me if anybody could do it—it would be Cabella!"

"Ain't nothin' wrong with havin' some kind'a ambition other than just puttin' his boots on and pullin' 'em off again," said McCall.

"Couldn't have said it better! said Colorado Charley with a wide-toothy-smile. Well gents' I hate t'a end this pleasant conversation were having, but I need t'a get back to the business at hand. 'Lookin like its gonna' be a busy day, so if there's nothing more for y'a today..?"

"I think we got everything we're gon'a need for now," said McCall with a nod in agreement from Lawson.

"Okay then!" said, Colorado Charley.

The buttons on the register began to click away as Charley began to tally up the grand total of their expense. When he'd finished, they paid him the amount he stated to them with greenback money. After paying it Charley instructed his clerks to arrange the goods by the entry door for the easiest method of pickup. It now appeared they were going to need a pack-horse to carry all of the supplies.

"Were gon'na need another horse," said McCall. If its not too much trouble were gonna' need a few extra minutes t'a get our supplies loaded."

"Not problem fellas! said Charley. Y'er things are just fine 'til y'a get 'em!"

"'Appreciate it Charley, said Lawson, with a smack of his hand on the counter top."

"Much obliged!" said McCall.

"I'm gonna wait here 'n browse," said Lawson.

"Okay, I'll go 'n get us a horse that can hall supplies. Be back in a few!"

"Go down to the livery, said Charley. Chappy usually knows where a good horse can be got. If he don't, come on back 'n we'll see what we can find for y'a!"

"We'll do!" said McCall as he turned and headed toward the door. He glanced the regulator clock in the corner. It read a time of 8:45 am. The door closed with a thick sounding—Whack! He was about five steps into it when, from over his shoulder, he heard a deep growl of a voice...

CHAPTER 20

"...Turn around real slow Luis."

McCall stopped in mid-step and threw his hands out at his sides. His heart jumped as the thought of being shot in the back raced through his mind. He felt a strange tingling sensation, back between his shoulders, where a bullet might possibly enter. He turned, slowly, on the heel of his boot, muscles tense and awaiting the bang, then entry of hot lead into his body that would kill him. He was feeling what he'd felt before—The Dead Man's Moment! As he turned a man came rounding into his view...

It was a wet-chilly autumn morning there at the edge of town. The man stood in the street where the buildings ended. Behind him, in the background, were hard timbers; The browns and blacks of tree bark and the green moss that clung to them were distorted by the smokey-gray of the drizzling rains. The open terrain rolled down and away in rich colors of red clay and copper, then ending abruptly against the base of the snow capped Rockies. McCall could see the man's breath on the frigid air. The stranger stood there, legs apart, his hand down low next to his side. His hair was black, shoulder length, and matched the beard that hung down past his thick neck—A big man but not fat. He wore a buckskin jacket that was pulled back to the side of the pistol rig that was tied down above his knee. The veins in McCall's neck bulged and his face turned red. His blood boiled when he recognized the big man—Buddy Hicks! But back east in Ohio they'd always just called him Bear. McCall's jaws tightened as his right hand moved slowly to position by his side... a claw next to the holster ready to hook and draw...

"Luis, I'm here t'a kill y'a!" said the man. "And I want that $10,000 bounty!"

"Well, that means you would have to kill my partner too..."

"Yep, that's the idea, just as soon as I'm finished with you."

"You'll never see Ohio again Bear, or any bounty! You made your last mistake coming here and right now y'er about one second from death—NOW DRAG IRON!"

Two shots rang out across the plains... crackled across the valley slopes, then faded away. Hicks had been knocked back, but was still standing. His gun fell from his hand and made a splat in the thick mud of the street. He looked down at his gun, then raised his eyes and saw the smoking muzzle of the Colt .44 in McCall's hand.

"Nooo..."mumbled, Hicks. He saw two shredded holes in his shirt front... short spurts of blood were pumping from each. He pressed one hand against his chest, clutching at the fabric, then fell straight back into the thick mud.

McCall's ears were still ringing as he watched Hicks fall and splat in the mud like a big-flat-rock that had just landed in it. McCall stepped down from the boards of the walkway and began walking toward where the man lay.

Hicks, lying on his back with raindrops forming pools in his pupils, felt a shadow fall across his face...

"Help me Luis," whispered Hicks, then he coughed blood from the corners of his mouth. "What happened?" A tear trickled down the side of his face.

"I killed y'a, Bear," said McCall. "I told y'a... y'a made a mistake comin' here."

"Help me, Luis," he said again choking up more blood. "I don't wanna' die..."

"'Nothin' I can do for y'a, Bear. Its hard medicine t'a swallow, but you're a dead man. I put two bullets through your heart; You should already be dead, but don't worry 'bout it Bear—I'll see to it y'er buried proper."

"Oh God, please... I can't die!"

"I don't think God is who y'er gonna' have t'a deal with Buddy."

Hicks tried to breathe, but he couldn't.

"Help... me..."

"Go t'a Hell, Bear!" growled McCall.

...Hicks was still lying on his back in the street. It was dark, he couldn't see. He felt funny, different. Then, he noticed ropes lassoed around his booted ankles. Suddenly, the ropes were pulled taught and the rocky earth began tearing into his back—he was being dragged! Ahead of him wheeled a fiery carriage where a black figure sat atop the perch and was cracking a whip across the backs of four flaming horses. Buddy Hicks began to scream when he saw the sign up ahead that read: "**THE GATES OF HELL**"
And the Devil was dragging him there by the heels of his boots!

McCall thumbed open the gate at the side of his Colt's cylinder and dropped the first spent casing into the mud, then clicked the cylinder around to the next empty casing and watched as it tumbled down through the air. He reached to his gun belt and pulled two fresh rounds from the belt and pushed them into the cylinder, then snapped the gate closed. He dropped the Colt back into its holster and looked down at Hicks's lifeless body that lay at his feet. McCall lifted the Stetson from his head, then ran his fingers through his thick hair as memories flooded his mind; Things he didn't want to think about right now. He stared out across the vastness of the land... north up the Rocky Mountain Range, then back to Buddy Hicks lifeless corpse. He thought of her... he thought of Clemens... then he got mad! He let out a roaring scream that echoed the entire valley! The kind of roar that would send Mountain Cats scurrying for their caves like frightened kittens! He replaced the Stetson back atop his head and turned. Lawson was standing at the steps of the boardwalk, his back facing McCall, Henry rifle gripped tight and pressed low against his side.

"You okay Lou'?!" he shouted back over his shoulder.

"I'm fine—but he's not..." said McCall, referring to the dead man at his feet.

McCall turned and began to dredge through the mud toward where Lawson was standing.

"'Y'a know 'im?" asked Lawson.

"Yeah, I knew 'im, alright... He's one of' 'em 'rode with Clemens. I knew 'im from back home. 'Name was Buddy Hicks."

McCall moved in alongside of Lawson and looked up the street for persons of interest. Lawson didn't know the name, Hicks, but he knew the name Clemens. He knew that when McCall crossed paths with Clemens, Hell's fire would be the least of the man's worries. McCall would crucify his flesh with a lead brand of his own before the devil would ever possess his soul! First he would pass worldly judgment on Clemens. Then, and only then, would he release him over to that conceited devil to be tormented throughout the ages!

"Here they come." said Lawson.

"Yeah, I see 'em..."

The marshal and two other men were running toward them in full stride. The sounds of boot heels hammered against the wood of the long walkway as they closed in. Just as the marshal reached RUSTY'S MORNING CUP the door swung open, suddenly, and the lawman nearly collided into it, but managed to stop his forward momentum just as a man came stepping out. The marshal froze, instantly, in his tracks upon recognition of who the man was—Doc' Holliday! Doc's hand swept up, quickly, and yanked back the weather flap on his long gray coat revealing the ivory handled Colt Navy Revolver hanging in a harness on his left side. His hand stabbed inside quickly and yanked out—a matchstick! He struck it with a thumb nail and lit the tip of a thin cigar. Holliday flipped the match away, then raised his eyes back to the lawman who had, suddenly, petrified in front of him like a prehistoric tree trunk. There was a disturbing silence for a moment, then the Doc' said:

"Why... what on earth is the matt'a marshall? You look as though you've just seen a ghost."

The marshal couldn't speak. It seemed to Holliday as though a cat had him by the tongue. Holliday took a long draw from his cigar. He blew out a thick cloud of smoke, then flicked the ash from the tip of the tip. He placed the cigar back between his teeth and glared the marshal with cold, pale-blue eyes.

"It was a fair fight I can assure you marshal" came the Doc'. 'Watched the whole event from the other side of that window (he gave a slight nod toward the glass) It was, of course, legal according to the Code of the West. It was by the "Code Duello."

Holliday stood patiently, his fingertips tapping lightly on the butt of the Colt that lay in wait for his hand to unleash it.

"We're going to go ahead and go marshal," said Slim, a thin man so thin that if someone were to squeeze a shot off at him his body would probably split the bullet in two!

"'Sounds like a fair fight" agreed the other "so called" deputy standing with Slim.

Finally, a stir of a sound from the marshal...

"Go ahead, said the marshal to his men. Get Whitey 'n tell 'im we got another t'a dress out."

"We'll do!" said Slim.

The two men turned (nearly falling over each other) and, quickly, walked away, not looking back. The marshal cut his eyes to where McCall and Lawson were standing in the street.

"I'm gonna need statements from them..." he said, barely, as if asking permission to do so.

"It's your funeral, said Doc', do as you will. Now, if you will excuse me I'll return to my previous affairs—Good day sir."

Holliday turned, then re-entered the cafe.

Lawson and McCall were cleaning their boots on the board edges watching as the marshal squirmed in the presence of Holliday.

"He looks a little confused," stated Lawson. McCall made no reply.

Colorado Charley had placed a throw blanket over the dead man mostly out of respect for the woman folk standing nearby.

The marshal was waving a hand in the air to signal his peaceful intentions as he sloshed through the sloppy gunk of the street. He stopped in front of them, his eyes browsing the stiff form lying under the blanket.

"'Anyone know the victim!"

"What!?" growled McCall. That scum ain't no victim! He's an accessory to cold blooded murder, and justice just found him!"

"Would you mind if I asked whom exactly it was that he "allegedly" killed?"

"My wife," said McCall, turning his eyes away.

Lawson had stepped over to the edge of the boardwalk and was rolling a quirly, his eyes stayed fixed on the center of town.

"That man there, said the marshal (pointing to the dead Hicks) he had a part in your wife's death?"

"That's what I just said... You got somethin' blockin' y'er damn ears mister!?"

McCall was tiring quickly of the gab.

"When was this?" asked the marshal.

"What the hell does it matter?! Look... he called me out in the street and went for his gun and that's the end of his story! Get him ready for burial and I'll pay for y'er trouble. Now, can I go? said McCall, turning, or are we gonn'a have a problem marshal..?"

In the time frame of a few seconds the marshal pictured his own funeral and It was taking place in McCall's glaring eyes.

"You gent's are free to go 'got problem with it! It will be on record as self-defense. But, would you please move on? You two have a lot of enemies here in town and I'm just tryin' to keep the peace."

"We're tryin'" said McCall.

McCall turned, saw Colorado Charley standing inside the open doorway, an arm propped against the thick door.

"We'll be back for our gear. 'Appreciate it a whole lot if

you would just keep an eye on our things."

"Your supplies will be here, 'got my word on it," said Charlie.

McCall flipped a $20 double eagle into the air and the sheriff snatched it up.

"That's for the burial expense. Don't make nothin' fancy out of it."

just as McCall, and Lawson, stepped down into the street the *pale-faced* undertaker pulled up in his wagon with *circus midget* at his side. Whitey raised a hand and gave them a broad toothed smile (as if appreciating their hand in the business) McCall threw up a hand and made a gesture with one of his fingers that left little to the imagination! The smile dropped away from Whitey's face when he realized what it was McCall was saying—Up Yours!

The town clock read: 8:50 am.

The two walked on in the direction of the livery. Across the street, where the boardwalk ended, a man came into view. Frank McPheron stepped up from the mud, stepped onto the boardwalk, then turned using the edge of the boards to clean off his boots. He then leaned back against the wall with a Winchester .44 carbine cradled in his arms.

"Howdy boys," he said.

"Well now, would you look at him," said Lawson with a surprised expression.

"'Heard the shots, said McPheron. 'Came down the back way to see what was going on—Who's the dead man?"

"Just some dirt I used to know, said McCall.

"Fertilizer for scrub cactus, said Lawson, 'matters'a factly!

"'Been watching town from my window this morning, said McPheron. 'Earps were out about sunrise, 'looked like they was headed toward the livery. 'Didn't see anyone leave town on horseback though."

"They're still here, said McCall. They're not leavin' town, not yet, not with that train carryin' sizable payroll. They'll stick around and wait to see who makes the first move. Wyatt's probably figurin' it'l be us, 'n were figurin' it'l be James."

"And you know what James is thinkin', came Lawson, he's got us figured as scapegoats!"

"We're gonna have t'a stop him from robbin' that train I guess. 'Looks like the only way to keep our asses out of it is by gettin' in it, said Frank."

"Well, it smells like a bunch'a shit t'a me," said Lawson with a look of disgust.

"like it or not, 'looks like we know what we're gonna have t'a do," said McCall staring down at his muddy boots.

"First things first though... Let's get y'er money Frank" said Lawson.

"Looks about that time don't it," replied McPheron. "We'd better make a move before some side-windin' snake comes slithering up and bites one of us on the ass!"
At that moment a young lad (about the age of twelve) chucked a bundle of newspapers up onto the walkway.

"Read all about it! Fresh off the press! Gunfight in Denver! Prizefighter killed! Read all about it..!"

The young lads shouting faded within the crowd of shuffling people as he continued on with his route. Lawson bent down and pulled one from the bundle. The front heading at the top of the DENVER REPUBLICAN read:

Monty Langford was gunned down in the streets of Denver yesterday after he had violently confronted two men with a shotgun. One of them being Frank McPheron, the other man, Wreck Lawson, nearly killing them both. A bystander took it upon himself to stop Langford's advancing assault. The man, Jim Phoenix, was exiting from the doors of Denver's, Wicked Eye Saloon when he stepped into the midst of the situation. Langford was wielding a double barrel shotgun, and had already squeeze off one barrel. Phoenix retrieved his own sidearm and dispatched the hostile, Langford, with one shot through the side of his head and another through his heart. Although the killing was ruled as justified, Wreck Lawson, and his associate, Luis McCall (not involved) were asked to leave town at first notice by Denver's, Marshal Tye Brooks.

McCall was looking back over his shoulder as Hicks's dead body was being loaded into the bed of the freight wagon driven by the bony ghoul and his midget sidekick. Lawson touched McCall's shoulder, he jerked and quickly spun around!

"You okay pard?" asked Lawson.

"Yeah, yeah, I'm alright!" said, the shaken, McCall—but he wasn't. Buddy Hicks had re-lit a flame that had been laying dormant and it was all flooding back to him now. He felt a sudden urge to leave Denver; to seek out the past and bring judgment down on Clemens and the remaining men responsible for his wife's death. He felt more than just the need to kill these men now, this would be a reckoning! Hell was waiting for their souls and Death was beckoning to claim them! McCall was becoming a legendary gunman, and was polished at the skills of his trade, as those bastards would soon find out.

On the opposite side of the street from them stood the man in the striped suit. He was eyeing a pocket watch attached to his vest by a thin-chain. Up a ways from him stood three men—The Earp's. Wyatt stood with his back facing them. Wyatt's brother, Morgan, was looking over Wyatt's shoulder and staring hard at McCall and his company.

"What the hell is that!" erupted Lawson.

"'Don't know, said McCall, "evidently one of 'em can't seem to let it go."

"Ahhh hell, they ain't scarin' nobody, said McPheron.

"It'l only take one to get the rest of 'em killed, or possibly even one of us, said Lawson."

"Let's move. Keep your eyes and ears open!" said McCall as he began to step away. They watched as the man in pinstripes met up with the Earps. The group of men walked away, then disappeared around the corner of building and onto a side street.

CHAPTER 21

On the floor of Phoenix's hotel room lay triangular-shaped-pieces of mirror shrapnel. One of them reflected the likeness of Jimmy Phoenix. It was staring up at a person who looked identical in reflection yet lacking of concern or emotion—Sand-yellow-hair flipped up on the shirt collar... parted down the side... the glass image showed a trace of concern building in its eyes as it stared up at Phoenix... then a boot-heel stomped the face into the floor!

The dream had jolted him—he had to shake it off! Phoenix was tough, there was no doubt, but he was lacking of experience, experience beheld by the likes and caliber of the men he sought—Storm McCall and Wreck Lawson. Men like those were seasoned and had formed hard callouses over their emotions, something earned over time and the loss of many layers.

"It was just a dream dammit!" he told himself. He went to the window and separated the thin curtains with his fingertips. Up the street a ways a man's body was being loaded into the back of a wagon. Phoenix wondered if the man was dead or just drunk. He couldn't help but notice the half-of-a-man (apparently a midget) who was helping a freakish looking goon carry the, obviously, limp body. Just below the window, across the street, strode three men—he knew them immediately! He stared intently as the three men passed... mingling in amongst the people who were jammed up along the boardwalk's length like herded cattle.

"We need to get out of here quick!" stated McCall. Something's not right... I'm jumpy 'n ready t'a shoot! I know were bein' watched and I'm not about to catch lead in my back!"

They walked on, rifles in hand. Slowly, Lawson turned eyeing doorways and windows on the opposite side of the street. His eyes fixed on a form in an upper window behind a balcony rail—Jimmy Phoenix—Lawson was sure of it!

Phoenix stepped quickly to the side of the window and leaned back against the wall.

"Did they see me?" he thought to himself.

The thought of having been discovered raced through his veins, but at the same time he was getting a thrill of excitement from it! At 17 years of age Phoenix was good —very good! He yanked the new Colt from its holster, gripped it and rolled it from side to side. It felt good like an extension of his hand—he felt Invincible!

The drizzle of rain had quickened mixing with the icy-pellets that were beginning to cover the streets in a thin blanket of tiny-white balls as the temperature dropped to below freezing. The pools of rain left behind now had a crispy white texture of freeze forming around their edges with a thick-chocolate-slushy center like one of those "Floaty shakes" you'd get at an ice cream parlor. By now a hundred people (or more) had begun moving about along the building fronts. Later on it would be a thousand, or more. They had chosen to stay in a hotel at the edge of town for a reason—easy escape! Now, in the middle of town, they could see why that had been such a wise choice for them. The streets were full with wagons and horse traffic, mostly spectators who had come to see the fight and were beginning to make their ways out of town. The hitch rails were full with parked animals, the boardwalks shoulder to shoulder with people of all walks and gender. This was definitely the red light district of Denver, and there were at least twenty saloons. Soiled doves lined the upper balcony's waving and cooing at cowboys who were passing in the street; luring them in to be rolled and robbed of their hard earned pay after they'd long-hauled their cattle up from Texas into towns such as Wichita, Abilene, and Cheyenne. Such acts were considered the highest of crimes by those men and it wasn't surprising to see the whorehouses lose one of their own working girls from time to time to a cowboy who'd caught one red handed in the very act.

On a corner where two streets intersected was the Wells Fargo Bank. It was a tall two-story building with large glass windows taking up most of its front. The three stopped at the buildings front entrance.

"What time y'a got Frank?" asked McCall.
McPheron glanced his time piece...

"Almost nine, Storm."

After a moment the blinds were raised on the bank's windows and a man unlocked the double-doors.

"Okay, I was just thinkin' about how it looks with us standin' here like this..." said Lawson, looking down at the Winchester in his hands.

"We are a little overdressed for the occasion aren't we?"

replied McPheron, also referring to the rifles they were carrying.

"The long guns are startin' t'a draw attention, said McCall. Folks are startin' t'a take notice."

"Frank, were gonna go across the street and stand at the corner of that building by the barbershop next to that big willow tree. You go ahead and tend your business, we'll be standing over there."

McCall looked up at the blue-gray-clouds looming overhead as freezing rain drops tapped and melted on the tight skin of his red face.

"Damn winter," he mumbled to himself.
Frank handed his carbine over to Lawson and said:
"See you boys in a few."

McCall, and Lawson sloshed through the muddy street placing their steps on higher areas of ground as they crossed.

Joining the ranks of the men, securing the safe car at the rail station, were the Earp's. They were brandishing double barrel sawed-off shotguns. Wyatt stood by the rear door. Virgil and Morgan were separated standing at opposite ends of the car. Among them were several men brandishing rifles and side arms. Wyatt was conversing with the man in the pin-striped suit—Allan Pinkerton "The Eye" of Pinkerton's National Detective Agency. Pinkerton had been on the trail of the James gang since 1871—It was now 1877. Up to present he had met with no success in bringing the James Boys to justice. He knew already of their presence in Denver and was readying his men at the rail station. Wyatt had been hired by the Río Grande Railroad to secure their interests after a notorious train robber had been hitting shipments along the Santa Fe Railroad. Earp (Railroad Detective) had been put on the trail of Dave Rudabaugh one year earlier. The hunt had started in Texas, at Fort Griffin, where Earp's acquaintance, Doc Holliday (a good friend to become) had clued him in on several of the trails Rudabaugh regularly frequented. Wyatt had rode out of Texas across the Badlands of New Mexico and touched points in Arizona, then finally headed North-East up to the Colorado Plateau where he recruited his brothers and incorporated a dragnet (working with the Pinkertons) in a final attempt to bring Rudabaugh and the James Boys to their final *Waterloo*. As with Pinkerton the Earp's already knew of the James's presence in Denver. Wyatt Earp had every area covered, so he'd thought. The only detail he had neglected to account for was the $80,000 in Gold Bullion that was awaiting shipment for mint by the United States government at Wells Fargo. Hell, the Earp's weren't even aware of its existence! The federal authorities had thought it best if no one knew about it, which would have been the smart thing to do, but someone found out and now the bullion looked like glimmering-gold candy in a baby's mouth with no one there to protect it. Wells Fargo was opening for business and all that gold was going to tempt the hell out of someone! A sign was turned in the window that read— OPEN.

Frank pushed on the elongated brass handle. The door swung open and he stepped inside. Across the room were three arched windows secured with steel-rod bars and wood-slat bifold shutters; a small counter in the front of each for the business of financial transactions. He stepped over to the window, furthest left, and waited. Within the short time of a couple of breaths the shutter rattled open. A man in a brown suit (silver hair gleaming like fine spun silk) with black-framed bifocals was standing on the other side of it. He cleared his throat (signaling his presence) then looked between the bars and said: "May I help you?"

"Yes, you may" said Mcpheron with a friendly smile. He reached inside his coat and pulled out his billfold, then handed the teller his proper identification papers.

"I'm Frank McPheron. I'm here to collect the prize purse for yesterday's fight event."

In another room, behind the counter, McPheron heard a scuffling sound and some indistinct whispers. The bank teller's eyes cut to the side where a shadow figure could be seen on the floor boards; it being cast through an unseen doorway. The teller resumed his business with McPheron.

"I'm sorry, sir... where were we?"

The gent' had a drop of sweat on his brow and was acting peculiar. McPheron caught shadow movement on a back wall and the outline of a shotgun barrel. Armed security was normal for a bank, thought McPheron, and he dismissed any further alarm. He turned his attention back to the business he'd come for. Another gent' (a bank cashier) came in and stood beside the first teller and gave McPheron a quick glimpse over the rim of his glasses.

"Excuse me for a moment please," said the teller. He then turned and left the window with McPheron's papers in hand. Again, McPheron heard indistinct whispering and one of them sounded strangely familiar to him. The front doors opened and two men entered the bank. McPheron turned, glanced them, then turned back to the teller's window. The bank clerk was approaching the window and, again, he glanced back over his shoulder as he did so. The man's face was flush-pink and McPheron couldn't help but notice the man's trembling hands. McPheron suddenly got nervous. The front door of the bank opened again and a pretty red-haired gal came strolling in. She was busty with curves, and green eyes like a cat. She threw a wink, then a smile at McPheron. He returned a nervous smile of his own. He recognized her; the pretty gal from the saloon, Lottie Deno.

One of the two men who'd entered a few minutes earlier was tall, thin, and wore a long black confederate style coat with fancy buttons running up the front length of the flap. His hair was dark, matched the growth of mustache and thick goatee that shadowed his face. Atop his head was a narrow-brimmed hat. The man accompanying him was shorter but not thin. He was dressed in the same style dress apparel. His hair, longer, but not as dark. Atop his head was a wide-brimmed hat. Both men fancied black string ties and fancy boots. The side arms they bared were housed in military style cutaway holsters. The two men stepped over to a corner and turned with their backs facing the arched windows. They appeared as though having a private conversation. All of a sudden McPheron realized where he'd heard the familiar voice—Jesse James!

The sound of racheting hammers spun McPheron around. The two men who'd entered earlier were now pointing gun muzzles at him. Their intent faces resembled snarling dogs with hackles raised; canine teeth revealing traces of white foam like that of rabid animals!

"Don't move!" shouted the thinner man. "This is a hold up!"

He moved over quickly to the spot where McPheron stood. The assailant threw the pistol straight out and leveled it at the tip of McPheron's nose, then stared a threatening glare deep into McPheron's eyes. The other bandit shoved the red-headed gal into a corner where she hit, then slid down the wall onto the floor on her rump. The sound of dead bolts being loosed from a side door grabbed everyone's attention. The door swung open and another man stepped into view wielding a sawed-off shotgun.

"We're the James Gang!" shouted the taller man in black.

McPheron recognized him now from wanted posters he'd seen before—Frank James!

"If anyone moves shoot 'em!" shouted Frank James as he moved swiftly toward the side door that led into the vault area in the back. On the other side of the barred window the bank clerk was trying to catch his breath, apparently in a state of panic as the bandits' shouted out curses and commands.

"Open that goddam safe old man! came a shout from the back; I'm not gonna' tell y'a again mister!" The gang member then planted the butt of his shotgun against the bankers forehead with a loud—Whack! It sent the man down into the floor, dead weight.

Jesse James sprung up beside the teller at the window, grabbed him by his collar and yanked him up into the steel muzzle of a Remington revolver laid across the side of his head.

"Now, open that goddam safe!" he yelled in the stunned teller's face, then jerked him back toward the vault. Kimble was there instantly and dropped both barrels of a sawed-off down between the steel bars where it rested on the narrow counter top and was pointed straight at McPheron's gut. McPheron threw out his hands and began backing away from the scatter gun. Lottie Deno had wrapped her hand around the ivory handles of a Smith & Wesson Pocket .38 concealed inside her handbag. She had it cocked and ready to be unleashed at her command. Steel boxes could be heard hitting the floor in rapid procession. Another door slammed in the back room, McPheron heard horses blow and whinny—the gang was going out the back! Wic Farley had entered from the side door and was wielding a pistol. He had a nervous, wide-eyed grin on his face.

"Eighty thousand in gold, boy!" he said to McPheron. "Man, that sure is a lot'a woman 'n whiskey!"

"Shut up Farley!" shouted Kimble. "You talk too damn much!"

"Don't tell me t'a shut up again Kimble!" growled Farley. (Kimble locked both hammers back on the shotgun)

"'You say my name again Farley 'n I'll blow y'er brains across that wall behind y'a," said Kimble with a cool-calmness in his tone. Farley, suddenly had nothing else to say.

The rest of the gang were unloading the Gold Bullion out the back door...

The front doors to the bank swung open suddenly! The man who was entering never knew what hit him; Kimble pulled both triggers on the 12 gauge and fire erupted out both barrels blasting the unsuspecting patron low in his chest! He was carrying two bags made up of coins and greenback notes. The blast of .0.0 buckshot blew the man backwards out the doors he'd just entered through. The bags exploded high into the air, then greenbacks rained down like confetti! Kimble popped the smoking shells out of the steel tubes and replaced them with two fresh ones. He snapped the barrels shut and locked both hammers back.

From across the street, McCall, and Lawson heard the canon-boom of a shotgun. They had watched as two men approached the front doors of the bank. One entered, but a split second later he was blown back out as if he'd been lassoed at the waist and yanked with tremendous force! The unfortunate landed on his back sprawled out in the mud. The front of his coat and shirt fabric were blasted away in shreds with a large area of flesh and bone missing from his chest cavity. The other man lit out as fast as he could run... slipping and sliding across the muck, trying to get to the far corner of the building. He slipped and fell down, then crawled on all fours around the corner where he stopped and leaned back against the building looking back once to make sure no one had followed him. People were running for cover in the street and along the boardwalks.

McCall jumped from the front porch at the corner of the barber shop and went splatting across the mud-hole street to the corner of a small cedar shed where he came sliding to a stop by slamming his shoulder against the side of it! He jerked the Winchester up, tightly against his shoulder. Aligning the sights he scanned the area for movement... Lawson had leaped from the front steps and was cutting across the street when another shot rang out from inside the bank. Wic Farley was backing out the front entrance with a pistol in his hand. He fired a shot into the interior of the bank, then a second later his upper body yanked around as he took lead in his shoulder from someone shooting from inside the bank. Lawson slid to a stop in the middle of the muddy street. He turned to face Farley when he heard McCall shout—

"Hey, stupid!"

CHAPTER 22

McPheron had dropped to the floor, then quickly slid over beside Lottie, their backs to the wall directly under the arched windows. Lottie had drawn the .38 from her handbag and had Wic Farley in her sights. He was backing out the door when she squeezed the trigger. The round hit the door frame and a chunk of wood disappeared from it leaving a rounded hole where the bullet had drilled deep into the thick wood! Farley continued backing away firing his Remington toward the bank entrance. The gun bucked in his hand and fire exploded from the muzzle sending a rushing cloud of white smoke between the front doors of the building. Lottie had sent another flaming round out the doors, this time hitting Farley in his upper shoulder and half spinning him around from the impact! Farley was momentarily stunned. Over his shoulder he heard a man shout—

"Hey, stupid!"

Farley snapped out of his dazed state. He turned to see McCall coming at him with an 1873 Winchester pressed tightly up against the side of his hip. In what appeared to be slow motion (to Farley) he could see McCall's hand levering the action of the rifle, feeding cartridges into the firing chamber. Farley raised his pistol to fire, but then caught movement from someone in the middle of the street. Lawson was running at him, a rifle barking and lashing out tongues of flame as he worked the lever action in a steady rhythm! Farley felt a hard kick from lead entering in the side of his left leg just as he squeezed the Remington's trigger sending a wild round buzzing past McCall's head! McCall continued firing; Farley was suddenly dancing... He didn't know why he was dancing, but his body was jerking to a strange beat as bangs of rifle-fire drummed out a timely rhythm. Farley's arm's were flailing about like they were attached to strings controlled by some unseen puppeteer. He was falling back... the street and buildings falling down and away from his sight, then his body splat down into the thick-wet surface of the street. Farley's eyes searched the sky above him which had now taken on an ominous yellow-gray hue. The icy-rain was soaking his face and mixing with warm tears that dribbled down from the corners of his eyes. His breath was slowing... suddenly he couldn't breathe. He began choking from the liquid gurgling in his throat—the rain he thought... he began to panic! His fingers clawed at the mud as he struggled to find air to fill his empty lungs. The wet earth oozed from between his clenched fingers, then his grip relaxed and he breathed no more. Farley had thought it to be the rain he was choking on but it was blood pumping up from his lungs into his mouth and sinuses, drowning him. He stared with lifeless eyes into the violet and ash-gray sky. His bullet riddled body turned muddy puddles into pools of dark crimson marmalade.

Inside the bank...

Frank James threw the hallway door open and started to step out when, McPheron and Lottie Deno opened fire on him and blasted several chunks of wood off of a door! James quickly ducked back into the hallway, avoiding any ventilation to himself.

"Let's go!" came a shout from the vault room. There was a loud ruckus—Then...

"Frank!" came a shout from the street—it was McCall...

"They're going out the back!" yelled, McPheron.

(It really was getting a bit confusing having two men named Frank running around at the same time!)

McPheron and Lottie lay still on the floor with muzzles pointing at the door that led into the bank hallway.

"Y'er pretty good with that pocket gun" said Frank to Lottie.

"Had t'a be," she said. (neither of them taking their eyes from the doorway) "When a gal runs the circuit with someone the likes of Doc Holliday, sooner or later she'll have to defend herself!"

"You were Hollidays girl?" asked McPheron.

"Don't know if I was "his girl" as you call it, but I never embarrassed him the way Kate Elder does."

"Maybe you can tell me about it at another time" said McPheron. Lottie gave a kurt nod in reply.

Something was happening in the back; sounded like a struggle was taking place, then the hammering of boot heels came from the narrow hallway. The silver haired teller was making a sudden break for the front doors when the back of his tailored jacket blew apart from a blast of . 0.0 buckshot at close range! The devastating impact lifted the man off the floor sending his careening body through one of the large sections of windows. Jagged angles of shattered glass followed his body out into the street where it landed face down in an awkward looking heap. The force from the blast had nearly ripped the man in half, his legs still jerking, the only sign of any life left in him.

"I need a gun! shouted McPheron. This Derringer is spent!"

"All I got are .38's" shouted Lottie.

"Were gettin' out'a here—Now!"

Before she could blink McPheron had her hand and both were racing toward the front doors. McPheron gave the hallway door a swift kick from his boot slamming it hard against its frame. Almost simultaneously the middle of the door exploded into wood fragments just as the two dove through the open double doors at the bank entrance. The killer of the bank clerk was standing on the other side of the door. He had unleashed the second barrel on his 12 gauge and was reloading. He scrambled to the rear door where his horse and the other gang members were getting ready to light a shuck and blaze the hell out of there!

There was no way James was going to allow the heist to go to spoil like it had in Northfield. Just one year earlier in 1876 the James Gang made a dire mistake in Northfield Minnesota. Cole, Jim, and Bob Younger had joined forces with "The Boys" and a few strays by names of Bill Chadwell, Charlie Pitts, and Clell Miller. The heist was bungled and the gang came face to face with the biggest shoot out of their lives. Three townsmen were killed and two of the gang members—Bill Chadwell and Clell Miller. A few days later Charlie Pitts was shot and killed by lawmen and all three younger brothers were captured. Jesse and Frank James high-tailed it to the Dakota Territory and then their trail disappeared near Sioux Falls.

McPheron landed on his side in the muddy street and slid to a stop. Lottie came down on top of him, then rolled away onto her rump and into a shallow puddle that was half frozen. In her hand was the pocket .38. She showed no hesitation as she squeezed off two more rounds placing both bullets through the bank's front doors. Again, McPheron had her by the hand and was yanking her to her feet leading her to a safer place across the street.

"I need a gun!" yelled McPheron.

McCall was thumbing fresh rounds into his Winchester and wondering where in the hell the marshal was. He watched as Lawson pitched McPheron's carbine through the air... McPheron caught it in both hands. He gently pushed Lottie back against the side of the building.

"Stay!" he said to her. The look in his eyes revealed more to her than his excited state; he was protecting her! She didn't move. Besides, she was out of bullets anyway.

Lawson had made the Bank's front doors and was standing to the side of them with his back pressed up against the building front.

"You be careful Frank McPheron!" cried out Lottie as he shot out from cover and went sliding back across the mud toward the bank.

McCall had just slid in opposite corner from Frank, he passed by right in front of Lawson as he did so. He thumbed the last cartridge into the receiver, levered it into the chamber, then turned and looked at Lawson.

He shouted a gnarly growl from between clenched teeth —"Flush 'em!"

When Lawson entered the bank he was firing bursts in a cross-pattern... the Henry roared and kicked at his side... tongues of fire uncurling, lashing out in search of flesh to seer! He fired left... center... right, then spread the pattern back blowing apart plaster and wood and creating a thick cloud of white dust that filled the room. In the hallway a man screamed out! A barking round had bitten deeply into his flesh. Lawson began pushing replacement cartridges into the Henry; he could hear men shouting at the rear of the bank...

McPheron was moving along the side of the building; for the life of him he could not understand why the marshal hadn't showed yet, but the three of them were doing what they had to do to stay alive, and keep the innocents from harm's way.

"You okay Wreck!" shouted McCall.

"Still here!" came his reply.

Suddenly, they weren't receiving any return fire. Lawson moved over to the hallway, then, slowly, he stepped inside...

The marshal's boots were crossed at his ankles and resting on the desk top, fingers intertwined at his belt buckle and he seemed to be totally at ease with the situation in Denver. The fact that the town was completely over run with notorious outlaws hadn't entirely registered in his brain—until now!

Slim (the marshal's deputy) were out tending to the affairs of the community after having been instructed to do so by the higher command. The banging of repeated gunfire rang a bell inside the marshal's ears.

"What in tarnation is that!" he exclaimed, aloud to himself. He quickly made the door where he saw Slim making his way toward him.

"They're robbin' the Wells Fargo marshal!"

The revelation had caught him off guard, then any kind of rational thought after that completely eluded his mind. People were running for cover as the relentless gunfire continued. Slim was dodging weeding around between folks on the boardwalk as he made his way, then, finally he came running up out of breath.

"They're . . . robbin'. . . the bank, marshal . . ."

"Who Slim? Who is?!"

"Not. . . sure. . . 'Think it's James, but... there are others too... what are we gonn'a do..?"

The marshal suddenly remembered his ace in the hole-- the Earp's! The panic stricken lawman took off in the direction of the train depot with the hope of enlisting the Earp's to assist him with his "sudden duty!" His hope was replaced with a tidal wave of fear when he saw the mega-steel wheels of the train turnover on the tracks. They caught traction and the train began to chug away, south, out of town in the direction of Pueblo. Wyatt Earp had not been hired out to protect the Wells Fargo gold and therefore could not compromise the security of the military payroll he had been entrusted to protect by the railroad. Besides, he couldn't protect something he knew nothing about...

The Denver Marshal stood and watched as the smoke breathing locomotive rolled away from the station. The Earp's had wasted no time in their decision to put Denver behind them before the threat could possibly turn toward the rail station and themselves. They had kept light on the idea that either Rudabaugh, or the James Boys could be using the bank as a decoy. Rudabaugh's main interest was usually Santa Fe Railroad payroll. Although wrong in their assumption the Earp's were wise to leave the area and not become involved in the confrontation now taking place at the Wells Fargo. The marshal turned his attention back to the mayhem taking place at the middle of town. He turned his eyes to his office where a gray horse was tethered in front at the hitching post. He began to move quickly toward that horse. He came to it and moved quickly up alongside it. He released the reins from the post, then booted the stirrup and swung up onto the saddle. Slim and some other local townspeople watched as he turned the horse around and spurred the animal into a quick gallop down the main street toward the east, out of town, never looking back...

Allan Pinkerton (Detective) had chosen to stay behind. He was crouched down behind a freight wagon watching as events at the bank were unfolding...

In the hallway Lawson could see a trail of blood leading into the back room (evidently from the man his bullet had found earlier. That man was now firing rounds from a pistol through the open back door and into the hallway where Lawson was standing...

At the rear corner of the building McPheron could see the gang, their horses wide-eyed with fear. Several of the gang members were now firing weapons through the back door into the bank's interior.

"Let's get the hell out'a here!" yelled Irv Kimble, then he began firing pistol rounds at the corner where he'd just seen McPheron peeking his head around. Another gang member joined in with Kimble and proceeded to blast the wood away from it. McPheron spun, quickly, protecting his face from the flying shrapnel. When they stopped firing McPheron stepped out and began blasting away. A spinning round of .44 lead hit Kimble in the leg and ripped his knee apart. The bullet drilled through soft flesh, hit bone, and exploded into fragments inside the joint. The Brown Gelding that Kimble was riding reared straight up and tossed the wounded outlaw off into the mud. He was up, instantly, limping and squeezing off rounds. Kimble's backup gun was bucking in his hand, lashing tongues of fire repeatedly lapping out of the smoking muzzle—he was confused, unable to find his target. McPheron fixed the muzzle on Kimble's chest and squeezed off two rounds both hitting him high in the chest. Small clouds of fabric popped away from his shirt front. He went down and didn't move again; the fabric still floating on the air where the man had just been standing.

Ned Drake witnessed what had just happened. He wheeled his horse around and smacked reins across the animal's rump—the horse bolted!

Jesse James threw open the flap on one of his saddle bags and pushed his hand inside it. When he jerked his hand back out it held five sticks of dynamite taped into a bundle. He struck a match on the tip of a bullet cartridge in his belt loop, then lit the fuse. He threw it through the rear door of the bank.

"Dynamite!" shouted McPheron as he ran for cover.

Lawson saw the bundle come whirling in... It hit the floor, bounced off a wall, then came to a stop at the tip of his boot with only a couple inches of fuse left. It lay there sizzling away in a brilliant shower of shiny, silver-gold sparks. Just as the TNT arrived at Lawson's boots he heard a man groan. The Bank Clerk James had buffaloed earlier was regaining consciousness and was attempting to get to his feet...

McCall had just caught sight of a man on horseback attempting to flee from the scene; Ned Drake was riding low and firing a pistol across his saddle. Lead was thumping into the wood of the corner next to where McCall was standing. McCall yanked up the Winchester, leading the rider until he drew the outlaw's face into his sites, then pulled the trigger and watched the top of the man's head disappear. The rider fell forward, then he slid out of the saddle and landed dead weight in a patch of Prickly Pear Cactus that sliced through his hide like the razor sharp claws of a Utah mountain cat. He lay there limber—Dead!

McCall heard a yell—"Dynamite!" He ran and dove for cover behind a pile of split wood that had been stacked between two trees, then covered his ears.

When the man stood up Lawson had him by the collar of his jacket and slung him out the back door. When they landed Lawson covered him just as the dynamite exploded. The building frame erupted from its foundation, bursting, sending splintered lengths of lumber high up into the air. The concussion force of the explosion hurled both men around like rag dolls. McCall's mind raced at the thought of his friend having just been blown to oblivion. Pieces of wood and shattered boards flew overhead, then began raining down. McCall's ears were still ringing and a huge cloud of dust swept in around him. In the distance he heard the quaking rumble of galloping horses. He turned in time to see what was left of the James Gang riding through the dark timbers and green pine forest at the edge of town—horses in a row hurdling, one after the next, over downed hardwoods that lay on the forest floor. In a blink the gang disappeared into the foggy-mist of ice and rain...

There hadn't been time to place a shot, so McCall stood there as a calm silence settled in—the shootout was over.

Frank McPheron rose up from behind a water trough. He saw McCall and flagged him, waving his hands in the air.

"Do you see 'im?!" shouted McCall.

Frank gave a quick look around, looked back and shook his head, no. Both of them began combing through the field of twisted rubble in hopes of finding Lawson, but doubting he could have survived.

CHAPTER 23

Only one wall of the bank structure was left standing. Part of the back wall was teetering inward at an angle looking as if it were going to fall at any moment. They came to the rear of the broken shambles where the body of one of James's men lay face down staring into the mud. Near him a brown colored Gelding lay on its side. Several long pieces of splintered pine wood had been projected through the air and was embedded deep into the animal's neck and side rib's. Streams of red ran from underneath the heavy beast; its ink-black eyes staring, lifeless, and empty. Some twenty feet away a lone boot lay. It was attached to a man's leg—Lawson! His upper body lay hidden face down in some brush pine littered by blast debris. Both, McCall, and McPheron were slipping and sliding in the mud frantic with the idea that he may still be alive. Frank reached him first, grabbed his legs and drug his limp body out from within the brush. Frank rolled

Lawson over onto his back just as McCall came sliding up.

"Is he dead?" asked McCall .

"Don't know yet," replied Frank in a low-even tone.

He leaned an ear next to Lawson's face, heard no breath.

"He's not breathing."

McCall, gazing on Lawson's lifeless body, suddenly dropped down and thumped Lawson hard in the chest with the side of his fist.

"You breathe boy you hear me!" He hit him again— Breathe!"

Frank's eyes were welling up. He smeared a sleeve across them.

"Wreck, 'ol boy... Now don't you go dyin' on me 'n Storm. We ain't gonna be doin' no plantin' today, so you'd best just wake up now. Wreck, did you hear me..?"

Frank grabbed Lawson by both shoulders and shook him several times, but he didn't respond. Lawson lay there, still, cold. Frank stood, turned to McCall with a lost expression hanging on his face.

"He's gone Luis..."

A sudden rush of air swept into Lawson's lungs! He was regaining consciousness; his eye's slowly opening to thin slits.

"Wheew!" shouted Frank all wide-eyed with excitement. He smacked McCall across his back, a big toothy grin pasted on his big face. McCall could only smile as he realized that his partner, Lawson, wasn't going to die today.

Townspeople were gathering around the sight of the aftermath. From beneath the rubble, a man crawled out and was standing to his feet—The suited bank clerk. Lottie Dino was now standing next to Frank, smiling, her arms wrapped around his waist with the side of her face pressed against his chest. The Pinkerton Detective came into, McCall's view. His gun was leveled and fanning from side to side.

"Don't anybody move... now drop those weapons!"

"Who the hell are you mister?" asked McCall.

"Keep your hands where I can see them!" My name is Pinkerton."

"Mister, you've got this all wrong, said Frank. We ain't done a damn thing wrong."

McCall turned, slowly, and squared off with the man.

"Pinkerton... if you don't turn that iron in another direction y'er gonna have more than you can handle! You do realize of course that James and his men are escaping while you stand here like a jackass pointing a gun at innocent people."

Lawson attempted to raise up, awkwardly, pushing forward on shaking hands. He was helped to his feet by Frank McPheron.

"Someone needs to get on their trail before they leave Colorado Territory, stated Frank. And just where in the hell is that marshal anyhow?"

(That was a question everyone was starting to ask)

"Leave those gentlemen alone, sir, came a voice. That man there (he pointed to Lawson) saved my life. If it wasn't for him I'd be dead right now," stated the dazed bank clerk.

"You know this man?" asked the detective in question of Lawson, his eyes shifting from McCall to Frank McPheron.

"Yeah, we know 'im," replied McCall.

"What the hell hit me?" asked Lawson, regaining some of his senses.

"Dynamite..." said McCall.

Lawson's mind flashed back to the "pretty sparkling fuse."

"Oh yeah, now I remember."

"As I stated, sir, these men are innocent, said the bank

clerk. And those robbers are getting away!"

The clerk stepped over to Lawson and said:

"Thank you for saving my life son. I've never seen such bravery in a man and I know its a rare quality to behold." He reached out and took Lawson's hand and shook it.

"Sir, I only did what any man would'a done given the situation."

"If you say so son," said the bank clerk, smiling as he let go of Lawson's hand and patted him on the back.

A large group of onlookers had gathered now. Mixed in among the many faces—Jimmy Phoenix. He was curious and amused to see how they were going to get out of this one! He stayed back away from their sight.

"Leave 'em alone!"came a shout from the crowd.

"Them boys are heroes! came the shout from a woman. I watched them, they defended our town today!"

"Let 'em go!" came another.

The crowd was getting riled. Pinkerton thought it best for his own personal welfare to lower his gun. Pushing through the crowd came the deputy, Slim. His gun belt hanging loosely from his waist, one hand securing it as he crossed over to where they stood. He looked like the kind of guy you would only permit to carry one bullet at a time —for safety purposes!

"'Marshals gone." he stated.

"Gone? What do you mean, gone!" growled Frank.

"I mean.. he spurred his horse and left town, gone is what I mean!"

So, who in the hell is goin' after James!" asked Frank, turning red in the face.

Slim turned his eyes away, said nothing.

"Dammit! Y'er the law boy—Do something!"

"We could send for the marshal in Pueblo. He'd be here

in a couple of..."

"No time for that now! demanded Frank. That was the James Gang that robbed the Fargo! They killed two innocent men in the process... We need to act now! If no ones goin' after 'em, then by God I will!" said Frank with boiling determination.

"Slim..." started Frank.

The thin man cut him off in mid sentence...

"How did you know my name?" he asked.

Frank stood silent, a puzzled look on his face, searching Slim's eyes for some kind of clue, but Slim didn't have one!

"Lucky guess I'd call it..." said Frank. "Slim, start puttin' some men together. All this talk is eatin' up time and it's time for action. Where's the mayor? I need ta' be sworn in as acting sheriff."

"Oh no you don't Frank, said McCall, were not gettin' involved any deeper in this one!"

"There is no *we* on this one my friend, said Frank. You'n Wreck got y'er own problems t'a tend with. I guess I'll be handlin' this one without the two of y'a."

Lawson started to object, but he saw the determination in the big man's eyes and bit his tongue knowing that any attempt at argument with the big man would be futile. Frank turned his attention to the detective.

"What about you Pinkerton? Where do you stand in all of this?"

"I know who these two men are" he said, indicating McCall and Lawson.

"And..!" jumped Frank.

"After what I've heard here today I've got to say that what these two men did here was not the actions of cold blooded killer's. 'Seems to me they should be commended for their heroics! I'm not going to interfere with them and their cause. I'll ride with your posse as soon as you have one put together Mr. McPheron." Pinkerton ended it with a "Bet y'er ass!" kind of wink.

Frank gave a nod and went sloshing through the mud toward the ex-marshal's office to await arrival of the Mayor, Lottie and the rest following closely behind him. McCall and Pinkerton stayed behind to collect the bank notes that were scattered about outside of the bank. $5000 of it was Frank's winnings.

Inside the ex Marshal's office the town Doctor was looking Lawson over. Lawson and Frank were discussing possible routes the gang could have taken while the group of townspeople were gathering outside the jail curious as to what would happen next. Slim and his similar looking partner came sliding up out of the muddy street and stumbled over each other as they came through the door.

"'Mayor's on his way, said Slim, his sidekick nodding his head in agreement. I got a posse put together for y'a. Those men'l be showin' soon."

"Start grabbing rifles and ammunition from the cabinet, said Frank to Slim.

"Oooh, hell no, not me!" said Slim.

"Not me either!" said his sidekick.

"Y'er supposed t'a be the damn law here son! shouted Frank. Y'er gonna' get y'er men and y'er sidekick there ready t'a ride... Then, y'er goin' after them outlaws—Got it!"

Ol' Slim was shaking like a Aspen leaf rattling in a strong Northern Wind—and looking just as yella'!

"You'd better snap out of it and do y'er job son, James is gettin' away!"

The *skinny* deputy's sidekick, Carl, was frozen stiff.

"Y... Y... Yes, sir" whispered, Slim, a frog caught in his throat.

"Hurry man!" barked McPheron.

Slim about jumped out of his drawers! He and his sidekick were out the door before Slim's boots touched ground again.

McCall and Pinkerton were just entering the office with the bank notes and coins they had gathered from out in the mud.

"Well, here's what we could gather," said McCall. "'Got most of it I think."

He dropped the burlap sack on the floor beside the desk. It sounded like a cash drawer full of coins when it hit. Frank opened the sack and looked inside.

"'Stuffs gonna' hav'ta be cleaned for sure," said Frank.

"It will have to be counted, and recorded also," said Pinkerton.

"$5000 of that money is Frank's," exacted Lawson.

"I'm well aware of that Mr. Lawson," said Pinkerton. "There's more than that amount in the bag. I'll tend to the cleaning and counting of the notes."

"Hey Pinkerton, if y'er through countin' before we leave I'd be obliged if you'd let Lottie hold my share." Frank turned to Lottie and asked: "Would that be okay with you Lottie?"

"If you trust me Frank. I'll do whatever you ask of me, she replied."

"Well, then, it's settled. You heard it Pinkerton. The Detective gave a nod of his head, grabbed the sack of money, then he went out the door

"Pretty good job on this bullet wound, said the doctor to Lawson. Who did the work if you don't mind my asking?"

"Well, said McCall, I think it was my dear ol' granny's healin' remedy of bacon fat kept against the wound; 'Draws out the infection; that and a good supply of whiskey." The Doctor raised a brow, scratched his head.

"...T'a keep the fever down, Doc'," said McCall, with a

wink.

"Oh... Oh! Of course... I knew that!" exclaimed the *knowledgeable* Physician. "Very well then... I think you'll live son."

He pulled out a tin of salve, told Lawson to apply it to the wound once a day, then packed his medical bag and headed toward the door.

"What about payment Doc'?" asked Lawson.

"Word is; you boy's are heroes. This ones on the house!"

With that he turned and went out the door.

"Nice ol' fella,'" said Lawson.

"I owe you boys my life, said Frank. And I wanna thank y'a both for bein' there today.

"Frank, that's what friends are for." said Lawson with a crooked smile.

"Okay, if you two are finished gettin' all mushy we got work t'a do," said McCall.

Lottie had stepped over next to Frank and placed her hand on his arm.

"Frank, I want to thank you for protecting me out there and for getting me in a safe place. Not many men could have handled me the way you did."

"Well, ma'am, replied McCall, 'don't mean to intrude, but you've never dealt with a man like Frank McPheron before.

"No, I guess I haven't." She turned to Frank. "But, I'd like the chance too."

She tipped up on her toes and kissed Frank right on the lips, then pulled back.

"Y'er a mighty beautiful woman Miss Lottie, and any man would be lucky to have you to accompany him."

Something was going on between them. Hell, anyone with eyes could see that!

The door swung open—It was Slim, Carl (Slim's sidekick)

and the Mayor of Denver. McPheron was immediately sworn in as acting sheriff. He went to the door and stepped out onto the boards of the office porch and the others followed. Funny thing about it; people just seemed to follow McPheron. He just had the natural aire of a leader.

"Frank, you need a badge pard'" said McCall.

Frank had just noticed it himself.

"'Got just the thing," said Lawson as he stepped over toward Frank. He reached into his shirt pocket. When he pulled his hand out he was holding a Lawman's Star.

"May I do the honors?"asked Lawson.

"Please do," said Frank, with a smile.

Lawson pinned the star to Frank's shirt front and the townspeople applauded their new lawman.

The posse was readied and not another minute was wasted. The men mounted and rode out. Frank rode tall in the saddle as his men followed. He was a capable man—A leader! For McCall and Lawson it was time to gather their horses, gear, and put Denver behind them. They went to the livery, then back to the hotel to recover their personal belongings. The last stop was Colorado Charley's to gather their goods. The pack horse would prove to be a wise purchase seeing how they'd traveled last without one. This time would be different for them. Comfort and convenience would have them traveling with some livelihood. Besides, the way they saw it; You only live once, and the end could come at any time for either of them!

"Might as well go out in style!" as Lawson would say...

Within a couple of hours they were ready to ride. The numbers of people in the streets had thinned out leaving, mostly, only Denver's regular citizens remaining. The town's citizens were friendly; smiling and giving an occasional wave of a hand to the heroes of the day. A man from the Denver Republic Press stopped them and asked for a photo of them together with the bank clerk, they reluctantly agreed to the request. The photo was taken with an explosive flash, rendering the bank clerk, McCall, and Lawson forever preserved in time. After the "pose" they remounted and continued on to the south end of town, passing the preserved body of Monty Langford displayed in a "pose" of another nature. Whitey had him propped up fancy-like. His hair slicked back, displayed in a pine box behind a large glass window at the funeral parlor and stiff as a board! Next in Whitey's "Freak Shop" lineup would be; Buddy (Bear) Hicks. The rest of the unfortunate stiffs would soon follow. Whitey's ghastly face suddenly appeared in the showcase window! A haunting entity from a spine tingling nightmare, startling both McCall, and Lawson in their saddles. He gave one last toothy smile and a wave of appreciation for both of their *selfless* donations. They stared him down, then turned their heads and rode on exiting the street at the edge of town, then back onto the Colorado Plains.

"That freaky bastard gave me the creeps," said McCall to Lawson while easing into his saddle.

"Me too, said Lawson. He shuddered as a chill ran up his spine. "I ever see him again, and... well, I better never see him again 'cause one of us'l be dead!" He thought about what he'd just said, then dismissed the notion, and eased back into the saddle. They was putting Denver further behind them with each rise and fall of the land. It wasn't long before both men reached for neck scarves and pulled their hat brims down to block the assault of the freezing ice pellets that had been stinging their faces red.

Jimmy Phoenix stood at the large parlor window gazing at his most recent trophy, Monty Langford... He'd missed his opportunity for a showdown with his two prospects.

He watched them as they shrank on the horizon, shadow figures fading into the gray-clouds of foggy-sleet. $5,000 each in bounty money would be enough of a reason to kill any man, but in Phoenix's mind the thought of the money seemed to slowly fade away. No, they had something more valuable than any reward would pay for them—Dead Or Alive! He had to take them down and he knew he could. That was the only reward he sought from them. They would pay him, with their guns, in the street. The men, their names, and their guns would die with them and the name Phoenix would rise to fame and spread fear in the hearts of men everywhere! Once he staked his claim as the fastest gun he would be immortalized forever. His name would be etched in history to be remembered throughout all time. He'd give them a bit of a lead, then set out on their back trail. Phoenix was in no real hurry to kill McCall, or Lawson—he had plenty of time! Turning the door handle he stepped inside where Whitey the Mortician was tending to the dead body of Wic Farley. Phoenix closed the door behind him. He stood and watched as the ghoul fixed orange colored hoses to dark-glass bottles containing a mixture of embalming fluid that he would ingest into the cold veins of the discolored stiff. Farley, laid out at length on a table (body riddled with deep-blackened holes) had become a lead-mine of bullets plugged into his face; chest; arm's; and leg's. Even the soles of his feet held lead! 'Reminded Phoenix of a piece of cheese; that yell'a kind the mice like so much... got holes all in it. Phoenix couldn't help but notice that the man had a pleasant smile on his face though—almost tranquil. 'Seemed kind of strange to him seeing as how he had Farley figured for already burning in Hell about now! Whatever place Farley was in now he wouldn't have to worry about bumping into McCall again—For the moment anyway..!

CHAPTER 24

Denver disappeared behind them like a bad dream, and for both of them it felt good to be awake and alive. Three hours ride brought them to a wide-shallow stream being fed from the nearby mountain range. The freezing rains had formed a coating of smooth ice over the terrain. Trees, rocks, and the hills glistened with a luster like fine crystal. Even the mane's of the steam breathing beasts they rode upon were matted with the frosty crystals. But, for the time being the freezing rains had ceased rendering only a few clouds over-head, but more blue-gray were looming off in the distance. The stream was washing its path across the land; It looked like a good place to water the horses and brew some hot coffee. No sign of recent rider's having been in the area, so they tethered the horses to a tree branch near the water's edge so's the horses could rest and partake of its cool wetness. Several mature trees lined the banks. Crispy autumn leaves shown the hew of rich copper shimmering in the breeze a midst the thick branches like shiny-pennies. In a flat-sand-bottom, they found a clearing and started a fire with some dried kindling and large pieces of dead branch they'd come across along the banks edge. Lawson dragged the ice layer from the surface of the sand with the side of a boot to prevent a wet-melt effect. With coffee under way, they leaned back (in the dry sand) against a bark-less old tree (that had fallen onto its side some years ago) and waited for the coffee to brew. Closing his eyes for a moment McCall drew in a deep breath and listened to the gurgling waters from the nearby stream mingling with the brushing leaves that were caught up on the chilled breeze. Thick tree branches creaked from the weight of the thick-ice-layer that had formed on them. An occasional leaf would let go, the laminates of ice shattering like delicately tinseled bulbs against the frozen bank. It reminded him of a place he'd been before, he just couldn't quite seem to put his finger on it.

"Quiet..." said Lawson.

"Sure is..." replied McCall.

"'Remind's me of somewhere, 'just can't put my finger on it" said Lawson, expelling his warm cloud of breath onto the frozen air.

McCall turned his head over his shoulder to find Lawson with his eyes closed.

"I know what y'a mean pard'" he replied back. "It's nice country. A place where a man could make peace with himself."

McCall stood to check on the brewing coffee. He filled two cups, handed one over to Lawson... he took a sip.

"Good coffee."

"Does hit the spot," replied McCall warming his hands against the warmth of the tin. They kicked back in the cozy spot and eased in as the world around them slowed to a comfortable yaw.

The whinny of a horse came in from the distance. Lawson stood, went to his saddle to retrieve his Henry from the scabbard, then levered one into the chamber. McCall released the thong from his Colt's hammer and waited as the sound of shod hooves drew closer. Coming down across a rounded slope appeared a rider. He cut down the steep grade, came to the edge of the stream, then turned the horse and came splashing across the rocky shallows towards them...

"Hello the camp!" shouted the stranger.

"Keep y'er hands where we can see 'em if y'a don't mind mister," said Lawson.

"Sure thing," said the man, stopping the horse in mid-stream.

"'Caught whiff'a the coffee from a mile out; mighty invitin' smell to a man lackin' in his own provisions."

He was a big man, but not fat—older—looked to be about sixty, maybe sixty five. His long-gray-hair was streaked with a hint of black from previous years of his youth. His thick beard matched, 'was cropped off at the top of his chest.

"I ain't lookin' for no trouble, just a warm cup of y'er brew.

He was an eye-full; dressed in a white tan-leather coat and pants. Lawson recognized the leather as Northern Caribou. No doubting the man had pondered some time deep up in the Northern Territories. Grizzly canine and claws wreathed his neck. A Colt Walker was shoved in behind his belt next to a sheathed Bowie. In the scabbard, on the saddle next to him, a Springfield .50 rifle. Serious fire power for stopping big game in its track's, or a man if he wanted to keep him at distance! After a moment of sizing him up...

"Come on in, said McCall in an even tone. Just keep y'er hands where we can see 'em."

"Thank y'a... thank y'a kindly sir" the man said as he eased the horse on across the stream. He dismounted and stepped off onto the sandy shoreline.

"Which way you fellas headin?" he asked.

"Oh, just headin' south a spell, said Lawson. 'Got some business t'a tend to down Fort Griffin way."

"'Don't say? That's a mighty long ride you got ahead of y'a'."

He said his thanks after McCall handed him a hot cup, then sat down on the end of the hollow tree trunk.

"'Names Zebadiah Cray. You can call me Zeb, 'makes it easier."

McCall and Lawson glanced each other after having recognized the name.

"I'm Blaine and he's Carson," responded Lawson, quickly cutting eyes over to McCall.

"Blaine and Carson; are those first names?" asked Cray, then sipped on his coffee, his eyes shifting from one man to the other.

"It's just Blaine and Carson if y'a don't mind," stated McCall, locking eyes with the man.

"No, don't mind at all! 'Mans got a right t'a privacy is what I believe. It's just that..." He hesitated, then took another sip.

"Just that, what?" asked Lawson, a slight irritation growing in his tone.

"Fellas, I ain't tryin' t'a come off unfriendly with y'a, but you two look mighty familiar to me."

"And why is that?" asked McCall.

"Well, I been up in the high country for a while. Prefer it that way really; safer for everyone if y'a know what I mean. Anyhow, I slid down into Pueblo a few days ago, first time in a while I'd visited a real town. There's a man there 'name of Rogan. He's lookin' for two men and showin' their faces around. Now, I ain't blind, and with a little more growth on y'er faces I'd say..."

"You'd say what?" gleamed McCall.

Cray tilted the last of his coffee, then held out the empty cup.

"'Mind I get a refill?"

"What kind of game are you playin' mister? If you got somethin' t'a say, then say it!" barked Lawson.

"I ain't the one lookin' for you boy's, son. But, I know who is, so maybe I can help y'a."

"Why would you want t'a help us even if y'a did know who we are?" asked McCall.

"'Don't rightly know, maybe it's the coffee." Once again Cray held out the empty cup.

McCall gave a nod, Cray stood and got his own coffee, then took a sip from the hot brew.

"Maybe I've been there," he continued. You two don't seem like the cold blooded killer's that bounty man was describing or I'da been dead before I crossed int'a that stream."

"Just who in the the hell do you think we are, mister?" came Lawson.

"Why... y'er Wreck Lawson. He turned his eyes. And you, y'er Storm, excuse me, Luis McCall."

"So, what are y'er intentions Zeb?" asked McCall.

"Like I said, you two ain't no cold blooded killer's. I've seen my share of killin' myself. There's a certain look in a man's eye 'says y'a can't trust 'im. Neither one of you got it. I've been accused of doin' things I never done before. Now, I've done my share, don't get me wrong! But, I never killed a man that didn't have it comin'. That's the way I got you boys figured. You've been wrongfully accused and I just can't stand by and let that happen to the two of y'a . So, I guess my intentions are t'a help you fellas in any way I can if you'll let me. Hell, I aint'a doin' nothin' else anyhow!"

"Zebadiah Cray, 'heard of y'a, said Lawson. 'Been tellin' Storm here about y'a for some time now. Y'er about as much legend as one man can be. Y'er the one been killin' all them Yukon Mounties' up Canada way ever since I was knee high to a sprout. Word is—Y'er plumb crazier than shit..!"

"Them bastards up in the Yukon tried t'a run me off 'a my claim back in "55." They took t'a shootin, 'killed my poor Annie..."

Cray's eyes welled up. He smeared a sleeve across them.

"Anyhow, I killed the bastards—every damn one of 'em! They never got the gold and never will and there's plenty of it! Got a ton of it stashed where they'll never find it!" His eyes drifted off, distant for a second, then he continued;

"Dumb bastards keep comin' though..."

Cray raised his head, 'seemed to come back from somewhere faraway.

"They never get too close I'll tell y'a! Me 'n that Springfield keep 'em at a distance. Most never know what hit 'em."

He gave a wide smile, then took a sip of the hot coffee. The camp grew silent...

The sun wouldn't set for a couple more hours. McCall threw more wood on the fire after they'd decided to stay put and stir up some grub, 'even invited their new acquaintance, Zebadiah Cray, to sit in on the fixin's.

After having taken their fill of grub the three men sat around the fire. The light of day began to fade behind the majestic Rocky Mountains that lay just to the west of them. Lawson went over to his horse and replaced the Henry rifle back in its scabbard. He had done it as a sign of trust. The way Lawson viewed it; if Cray knew anything about them he'd be a fool to reach for that Walker.

"Can we trust you Zeb? Or the first time we turn from y'a are y'a gonna' shoot one of us in the back?" asked McCall.

"Wouldn't make much sense to shoot one of y'a in the back!" Cray stated, bluntly. "I'd still have t'a tend with the other of y'a and we all know I'd be dead before then.

"Hey, you know, you've got a point there!" said Lawson with an air of confidence.

"Besides, finished Cray, I could have taken at least one of you fellas out from the top of that ridge line back yonder if I'd wanted too. I never miss with that Springfield—Ever!"

Lawson narrowed his brow having lost some of his sand. He knew that what Cray was saying had substance. If legend held true, Zebadiah Cray could have killed both of them in two blinks!

"What do you want from us Cray?" asked Lawson.

"Not a damn thing son, 'cept maybe a chance t'a right some wrongs. I don't believe what they're sayin' about y'a. 'Seen my share'a lies. Besides, 'ain't had no company for a spell, 'be kinda' nice t'a ride with men again. 'Won't stick around forever mind y'a! just long enough t'a see y'uins through is all. Then, we can say our goodbye's."
McCall was thinking it over...

"What'a y'a think Wreck?" he asked.

"I don't know... he sure does eat a lot!" said Lawson just as Cray was taking a bite from another biscuit, making it his fifth! Cray stopped chewing, had a puzzled look on his face.

McCall, and Lawson both cracked up! The look on Zeb's face (biscuit crumbs dribbling from the corner's of his swollen jaws) had them both teary-eyed with laughter. After a minute, Lawson said;

"Ahhh, hell... I don't care if you don't Lou'."

Cray smiled, finished chewing his biscuit.

"A third man at this point ain't such a bad idea; 'Balances the odds a little better in our favor," continued Lawson.

Cray swallowed, said; "'Didn't mean t'a be a glutton there."

"Y'er fine Zeb," said McCall. "We got plenty."

McCall got serious.

"Y'a seem like a descent man Zeb... You cross one of us 'n It'l be the last thing y'a do."

"I can understand y'er concern. Like I said... just wan'a right some wrongs, maybe help you fella's out a bit."

"Alright Zeb, y'er in. Just don't go gettin' y'erself killed on account of us!" said Lawson.

"'Don't intend t'a die no time soon," said Cray with a thin smile.

CHAPTER 25

Daylight was fading as the snow began to fall... Within minutes the large flakes were covering the land in a blanket of powdery-white. McCall caught a shiver and pulled up the color on his coat after several of the flakes landed on the back of his neck. The flakes ,big, were spinning around on the wind like moths flapping their frosty wings against his face. The flakes stuck for a moment against his skin, then melted away leaving his face bright red and cold. With the gear packed away, the three men booted stirrups and remounted.

"This stuffs really startin' t'a come down, said McCall. 'Better git on the trail before it becomes a white-out. Let's stay with these foothills, 'pro'lly be best if we would need to find shelter. What do you say Zeb? You just rode up from way of Pueblo. How's about we just follow your trail?"

Both, Lawson, and Cray gave a nod of agreement.

"Let's go!" exclaimed Cray.

The three wheeled the horses around, and nudged them into the icy-waters of the stream, splashed their way across to the other side. The water was deeper there, coming up to their booted stirrups. One by one the wild-eyed animals lunged up out of the icy-depth and broke out onto the steep embankment, necks stretched out long, shod hooves digging deeply into the cold earth.

"Heee yah! shouted the three horsemen as they pushed the animals upward...

Coming to the top, a midst the hard timbers and green hues of Spruce Pine, the horses wheeled with excitement and stomped their steel-shod hooves against the frozen earth...

Jimmy Phoenix had been downwind of the camp when he smelled the trailing smoke of a fire. He climbed down from the Gray's back and walked the horse, leading it by the reins to the edge of the foothills, then moved up to higher ground. From there he would be able to get a better view of the man, or men, who would be at fireside. He ground staked the Stallion in good cover, retrieved a retractable looking-glass from one of the saddle bags, then worked his way to the edge of a sheer bluff. Nestled back inside the thick pine cove he spotted the glowing light of a campfire. He knelt down on one knee and pointed the lens at the flickering light below. Phoenix was amazed! He could actually see the glowing embers of the fire; the smoke rising into the air. Yes, the looking glass worked very well indeed! There was no doubt in his mind who the two men were, he could see them clearly through the glass. But, who was the third? An oddly dressed, grizzly looking man had taken up with them. That changed his plan—now he'd have three to kill! He watched as the men mounted up, then turned the horses and put them across the wide stream. They ascended up a steep hillside, then they vanished over the curve at the top of its ridge line. He pushed both ends of the scope together and went back to the horse and replaced the *spy* glass back in the saddle bag. He remounted, turned the Stallion around and rode back down to level ground and pointed the horses long face in the direction of the campfire. As he approached he pulled the new Winchester from leather and levered a round into the chamber.

"Hello the camp!" he shouted, but got no response.

Phoenix was nervous. The smoking embers left from the fire glowed brightly on their ends as a gust of wind rushed over them. He turned to step down from the saddle when one of the cinders popped loudly sending chunks of red spark shooting out in all directions. Phoenix flipped back over the saddle, landed and rolled onto his stomach with the rifle muzzle pointed at the fire, wide-eyed, his heart thumping wildly inside his chest. Sensing no-one there he stood, planted the heels of his boots in the icy sand and replaced the rifle back in its scabbard. There for a moment he'd thought for sure he was dead!

After gathering some dry wood Phoenix soon had the fire blazing again. He leaned back against the hollow tree and grinned, chuckled to himself at how sly he was—and they didn't even know he was following them! The confidence he was feeling was clouding his ability to think the situation through; Being a deadly-fast gun was one thing, but Phoenix lacked the experience required to successfully track the kind of men he was trailing without being discovered. He was learning the hard way...

McCall and Lawson were just doing what they'd done so many times in the past; Riding just out of sight, then turning to check their back trail. Zeb stayed with the horses while the two went back to scout the rim edge of the steep rise. Kneeling down behind the tree line they watched as the stranger below them stoked the fire they'd left only a short time ago. They couldn't see him well enough to identify him, but one thing for certain—they were being followed!

Lawson whispering...

"I could take him out from here," referring to the Henry rifle resting across his knee, a .40 cartridge in the chamber ready to—Bang!

"Who the hell is he?" whispered McCall.

"I don't know, replied Lawson, but he's got a set'a balls on 'im doesn't he?"

McCall thought for a second...

"We should shoot the bastard. Only problem is..."

"I know... It's kinda' like shootin' 'im in the back, huh?" said Lawson.

"Yeah, kind'a. Y'er right we can't do it. 'Don't seem right," said McCall.

"We should though!" snarled Lawson.

"I know dammit!"

McCall pointed a finger down at the stranger beside the campfire and said;

"Y'er one lucky man today whoever you are..."

The *Gray* Phoenix was riding whinnied and blew having caught scent of the two men up above on the ridge. Phoenix was quickly on his feet! The orange glow of the fire dancing in the blackness of night was casting flashing glimmers along the shiny muzzle of the .45 he held in his hand.

"Let's get out'a here before I change my mind!" whispered Lawson.

Standing, they turned and disappeared into a row of pines, then faded into the blackness of night. The snow was getting deeper like a tossed blanket of white covering the land in all directions. On the air float a perfect silence as the three men rode on into the depths of night; horse breath and snow packing under shod hooves being the only sound rendered. Only one thing weigh on McCall's mind now; Pueblo was drawing nearer, and there he would find a man called Rogan. If that man refused to cooperate of his own will, McCall would use whatever force necessary to get the answers he was seeking!

McCall adjusted the thick-flannel scarf around his neck, leaned his weight into the stirrups, then pushed the red horse onward into the black and white...

SHOOT 'EM T'A HELL!

AFTERWORD

"The Noose" and his eastern associates were waiting on word from Cliff Rogan to arrive from Pueblo concerning the demise of McCall; Lawson was a freebie they'd thrown in for entertainment purposes.

The Ferrell gang was headed for Santa Fe soon to meet with Neusom. They would ride out of Yuma by next week's end. There they would be joined up with a new acquaintance; an Easterner looking to settle a score of his own with a man by the name of McCall!

Jimmy Phoenix pushed on... losing his way at times. The whiteout would soon stop him in his tracks and before nights end a small fire would dot the blanket covered scape. Centered in the midst of some snow covered pines Phoenix lay back, thinking...
"I'm the fastest gun that ever lived..!"
The three men he'd killed, and the horse he'd stolen, never crossed his mind.
Myles Forte' had learned that his prize Stallion was being ridden by a man going by the name of Phoenix'; Forte' wanted that horse back!

304

Near the Colorado, Nebraska line

Marshal Frank McPheron and his posse had the James gang pinned down in an old rustic cabin built into the face of a dirt hillside. A thin swirl of gray smoke was rising up from the sod grass roof...

"You'll never take me alive! shouted James. "Ain't a prison made 'could ever hold me!"

"Throw down y'er arms 'n come out with y'er hands high, or we're gonna' open fire! I'll give y'a one minute t'a decide!"

"You'll hav''ta burn me out first—Law Dog!"

AUTHORS BIOGRAPHY

Nick L. Shane grew up in the rolling hills of South-Western Ohio where the local woodlands grew thick in the summer with the smells of sweet-ripened black berries. As a young man Nick hunted those hills alongside his father (Veteran of the Korean conflict) who'd educated him in the ethics of weaponry, gun safety, and his personal responsibilities concerning the right to bare firearms.

In 1979 Nick went west to work for a company out of Tulsa, Oklahoma. It was there that his fascination with the American West would take seed. Ultimately that inspiration would direct his paths over a vast terrain to arrive where he is today—A Western Writer.

Nick has lived in Dallas, Austin, OKC, Denver, Wichita, and Santa Fe, just to mention a few. It was the enchanting lands of New Mexico that would embed the spirit of the West in a young man's soul that would remain for a life time.

He entered the rodeo arena at the age of 19 and competed in bull riding events around the New Mexico Territories. At one point he actually came close to considering himself a "True Cowboy."

He has worked as a Tradesman in the building industry. Also worked the shipping harbors in Tampa Bay and has had his hands on many other dubious helms throughout the youthful-roaming-years of his experience. Nick believes that the greatest honor he has is in remembering the spirit within the places he's seen on the Western Panorama and being able to share that spirit with others, like himself, and you, who still recall *The Spirit* of the American Wild West!

NICK L. SHANE

DON'T MISS THE NEXT EXCITING ADVENTURE
IN:

THE GUNS OF INFINITY

VOLUME 2
SIX BULLETS 'TIL MIDNIGHT!

THIS TIME DEATH WILL BE THE LEAST OF THEIR FEARS,
AND TIME IS RUNNING OUT...

I want to take the time to thank each of you, personally, for your encouragement and support. When I first started the writings I had no idea how vast a plain I was stepping onto. It has now become a personal journey to say the least. My hope is to entertain you with a quality read, and to give you something back for your invested time. I hope you enjoy the story and the depths of its content as much as I have during the unfolding of its creation. Thanks again for your time, and your attention, as you discover the span of ages from cover to cover that have now come to life within the pages of

THE GUNS OF INFINITY!

-Nick L. Shane

SHOOT 'EM T'A HELL!